"I'm willing," she had said. So much harder to take it back once it was spoken. *I said yes,* her inner voice was astonished and elated at the same time. *Yes, I said, yes I will.*

And then there was a mouth covering her mouth, a tongue touching the edge of her teeth lightly, probing. Rachel felt her heart beating again, not in panic this time, but in anticipation — *thank you, thank you, thank you* — each beat more pronounced. She needed to be touched, touched in her body and in her heart. It was time. Even if it had been hard to say, she was willing. She knew that like she hadn't known anything in years, knew it viscerally, without explanation or apology. She wanted Susan, wanted her body, her touch.

About the Author

Judith McDaniel lives in Tucson, Arizona, where she writes and teaches writing and communications courses. She has just completed *A Lesbian Couples Guide* (Harper/Collins, 1995). Other books include the novels *Winter Passage* (Spinsters Ink, 1984) and *Just Say Yes* (Firebrand, 1991), and several collections of poems and essays.

YES I SAID YES I WILL

Judith McDaniel

THE NAIAD PRESS, INC.
1996

Printed in the United States of America on acid-free paper
First Edition

Editor: Christine Cassidy
Cover designer: Bonnie Liss (Phoenix Graphics)
Typesetter: Sandi Stancil

Library of Congress Cataloging-in-Publication Data

McDaniel, Judith.
  Yes I said, yes I will / by Judith McDaniel.
      p.   cm.
  ISBN 1-56280-138-4 (alk. paper)
  I. Title.
PS3563.C3538Y47   1996
813′.54—dc20   96-8547
                                                                    CIP

for Jan
and a lifetime of yes

Books by Judith McDaniel

Just Say Yes, a novel

*The Lesbian Couples Guide: Finding the
Right Woman and Creating a Life Together*

Metamorphosis: Reflections on Recovery

Sanctuary: A Journey

. . . a womans body yes that was one true thing . . .
and then I asked him with my eyes to ask again
yes and then he asked me would I yes to say yes . . .
and first I put my arms around him yes and drew
him down to me so he could feel my breasts all
perfume yes and his heart was going like mad and
yes I said yes I will Yes.

James Joyce, *Ulysses,* 1921

. . . there were only a few dozen new romances a year,
and once you'd read all the reprints of the dyke
novels from the forties and fifties, well, what was
a girl to do? Change the pronouns.

Angie in *Just Say Yes,* 1991

CHAPTER ONE

Water roared down the gorge where the Ausable river narrowed and deepened. If the two women looking upstream at the boulder-strewn falls had wanted to speak, they could not have been heard, but they were content to watch in silence, letting the autumn sun, bright but cold, splash on their faces. After a while, the taller woman took the other's hand and led her away from the precipice, back into the woods where the roar lessened and, gradually, Rachel could begin to distinguish the call of birds, the rustle of wind in the crisp autumn leaves still clinging to branches.

Susan paused then, turned toward Rachel, leaned toward her. "I want you," she said, her voice a whisper closer to the rustle of leaves than the passionate roar of the river.

Rachel heard her, hesitated. She had been about to look at her friend, about to make a joke, a light-hearted statement, something to ease the tension she had felt building all morning. Now here it was, out in the open. She couldn't pretend anymore.

Rachel kept her eyes on the forest floor for a moment longer, as though the patterns of fall leaves fascinated her beyond hearing Susan's voice. If Susan could hear her thudding heart, she thought, then speech would be unnecessary. But it was time; she had known it was time.

Finally she looked directly at Susan and drew a deep breath. "I'm willing."

A slow smile began at the corners of Susan's mouth. "I needed to hear you say that."

Rachel would always remember the warm breath on her cheek, the tension heating Susan's skin under her shirt, radiating out, drawing her fingers to its smooth warm surface.

"Kiss me," Rachel demanded, then added softly, "please."

She took the leap and thought it part of an extraordinary season in her life. A northeastern autumn had stunned the late September landscape, splashing the oaks and maples with red and gold almost overnight. Some years the color came slowly, Rachel thought, imperceptibly, tree by tree, until she awoke one morning surrounded by color. But this year there had been late summer rainstorms, a sudden killing frost in early September, and a few days later the northern mountain slopes of the Adirondacks broke out in color overnight. She hadn't seen color like this since she'd been a child, scuffing through leaves on this same dirt road that led past the gorge and along the river to the falls. Or was it only that all of her senses seemed alive this particular autumn, alive and vibrant, connecting her to the landscape around her in ways she hadn't felt since she was a child?

They had driven up to the mountains that morning from Albany — to a cabin that had been in Rachel's family since it was built at the turn of the century, a cabin on the edge of a private estate, jointly owned by several dozen very wealthy families, families like Rachel's.

"Did you spend a lot of time here when you were a child?" Susan asked as they walked out the old logging road toward the gorge.

Rachel looked shyly sideways at the woman walking beside her in a soft, contemplative silence and nodded. "My mother and I came up, mostly. It was her retreat, I think. My father sort of left it to be her place. And when he wanted to get away, he went south, to New York City. It wasn't too far from Saratoga to come up to on the weekend, just about an hour and a half." She looked at Susan, wondering what she was really asking.

"I can't imagine having a place like this to ... well, to ground me," she said slowly. "Was it like that for you?"

Was it? Rachel wondered and dragged her feet through the leaves, watching the bright colors cascade to the side as she passed. "I guess it was," she said finally, searching this face that was becoming familiar, so familiar. Certainly there had been no person to root her in that way, no brothers and sisters, no aunts, uncles, cousins, nor even any grandparents by the time Rachel was six. Just her father, her mother and Rachel. "I loved coming up here, even when it seemed lonely." Susan looked a question at her. "My mother liked to come when no one else was here," she tried to laugh off this explanation. "She never liked to socialize, so we didn't come up much in July and August when the pool and tennis courts were open and a lot of the other families were up for the summer."

Rachel took a deep breath. How much to reveal? When to say it? And which among her memories of childhood were relevant? Which were even real? She knew the tricks of memory intimately. Sometimes she had actually believed the childhood she'd made up for herself years ago. "When I entered seminary," she said finally, "I had to learn how to be a social person. It wasn't part of my upbringing."

Susan nodded silently, smiling in understanding. They had walked out to a bluff looking down over a small, fierce river that raged down the gorge. Since they met in August, just the month before, they had been talking about their lives, about relationships, what they wanted for the future, what the past had been like, what had worked and what had failed. The conversations had meandered in and out of Rachel's waking thoughts like a plains river wanders, acting as though it had nowhere in particular to go, no ultimate destination determined by gravity pulling the water deeper into the riverbed. And yet, they were carving out a possibility with those conversations, just as surely as the torrent before them had carved out the gorge.

Rachel realized almost at once what these conversations were doing. They were creating a place where she and Susan could meet across their differences. For they were nothing alike in the faces they presented to the world. They were both over forty, with fully lived lives behind them. Several lives at least, Rachel thought, and no shared experiences, none. Only in their deepest sense of who they were, the women they had become as a result of those lives, and of future dreams, dreams of a daily life they could share with someone, did she begin to understand what was drawing them together.

Trust. Rachel could sense that was the issue for Susan. She had gone slowly, tested the first few steps, as if she sensed there was a place very near the beginning of this journey that was marked "No Turning Back." And so she gave Rachel the most difficult bits of her history, encapsulated but accurate, and watched for Rachel's response.

"If you read my drug history," she began the story for Rachel over dinner in one of the small restaurants near the center of downtown, "the one you have to give when they do an intake at the detox center, if you read that profile without meeting me, you would have gone with the stereotype and assumed I was a black, urban, teen mother." Susan had kept her voice low and dispassionate, but she was watching Rachel's carefully. Rachel had nodded, sipped the after-dinner coffee, keeping her expression calm, accepting, and so Susan went on. "I was an IV drug user at twelve, a heroin addict at thirteen. I was locked up for a year under a PINS petition when I started selling heroin in the schoolyard. It was 1962. I was a little ahead of my time." She had smiled ruefully then and paused. Rachel had known Susan was in recovery, but Susan had been deliberately vague about the details, waving away inquiries by referring to her fifteen years clean and sober.

In her heart, Rachel was surprised, but for many years, as a minister and confidante, she had listened to stories that she hadn't expected to hear. "I don't suppose there was any reason to think the white kids would escape it when heroin started flooding into black neighborhoods...as a...well, probably as a way for the government to counter the Black Power movement," she said quietly.

Susan nodded. "It was about that time, actually," she said, "and it was true that being middle class, white and half-Jewish from college-educated folks didn't protect me the way it was supposed to."

"Were you in prison?" Rachel knew she had to have been. The profile was fairly standard. She hoped the questions would let Susan continue her story.

"Oh, yes. Several times. Never for more than six months. Once for disorderly, twice for possession. I was lucky. I was young and I never got trapped by the feds. The local sheriff, the county prosecutor, really didn't want to lock me up forever." She was trying to be casual, Rachel thought, but the tension showed in her shoulders and hands.

"When was your son born?"

"I got pregnant while I was in the juvenile lockup." Susan's smile was ironic. "I was a stubborn kid. Didn't tell anyone I was pregnant for a long

6

time. Wouldn't give the baby up for adoption." She'd stopped the story there that day, as if saving a layer of her protective shell and hoping she wouldn't need it. Rachel let it drop.

Over dinner another night, a quiet dinner in Susan's small kitchen with a single candle illuminating the late summer-light, she went a step further. Relaxed, holding a warm mug of cinnamon tea, she had told Rachel the hardest part.

"I went back and forth for years. Sometimes I could get away from the drugs and cope with life. I managed to finish college after eight years of trying." She shrugged. "But finally I couldn't pull away from it. I took Jacob back out on the street with me for a while. When my parents found out, they got legal custody of him." She stopped, her knuckles white as she clenched the mug, waiting for Rachel to speak. No doubt — this was the part she seldom shared with anyone.

"That must have been awful for you." Rachel reached across the table, inviting Susan to continue. Susan waited for a moment, then set down her mug and put one warm hand in Rachel's.

"Yes, but the alternatives were probably worse," she admitted finally.

Now, standing on a ledge back away from the roar of the river, Rachel and Susan were silent. The lesbian minister-theologian and the closeted state worker. The child of inherited wealth and the recovering drug addict. They stood a few feet apart, not a casually chosen distance. They were at that pivotal moment that happens only once in any relationship, Rachel thought, when they both knew what could happen, they had both acknowledged the desire, but not in words, and they had both stopped just short of physical intimacy. The erotic tension between them, if it could be translated into some other currency, if it could be measured, if it could be . . .

She watched Susan crumble the dry leaves she had been playing with, sift them between her fingers, letting the flakes float out like the years that had passed in their lives. That was when she said the words, *I want you*. And Rachel had raised her face, looked at Susan and agreed.

What have I done, Rachel asked herself. She had never said her permission out loud like this. Always before the request had been physical, had been intimated rather than spoken, so that retreat would not cost so much. Rachel knew how to answer those silent requests — either by moving away or by returning a kiss, touching her hand to another woman's face, moving her body into an embrace.

"I'm willing," she had said. So much harder to take it back once it was spoken. *I said yes,* her inner voice was astonished and elated at the same time. *Yes, I said, yes I will.*

And then there was a mouth covering her mouth, a tongue touching the edge of her teeth lightly, probing. Rachel felt her heart beating again, not in panic this time, but in anticipation — *thank you, thank you, thank you* — each beat more pronounced. She needed to be touched, touched in her body and in her heart. It was time. Even if it had been hard to say, she was willing. She knew that like she hadn't known anything in years, knew it viscerally, without explanation or apology. She wanted Susan, wanted her body, her touch.

In the last few days Rachel had been able to

8

concentrate on little else, and now she had the permission she wanted, permission to slide her hand up the soft cotton shirt sleeve, feel the firm muscles, the strong shoulders.

Susan shuddered under Rachel's touch and drew her head back from the kiss for a moment, breathing deeply. "You like to kiss." She nibbled up Rachel's cheek to her earlobe. "I'm glad." Their mouths came together again. Rachel's tongue flickered around the edge of Susan's lips, tickling, teasing, then moved deeper into Susan's mouth.

Yes, Rachel remembered, she liked to kiss and to taste and smell. She breathed in, imprinting the scent of Susan's skin the way an animal might, knowing as she inhaled she could never mistake this woman's body for another. Once she knew the scent of her, she would roll over in the dark and know Susan was there without needing to see or even to wake up. For Rachel, it was the beginning of intimacy.

Susan pulled away for a moment. "Let's go back to the cabin."

Rachel laughed. "Yes. We aren't young enough to ignore the cold ground and the stump roots in our backs."

"Young enough or drugged enough," Susan agreed. They walked back up the road, hip to hip, arms around each other, savoring their anticipation.

Rachel could barely watch her footing. Her gaze kept wandering to Susan's face, her cheek. She was forty-seven years old and had thought that this passion for another woman's body might not happen to her again. She had grown too cautious, learned too well the lessons taught by broken trust, by thwarted desire, by indifference and inability. If she had

9

learned one thing for her maturity, she told friends, it was how to take care of herself. Oh, she wouldn't call it self-protection in the negative sense, but she had found intimacy in caring friendships, in lifelong commitments that weren't sexual partnerships. Her role in the community she had just left, her role as a minister or spiritual leader, call it what you will, was to model a different way of being whole. She believed that and could hear the voices in her head, warning, cautioning, yet she ignored them.

In the warm cabin, they stood awkwardly for a moment. Then Rachel felt Susan pull away from her slightly and take her hand. She let herself be led into the bedroom.

Lying side by side, Rachel caressed the fabric over the swell of Susan's breasts and then found her already erect nipples. Susan's breathing came shorter, shallower. "Yes," she whispered in Rachel's ear, "yes, yes, yes."

She slipped her hands under Rachel's shirt, then changed her mind, raised herself from the bed, and began to tug Rachel's jeans down over her hips.

Susan was finished with the preliminaries, Rachel realized, smiling to herself. And this was what she wanted, a lover who would take the lead, a lover who knew what she wanted and wasn't afraid to go after it. She moved her body slightly, but let Susan pull her jeans and underpants off, luxuriating in the lingering touch of fingers on her thighs, the brush of a hand across her pubic hair. Susan knelt, one knee between Rachel's bare open thighs, and began to unbutton her own shirt.

Rachel let herself see their bodies as though she were a spectator. Her body had always been a friend to her, easy to take care of, comfortable in its average size and average weight. If she exercised it and fed it moderately, she never had to think much about her body. Since she'd turned forty, she watched with interest as her body aged — deepening wrinkles around her eyes and mouth, a slightly spreading waistline, the gray in her hair more than a highlight. Rachel had never thought of herself as beautiful, and this aging was more interesting to her than problematic. But now, seeing herself and Susan, frozen for a moment as if in an erotic vignette, Rachel believed herself beautiful. The curve of her belly was smooth under Susan's hand and the soft fold of her shirt fell open to show another curve. Susan slowly slid her shirt off her shoulders and invited Rachel to look, her hands pausing for the moment. Her breasts were small, emphasized by the well developed muscles in her chest and shoulders. Susan was gorgeous, she thought, simply gorgeous. Who was this dark, curly-headed woman kneeling so deliberately between Rachel's open, naked legs? Rachel had said she was willing, and now she knew there was more to say.

"I want *you*." She raised herself slightly and gripped Susan's shoulders, pulling her down toward her. "I want you. I want you." And then Susan's weight was full on her chest and her face was next to Rachel's, and Rachel was no longer a spectator.

CHAPTER TWO

Susan leaned back against the seat of the Toyota and tried to stretch. The two-and-a-half hour drive to Albany, down from the mountains with Rachel, had flown. They had floated, it seemed, down the Northway through the foothills, past the lakes to the north of Albany. She dropped Rachel off in front of the fashionable, narrow townhouse where she was staying, only a couple of blocks from the Capitol building itself. Now, on the short drive through downtown to her own house, Susan had to fight to keep her eyes open. She gunned the car through a yellow light, using her peripheral vision to watch for cops. Only a few more blocks to her house. How could traffic be this bad on a late Monday morning? God, she wanted a cup of coffee, she thought as she forced herself to concentrate on the road.

Yeah, right, coffee, her interior voice chided her. Maybe a little sleep this weekend would have helped too. And beneath the exhaustion, Susan couldn't stop smiling. How could she walk back into her office like this? She'd told them she'd be in after lunch so she wouldn't be docked another vacation day. A quick stop at her house to put on work clothes, corporate drag as she called it, then she was due at work. With the scent of Rachel on her hands. "Don't you want to wash?" Rachel asked sleepily as they had prepared to leave the cabin that morning. "I can heat some water." No, she hadn't. Leaving was hard enough. She wanted to keep Rachel with her as long as she could.

Susan knew she would never have dared this a year or two ago, dared to court a woman like Rachel, a woman who was so sure of who she was in her world, so "out" as a lesbian to the public, a woman whose entire experience was foreign to Susan. Except for this. The physical connection.

Remembering Rachel's fingers exploring her body, moving from her nipples up to her face and then ranging through the soft curly dark hair, then back to her breasts, Susan wondered how she ever doubted the connection. Had it really taken her eight weeks to say to this woman: I want you. Now, she was going further, taking the risk she hadn't allowed herself in years, because she suspected she could hold nothing back from Rachel. She wanted to hold

13

nothing back from Rachel. She wanted it all on the table, right out in the open. Even her terror.

She pulled the car into a parking place at the Quik Market around the corner from her house. She swung out of the car and strode across the parking lot, oblivious to her surroundings. Two businessmen stopped prying the lids off of their coffee cups as she walked by, both following her movements for a moment, then returning to the coffee. Susan knew she was attractive, knew that when she chose to dress to impress, she could be very effective. It had been a part of her mother's training in her earlier life that she'd rejected but never forgotten, and she made good use of it in her work. This morning, dressed in blue jeans and a cotton shirt, comfortable as she walked, Susan felt more like a college girl than a government executive or a forty-four-year-old grandmother. Young. Scared. Vulnerable. And very much in love.

Back in the car, Susan gave a deep sigh, took a gulp of the bitter black coffee and wished desperately for a cigarette. Funny. When she was tired, she wanted the cigarette more than she wanted the coffee, and it had been six years since she quit smoking. Some things never change, she thought ruefully.

But Rachel, now that was a change. She started the car and the voices in her head picked up where they had left off.

You can't do this, Susan, you can't carry it off. That voice came through first, and since it was one Susan had known since her childhood, she let it play through. Her mother's voice had long since ceased to haunt Susan, but — like the instinctual craving for a cigarette — it was still there, still a part of the interior landscape. Originally she'd thought therapy would make the voices go away, but it didn't; it only changed her responses to them, and that was enough to give Susan the room she needed to live her life differently.

Too late for the voices that said she couldn't do it, Susan thought ruefully. *I've done it. I said yes. And not in rebellion this time, not like when I was a kid, not just because I always have to push against the voices that say no. This time is different. I've done it out of desire, because I want her.* Susan felt as though she'd swung out over the chasm on a grapevine and let go just as her feet touched ground on the other side.

"I'm not interested in a casual affair," she'd said to Rachel as they stood in the cabin's tiny kitchen trying to fix dinner on the second night of their weekend. Trying. Every touch, every gesture was an invitation to continue making love. She'd said it seriously enough, and then the ludicrous tone of it struck them both and they began to giggle. Nothing they were doing was casual. The intensity of their attraction to each other, the bond that had been forming for weeks earlier in their conversations, Rachel's softly breathed "I love you" caressing Susan's ear early that morning — nothing about this was casual.

Susan drew a deep shaky breath as she remembered Rachel's voice. That strong, calm, vibrant voice was part of what had taken Susan to a new place and made her pulse race with tension as she thought about the future.

You can't do this, you can't live this way had kept

Susan closeted all during her career rise through the state system. Today she was close to the top, closer than she'd ever dreamed back in 1980 when she decided to give it a shot and said yes to a job as an education aide when the New York State Divisions of Alcoholism and Substance Abuse had been joined into a single agency. Today, she was a deputy commissioner with a staff, a budget that grew every year as she fought with the legislature and the governor to make them understand how essential the education component was to stopping alcohol and substance abuse. For years she'd spent a lot of time in high schools, talking with youngsters about their experiences, traveling all over New York State from her office in Albany, and now her staff continued that work. Being out as a lesbian had not been even a vague possibility during those early years, and Susan hadn't minded. At first.

"If we spend a lot of time together, well, it would change things for you." Rachel's voice was tentative, suggestive.

"I'm ready for that." Susan knew what she meant and leaped over the boundaries to the center of the issue. "I've wanted to be more out in the community and at work for a couple of years now. I'm ready to deal with that. I could hardly expect you to pretend to be someone else. You'd have to change your name. You're too well known as a lesbian minister and theologian." Susan had swallowed her hesitation as she spoke. She had told Rachel it didn't matter to her, this very Christian association. But in her heart, she wasn't sure yet how she felt about it. Even so, she'd told Rachel, "That's the work you do, the new book you'd be working on. I wouldn't change any of that."

Nearly overwhelmed, she sat for a moment in her own driveway, bending over the steering wheel in fierce concentration, and felt the enormity of what she'd committed herself to. It wasn't just the religion thing. Susan felt she and Rachel could work that out — hadn't they talked easily about almost anything? But being out? Now there was a challenge. A new challenge. Could she keep her career and have her life out in the open? That was the question, and Susan wouldn't know the answer until she had risked it all. No easy preparation for this one, no dry run; she could see the grapevine swinging back and forth over the abyss, just out of her reach.

On the other hand — she drew a deep breath and began to talk back to the voices — on the other hand there is nothing I wouldn't trade for some time with this woman. I don't know why, but it's that simple. Years of my life, career, reputation, friends. Why? How do I know it this clearly this soon? Susan shrugged. Knowing why wasn't that important to her. But she did know it. In her heart she was quite sure of it.

She kept her assertive, nearly pugnacious stance as she heaved her suitcase out of the car trunk and climbed the front porch stairs to her house, a tiny bungalow with a huge backyard in a working-class Italian neighborhood. She had lived here for eight years, bought the house as soon as she felt secure in her job, and now it was so familiar to her she scarcely saw her own surroundings.

She was tired, her muscles complained a bit and

she felt slightly stunned to be back in her own life. The key turned easily in the lock, and she swung open the door, her mind still back in the cabin she and Rachel had shared, the bed they had shared. Never mind. A quick shower and then she'd be at work for several hours. That ought to acclimate her. Nothing like a dose of workplace reality to let you know your vacation is over.

Susan felt a vague discomfort settle down on her as she looked around her bedroom. She sniffed. It didn't smell like her space. What was it? Probably she'd just gotten used to the smell and feel of the woodsy Adirondack air, the musty, nearly mildewed odor of the old furniture.

Warmed by the shower, Susan pulled a silk shirt and skirt out of her closet and wandered around her bedroom, choosing earrings and a necklace to go with it. Half dressed, she called the office to check in and let her staff know she was on her way.

"Everything holding up after the weekend?" She could picture Martin stretched across his chair, his long legs looking for more space than ever existed under a government-issue desk.

"Well, that's not exactly how I'd put it." His voice came back at her slowly, and all of Susan's warning lights came on.

Oh, shit, she thought warily. She didn't want to have to deal with trouble today. "So what's up, Martin. Fill me in quick."

"You've been out of town, haven't you?" He knew she was. What was this about? "I think you'd better come into the office. We've got a big one here to deal with, and I don't want to talk about it on the phone."

"Martin, for God's sake..." She started to protest, then realized he was telling her something about the telephones. Tapped? This was ludicrous. What could be going on? "I'll be there in half an hour," she said abruptly and hung up.

Her mind raced through the possibilities, but only one clue struck her. You've been out of town, Martin said. She slipped into her heels, grabbed her briefcase and purse and ran down the stairs. She'd get the local paper at the drugstore on her way in. Why hadn't she thought to pick one up at the Quik Market? Something must have happened here that she'd missed while she was up in the woods.

Adrenalin carried her out the front door and back to the Quik Market where she grabbed the next to last paper on the shelf. Susan held her body rigid as she read the headlines. DRUG BUST OF HIGHEST DASA PERSONNEL. Several high administrators, perhaps implicating even the Commissioner of the Department of Alcohol and Substance Abuse. Some of his staff were named in the latest series of indictments from the grand jury. Five high-placed officials named for conspiracy, two of those with possession with the intent to distribute, and nineteen for possession.

Oh, shit. Susan took a deep breath. No wonder Martin didn't know what to say to her on the phone. Who were they talking about? Selling? She knew some who might have been using, but selling? What evidence could there have been? She felt safe herself, and yet strangely threatened. She hadn't used drugs for more than fifteen years. Socially, she'd come nowhere near places where she might have known or suspected illegal drugs were being sold. Probably, she told herself, she was responding to the generalized threat — the entire structure of DASA was at risk. But beyond that, there was always the "what if?" And her history made her vulnerable at the same time her revulsion from drugs made her safe. What was to stop people from assuming she'd "slipped" or gone back to that life?

She parked the car in the underground lot and walked up the hill toward her office, holding the newspaper and her briefcase tight up against her chest like a shield. In the entryway, deserted just after lunch hour, Susan turned away from the escalator and went toward a bank of phone booths in a secluded corner. She shoved a quarter in impatiently and dialed quickly from memory.

"Debora Feldman, please," she said urgently to the secretary who announced that she'd reached Feldman, O'Grady and Clark. "It's Susan Myers calling." She had a desperate need to touch base with her best friend. They usually spoke every day, in the normal course of things. She longed for Debora's good sense to help her process this turn of events.

"Hi, Susan," Debora's answer was almost immediate, as though she'd been waiting for the call. "I'll bet you're not calling to tell me about your weekend in the mountains, are you?"

"Debora. Don't joke about this. What do you know? Who's involved?" Susan took a deep breath, waiting for the scoop.

"Where are you calling from? Have you gone to your office yet?" Debora could be maddening. Why didn't she just tell her what was going on?

"No. I'm at the phonebank in the lobby. Why?"

Debora took a long noisy breath, held it for a

moment, then sighed. "Susan, go up to your office. If there's a message from the D.A.'s office, call them and then call me." She ignored Susan's half-uttered protest. "If there's no message, that's good. Then call me anyway and tell me about your weekend, okay?"

"Why would I have a message from the D.A.'s office? Why do I get the sense you're not telling me something? Are you my best friend or what?" She could hear the anger rising, inadvertently, in her voice.

"Yeah, I'm your best friend, and I may be close to being your best lawyer, too. Go find out, Susan. Damn it, I can't be sure," she said angrily, "but I got some really bad vibes when I tried to get some info this morning."

Susan was silent for a moment. "Okay," she said finally, her heart sinking. A moment ago she had been worried about her reputation as a manager — that people on her staff might be involved in this and that she should have known, should have dealt with the problem. Now Debora was suggesting something else, something that Susan had been fighting not to let into her consciousness. It was too much to comprehend all at once.

"Susie?" Debora sounded gentle. No one else was allowed to call her by a nickname.

"Yeah?" Susan's voice was choked.

"So, was it a good weekend?"

"It was fabulous." She smiled in spite of her anxiety. Remembering the weekend sent her emotions back up the other side of the pendulum swing.

"Hold on to that. And call me."

CHAPTER THREE

"So, Rachel! I haven't heard from you for days. Where have you been? Why haven't you kept me up to date? Something must have come of this, right? All the time you've been spending with her? It's more than conversation, right?"

"Right, Carmen." Rachel instinctively pulled back from the phone as Carmen's voice boomed across the wire from Boston. She had just walked into her own rooms in Richard's house when the phone began to shrill. The sudden transition from Susan's whispered farewell jarred her.

"So?" Carmen changed her inflection, sensing Rachel's mood. "I want to hear all about it, sweetie. Give me all the details. You like her?"

Glad that Carmen had finally given her something specific she could answer, Rachel laughed. "Yes, I like her. More than like her. She's incredible, I mean, this is *major*, Car."

"It must be." Carmen was laughing at her now. "Three cliches and one 'oh, wow' and you didn't even pause to take a breath. It *must* be love."

"I think it is, actually," Rachel acknowledged, letting the conversation slide into serious. "I miss you, Carmen. I want to see your face when I talk with you."

"Then drive on over. It's only three hours. Come and have lunch tomorrow."

"Maybe." Rachel hesitated.

Going to Boston ought to be easy. Richard didn't have any doctor's appointments tomorrow. When she'd agreed to come and live with him this year, he'd been quiet about her keeping her own life. "You're coming here on sabbatical," he insisted. "You've got a book to write, and you have your own life. I'm sick. Sometimes at night I'm afraid, and I want someone in the house, someone I can talk to. But you won't be my nurse, do you understand? I have a buddy who helps me, a home health aide, lots of friends . . ." His voice had gone still, and it was then that Rachel thought she might do it, go and live in Richard's house, away from the tumult of her own life in Provincetown, go and be in a place where she could rest as well as write. "But the house," Richard found his voice again, "the house is so large for one person. And there is so much of Colin here."

23

Colin. Rachel had loved him, too. Richard and Colin were family, part of the intensely connected network of gay and lesbian religious workers. Colin had been an Episcopal priest who died from AIDS last year. Richard, a church musician first and then a social worker for Catholic Family Services, seemed to have lost his will to fight for his own life.

Albany, Rachel thought, a city so close to Saratoga and the life she left behind. She didn't promise immediately, but inside she'd already said yes to the loneliness in Richard's voice.

"Why maybe?" Carmen heard Rachel's hesitation and pushed. "Get on over here. I want to hear how the book is coming, too."

"Oh, God, Carmen, it's not coming," Rachel moaned. "What seemed like good ideas when I was thinking about them, well, they just won't work on the page. It's impossible. Why did I ever think I could write a book?"

"Rachel, you've only been in Albany for eight weeks, and from the way it sounds, most of your time has been with this Susan, not working on a book. Give yourself some space, you hear? Don't push so hard. Let it come natural. You've done lots of writing, good writing."

"Yes, I'll come have lunch tomorrow," Rachel said suddenly. "I need to see you. Tell you about Susan, too."

"What about Susan? What aren't you telling me? Didn't you tell her you've got money? That you aren't ashamed of it?"

"I told her that," Rachel laughed. "And we stayed at my mother's cabin up at Keene Valley. Tomorrow," she interrupted Carmen's expected response. "Tomorrow you'll get the whole story." And Carmen had to be satisfied with that.

Rachel smiled as she hung up the phone. She and Carmen had been seminary students together fifteen years earlier, when there were only one or two women in each class, and after a rocky start had managed to become allies first, then friends. Carmen was black, married, five years older than Rachel and widowed in her first year at seminary. She had been born in rural Alabama and raised by parents who would never forget the Depression. Rachel had been thirty-two, unsure of her sexuality and at a loss for something significant to do with her life after too many years of upperclass leisure in her family home in Saratoga. She was the only child and, when her mother was diagnosed with lung cancer just before Rachel's graduation from college, it had seemed that she ought to go home, help out. Three weeks before her mother's death, five years later, her father had a stroke, the first in a long series, and he never left the house again.

Rachel had been intrigued by Carmen, and over and over they had been thrown together by their exclusion from the men's club. Giving and taking advice had become a habit, one they'd clung to as their careers took them apart and brought them together again many times. Recently called to a large urban Methodist church in Boston, Carmen had left the South gladly, permanently, she insisted, and she and Rachel resumed the easy habit of being nearly neighbors.

When Rachel applied for her leave of absence, she knew Carmen would approve. For months, Carmen had been telling her to take a break, not to let the exhaustion and depression of working with the AIDS Project in Provincetown turn into burnout. "Don't let them beat you down," Carmen fumed. "Running between that fancy board of directors and people so down you can't pry them up. That's not the way to do it and you know that. Aren't you the one who wrote the book about folks getting empowered and taking on life for themselves?" Carmen was right, Rachel knew that in her bones. It just took her a while to act on what she knew.

Rachel was pensive as her thoughts went from the guilt of leaving her work in Provincetown to Susan. Three days. She and Susan had been lovers for three days. For three days they had been together every minute, away for a long weekend in a remote cabin in the Adirondacks. They spent much of that time making love, lying together in bed, touching at every possible place, talking. And talking. Rachel felt like talking to Susan now and laughed at herself a little. Let the woman alone, for goodness' sake. She's only gotten into work and already you need to talk with her.

Rachel wandered around her room, putting away her backpack, tossing dirty clothes in the direction of her laundry basket. Then she went down the hall to the office. It had been Colin's workplace, and Richard had urged her to make it her own. The computer, the desk and file cabinets stood just as they had when Colin used them, but Richard and some friends had cleared out Colin's papers and made the place ready for Rachel and her new book. She began sorting through the mail that had arrived in her two-day absence and finally noticed her stomach growling angrily. It had been too many hours since her last meal. She wandered downstairs to fix herself some lunch.

The whir of the blender in the kitchen told her that Richard had the same idea. "Gourmet liquid protein," he said cheerfully as she came through the door. "Want some?"

"I think I'll try something gross like a toasted bagel." She touched his shoulder gently as she walked by on her way to the refrigerator. "Thanks, anyway."

When the blender stopped roaring again, Richard held the glass canister up to the light to check for lumps, then poured the pale orange mixture into his glass. With a smile Rachel watched his performance, concealing the twinge of grief as she saw how thin his hand seemed, how translucent the skin. They were the same height and had once been about the same weight, stocky but not fat. Their hair, ten years ago, had been the same sandy brown and today they had grayed in about the same proportion, and they had a similar gentle, serious demeanor. People meeting them for the first time often asked if they were brother and sister, which pleased her. She would have liked a brother, she told Richard often, and he would do just fine as her brother in this life.

Catching her meditative look, he turned toward her, lifting his glass in a mock toast. "You look a little stunned," he observed wryly. "May I take it that means we should celebrate?" He held one hand up. "You have a right to remain silent and all that. Or a right to throw that bagel at me." Head to one side, he waited for Rachel's response.

Richard would never fall in love again, Rachel knew that. He didn't have enough time and he wasn't one to do things by halves. She also knew he would be genuinely glad for her. "I think it's a celebration," she said softly, bending forward to kiss his cheek. "And yes, I guess I am a little stunned and a little scared."

He nodded, glancing away. "Give me that bagel. You'll cut your hand off, slicing it that way." He took the knife away from Rachel, who had been cutting bagels for nearly forty years by holding them in one hand and cutting toward her palm with the knife.

Rachel appreciated his reticence. Richard didn't know everything about her family, but he'd known about the painful years she'd cared for her parents during long illnesses. They both knew when she said yes to staying with Richard that she would be living through an old scenario, but living through it differently this time, they promised one another.

"I think I'd better look at my notes for this book," Rachel's bagel was history and the empty afternoon was staring at her. "I told Carmen I'd drive over to Boston tomorrow for a consultation."

"Ah ha. Better bone up. Carmen will do sixty questions. Unless you can distract her with news about Susan."

Rachel sat at her desk and stared at some of the correspondence that had piled up. She tried, she really did try to look at her notes for the book she was writing, but images of Susan interrupted her thoughts.

For a moment she was back in her mother's kitchen in the cabin — their second day. She'd awakened alone in the bedroom and smelled coffee brewing, then pulled on an old robe and walked into the kitchen. Susan was standing by the sink, looking out the window. Nothing, thought Rachel, would ever be etched as clearly in her memory as the look on Susan's face as she moved toward her, as the feel of Susan's hands as she pushed her gently backwards until Rachel stood leaning against the pantry door. And then Susan went down on her. There. In Rachel's mother's kitchen with the red plastic clock ticking loudly. Susan kneeling. Pushing Rachel's knees apart slightly. Eyes closed, Rachel could feel Susan's fingers open her, Susan's warm tongue move against her clit, up, down again. Rachel had come in about thirty seconds. She was surprised it took her that long.

Shaking her head to clear the memory, returning reluctantly to the present, Rachel looked at her watch. Nearly three p.m. Susan would have been back at work for a couple of hours. Rachel wondered if Susan was as exhausted as she was after their three days together. It had been glorious, but it also let her know she wasn't twenty anymore or even thirty — sleepless nights just hadn't taken that much of a toll in those days.

Giving in to impulse — the urge that had been sitting on her shoulder all during her talk with Richard, hovering around the edges of her unanswered letters — Rachel picked up the phone and dialed the private number Susan had given her. "You'll usually get me in person," Susan said. "I don't let many people have this number. But you shouldn't have to go through my secretary."

The phone clicked, rang once, and then a crisply efficient voice Rachel didn't recognize said, "Deputy Commissioner Myers' office. How may I help you?"

"I'd like to speak to Susan Myers, please," Rachel said softly, chagrined that she had to ask.

"I'm sorry, she isn't available today. If you'll leave a number, I'm sure Ms. Myers will get back to you."

Rachel paused for a moment, not sure whether to leave her name or not. This voice sounded so official, so unlike the Susan who had shared Rachel's bed, whose scent still lingered on Rachel's hands.

"Thanks, I'll try later," she said and hung up the phone. Probably she was in a meeting, Rachel thought. Never mind. She'd call her later, tonight after she'd fixed some dinner. Watched the news. She needed to hear Susan's voice again.

CHAPTER FOUR

Susan went down the long hall from the elevators to her office with her head tucked down, looking neither right nor left. She felt besieged, although she met no one. The panic in her chest was rising to her throat. What had a few moments before been an unpleasant threat to her competence as a manager suddenly had the potential to blow up in her face. Voices coming from the nearby offices were muted, unnaturally low, she thought, as she walked the final stretch to her office.

Martin, her secretary, met her at the door, saw

her newspaper with the glaring headlines and stepped back.

Susan stopped, afraid to ask, but he told her. "The D.A.'s office left a message for you to call."

"Shit." She let a long breath out, unaware she'd been holding on to it, and stared at him.

He nodded.

"Who else got the message?" she asked, fighting the impulse to scream, to run, to strike out at Martin, the bearer of terrible news.

"John. Eduardo. Tom. So far. No one but me knows you've gotten a message too. And I don't know who got the fifth message. John and Tom have already called and been invited to turn themselves in at three p.m. Instead of being hauled in by the cops, you know?" Only the edge of sarcasm in his voice let Susan know how upset he was.

"Three p.m.?" She could barely take this in. Something was wrong, very wrong. She'd been a good citizen for years. Turn herself in? For what? Where had this nightmare started? She wondered if she were still asleep, fighting her way through one of those interminable dreams about being back in prison. She hadn't dreamed like that in years, though. And here was Martin, standing in front of her, his wire-rim glasses sliding down his nose. Alive. No dream.

"Yeah," he was saying, "three p.m., just in time for prime news coverage. Somebody's up for re-election. You can count on at least one speech about drug dealers and betraying the public trust." He ran his fingers through his hair. His edges must really be fraying, Susan thought. Martin paid far more for his hair styling than she did. But he was only twenty-eight, and she had worked closely enough with him in the year and a half he'd been her secretary to know he tried hard for an air of quiet, competent maturity. Left to himself, she'd bet Debora once, he'd probably rather do full-blown hysteria.

Susan looked at him and forced her attention back to his announcement. "Martin, three o'clock is in one hour and thirty minutes," she said inanely.

He nodded as though she had made an important point, took her briefcase from her and led her through his office into her own. "I'm sorry, Susan." He deepened his voice with responsibility. "I'm sorry to have to break it to you like this. I don't know what's going on, but it's big and it's messy. They may have implicated the Commissioner himself, but if so, apparently they don't have enough on him yet to get a warrant. This may all be fishing. None of my sources knows."

Susan looked up sharply. "None of them?" She wasn't joking, but it had been a joke between them when Martin first came to work for the division.

Even then, his grapevine resembled Susan's Grandma Yetta's — and she had been head yenta in her crumbling Bronx neighborhood, her kitchen window facing both entrances to the elevated subway and a small park. If Yetta didn't know about it, it probably hadn't happened yet. Martin's kitchen window looked out over his walled private garden and reflected nothing more than a compulsively neat cobblestone walk and raised beds of perennials. His information depended more on knowing every gay professional working for state or city government and every recovering alcoholic within a thirty-mile radius. Martin was a natural schmooz. Much more than Yetta, Susan knew. Yetta wanted information because it was power and safety. Martin wanted people to like him, and he really wanted to know what made them tick. He usually found out. Susan was never sure if he knew about the power and safety factor in having lots of information, or whether those were just happenstance byproducts for him.

"It's a mistake, Martin, it has to be. There can't be a shred of evidence. I haven't been near the stuff, and I avoid users like I used to avoid my mother's meatloaf on Tuesdays. Any excuse would do." She was getting side-tracked.

Martin shrugged. "I hope you're right. There's only one way to know." He gestured toward the phone.

She wasn't right. An officially polite voice told her she had been named in a grand jury indictment. Conspiracy. There was a warrant with her name on it. It would be helpful if she would appear at 3 p.m. at the County Courthouse. Judge Scarlatti would be sitting. Susan stifled a groan. Scarlatti was the only judge still working in the state who she'd seen before — sixteen years ago when she'd clocked her last D.W.I.

Susan put the receiver down and stared at it. She was aware of Martin on the other side of her desk, watching her sympathetically. "I'll be leaving at two-thirty. Will you walk over with me?" Her voice was carefully controlled.

"Of course," he nodded briskly, as though she had asked him to bring in the mail, and went into his own office, closing her door behind him.

Susan sat quietly at her desk. Debora. She said she would call Debora. "I've been invited to turn myself in at three o'clock."

"Oh, shit, do you —"

"No," Susan interrupted. "I have no idea. This is so far out of the realm of what I would have thought was possible yesterday that I still can't really believe it. And that's the truth."

"Okay," Debora said slowly. "Maybe it is a mistake. But it's a weird kind of mistake."

The uncertainty in Debora's voice unnerved her. It was at least as bad as Martin's hushed, concerned attitude. Debora was not an uncertain person. Caution was not her middle name, and Susan heard the hesitation, mirroring her own fear.

But Debora recovered her authority quickly. "I'll be at the court. Meet me on the corner before you go in. I'll handle the press. Don't say a word until you tell the judge you're not guilty. I don't think bail will be a problem. It's not like they can argue that you're a risk to the community. We'll get own recognizance and take it from there."

The time she'd just spent with Rachel seemed light-years away. Her hand moved toward the phone, responding to a deep urgent need. She wanted to hear Rachel's voice, to know that she hadn't imagined the last few weeks, particularly the last few days. But what would she say? How could she explain what was happening? She didn't *know* what was happening.

She sat at her desk and fought a despair she hadn't felt since her first days off drugs, days when it seemed as though she had ruined her life and there was no way back. You haven't done anything wrong, she told herself again and again, you haven't done anything wrong. She was beating back waves of old guilt as she sat there, fists clenched, staring at the telephone. Then, there had been a reason for the guilt, at least it seemed that way. She had chosen the drugs, the rush, the sense of power and omniscience. Knowing the reasons for her rebellion hadn't made her choices any less hers.

But now? She'd been enjoying her life. And she thought she'd been living it well. The guilt that rushed in at the first hint of an accusation was old stuff. She wasn't guilty. Susan knew that. She took a deep breath and hoped that Rachel would know it too.

Her mind began racing to find scenarios that would explain the call from the D.A.'s office. She wasn't *that* surprised at a couple of the arrests. Martin had reported some rumors that unnamed people on the street had seen some unnamed exec types from DASA — no one could say from which office — buying drugs down at the pit. It had been on Susan's list of things to find out more about just before her attention focused so single-mindedly on Rachel.

So John and Tom had been trapped by this drug sweep. She could believe that. But Eduardo? He hated the stuff, hated what it was doing to his community. Would he really have been selling? Had she been duped by him? She didn't think so, but she couldn't be sure. And then she realized that was probably what everyone in her office would be thinking about her, wondering when her slip started, how long it had been going on. Shaking their heads silently, as they talked about all of her trips out of town for long weekends in the past few months. Trips with Rachel.

Susan felt her cheeks start to flame. It wasn't

about guilt, she realized then, it was about her privacy. The thought that anyone might know about Rachel, the part of her life that felt most private, the part she would want to protect against prying eyes. That was her problem with being out, she realized, with being known publicly as a lesbian, specifically as Rachel's lover. The prying eyes. The judgments of people who didn't, couldn't know her. Her life had been exposed to public scrutiny once — when a judge had examined her life and decided she was unfit to raise her own son. Whatever she might think about the decision today, she had never forgiven her parents or the court for exposing her like that. She'd talked about it for months, years, in therapy, after she'd gotten sober, but her only reconciliation had been a vow. "I'm never going to read about myself in the newspaper again," she told her therapist, who had smiled and asked, "Never?"

She'd stayed closeted on her job but allowed herself more freedom in the gay community, starting to go to lesbian events and concerts in her own town now and then, rather than only when she was on vacation. Even that hadn't been easy. Once she'd seen a coworker at a Holly Near concert who thought she could make some assumptions about Susan's presence there. She was a woman Susan liked, someone she worked with fairly easily, but she'd been uncomfortable seeing her out of the office, more uncomfortable the next morning in the office when the woman had invited her to a weekend party. "Bring a friend," she'd urged Susan, "you know, a guy friend, a girl friend, whatever."

Susan had favored her with a perplexed look that allowed no more assumptions and the relationship withered. It wasn't that her coworker was going to publish the details of Susan's life in the newspaper, she'd protested to Debora. "What? I'm going to take a date someplace where I don't know who I'll see or what they'll think?" There it was again. The privacy thing. Rachel was a public figure. That was all. It wasn't that Susan minded being out, she assured herself, but that people she didn't know would be looking at her life.

Somewhat reassured, Susan reached for the phone again to call Rachel. But then she remembered. Today wasn't about being out. It was about going to court. She put the phone down, opened her desk drawer and put her toothbrush in her purse. She didn't think of herself as a pessimist, but she was nothing if not practical. Then she picked up the phone and pressed intercom for the receptionist's desk. "Terri, Martin and I will be out of the office for the rest of the afternoon. Take my calls," she said quietly, "and tell them I'll be in tomorrow."

She picked up her briefcase, looked once more at the phone, shook her head no and went into Martin's office.

"Let's go," she said. "I want to know what this is about."

An hour later Susan was being handcuffed and led from the courtroom to be fingerprinted, mugshot and processed for the county jail. The original warrant for her arrest had been on conspiracy charges and Debora told her that if it had been only that, they wouldn't have a problem. But a search warrant — issued that morning and carried out just after she'd gone into work — had turned up nearly a kilo of pure cocaine in her house, cut, bagged, and ready to sell. When Judge Scarlatti set her bail at $100,000, Susan slumped in her chair, too stunned to summon anger. "Do not pass go," she muttered to Debora who was sitting beside her, rigid with anger. "Go directly to jail."

"Do you want to post bond?"

"Waste $10,000? Not if we can raise it any other way."

"I'll do what I can," Debora had said through clenched teeth, and then Susan was on her own, trying to maintain her dignity as the past came crashing in on her.

She hadn't been in jail for years, long enough so that she'd actually lost track. But some things were too familiar. She let her hand go limp as her fingers were being pressed into the ink pad and then turned carefully onto a blank card. "Right," said the soft-voiced uniformed boy who held her hand. "Keep it limp. That will help me get it right the first time." I knew that, Susan thought to herself. He didn't have to tell me. "Thanks, Ms. Meyers. You can wash up at the sink over there." He gestured toward the door where a matron was standing, waiting to take her to the next stop on this journey.

Susan realized that she had never before gone to prison stone sober and dressed like an upstanding citizen. In one sense, it was better. She was being treated with a quiet respect she'd never experienced in her drugging years, and that moved her in surprising ways. On the other hand, as the handcuffs were refastened to her wrists, being sober, she reflected, meant noticing everything. "Where was a good black-out when you needed it," she imagined herself commenting wryly to Debora once this all got straightened out. She would not let herself think about Rachel, not yet. Mentally, she felt as though she had two hands and the entire weight of her body leaning against the door which would open into her feelings about Rachel.

CHAPTER FIVE

The river in the gorge, churning and raging around boulders in midstream, pushing up against the steep cliff banks, was in Rachel's mind during that long afternoon. It scared her, this raging torrent. Not in a major way. She wasn't panicked, not yet, Rachel reassured herself. But she had let herself go. She was committed in a fairly serious way. Not just committed, she was in love. She loved falling in love with Susan, but at the same time, she had to remind herself that she *was* the same woman who'd lectured her friends for years about how dangerous it was to lose control, how women lose themselves, their lives, their goals, when they fall in love and merge instantly with another person. All of this had been theoretical, of course, since Rachel herself hadn't been losing too much control during those years.

So even during the most wonderful part of that weekend, Rachel had been aware of the pitfalls, noticed when the fast-rushing stream went around a bend and slowed. She'd whispered "I love you" in Susan's ear as they woke together the third morning, and then asked herself what the hell she thought she was doing, saying that to somebody she barely knew.

Her hand still on the phone after learning that Susan was not in her office, Rachel wondered if she ought to slow down, move toward this relationship a little more cautiously. Then she pushed the question away.

Irritated with herself, she yanked her jogging shoes out of the closet, changed to running shorts, and headed out to run a few laps around the lake in the park. She walked up the hill toward the park, past the rows of renovated town houses with ornate wood decorations under the eaves of the roofs. At the edge of the lake, she sniffed the damp autumn air, stretched her legs quickly and began a slow jog.

"Yes," she had assured Carmen earlier that same day, "I told her where I came from, that my mother drank." But what else, the voices asked, what else did you tell her? What else, indeed? Her running shoes made sucking noises in the mud, frightening three ducks pecking for crumbs at the water's edge. They took flight, squawking angrily.

"Right," Rachel muttered, glowering at the ducks, angry herself. "So sue me." She hadn't told Susan that they never talked to one another about anything, that they never told anyone outside the family about themselves, that she was taught to keep secrets, not to reveal herself. "But I've worked on that," she said to the ducks as she passed them again. And she had. Her pace picked up with her spirits and she did a sprint on the final leg of her last lap.

Rachel walked back toward her home, pleased with the run, wondering what she should have for dinner, wondering when she would talk to Susan again. She puttered happily around Richard's kitchen, finding what she needed for an omelet. She took his shining omelet pan down from the hook where it hung from an open rafter and admired the thing. She couldn't imagine ever buying a pan for something so specialized, but she'd be glad to use it. The small television was on and she caught bits and pieces of the end of a talk show as she chopped an onion. She heard the local news lead-in, something about a big drug bust that implicated state workers, and made a face. But when she heard "Department of Alcohol and Substance Abuse," she moved toward the television, riveted.

"A county drug investigation culminated today after nearly a year. Five warrants were issued this morning for top DASA officials," the newscaster intoned gravely, "and nineteen other warrants were served on lower-level state workers. Named in the warrants on suspicion . . ." Rachel hardly heard the names as a picture of the indicted flashed on the screen and she caught a glimpse of Susan, just a fleeting glimpse of her face as she went into the courthouse walking next to a petite, determined-looking red-haired woman. The newscast was continuing, making it clear that Deputy Commissioner Susan Meyers was one of the accused. She had a history of previous arrests for drug related problems.

Without thinking, Rachel leaned over and turned off the stove top under the omelet pan, and when the news coverage of the arrests was finished, she turned off the television, her hand shaking only a little as she pulled it back to her side.

As a young woman, Rachel couldn't tolerate silence. She played the radio, the television, any kind of music or chatter, day and night in her space, anything at all to keep away the sound of her own thoughts. And the voices of others as they came into her thoughts. It took years before Rachel understood why she'd had such trouble living in silence — it was that she never experienced silence as an absence. For Rachel, the absence of external noise was only a door, the other side of which was the roar of her own thoughts. And so she had been terrified and covered it with noise, draped a blanket of sound over the open door of silence.

Now she stood in the quiet kitchen and willed herself to recall Susan's face as she had kissed her goodbye earlier in the day. When she did that, there was no doubt. None. She knew Susan had not lied to her.

When Richard came through the door a half-hour later, Rachel was still standing in the darkened kitchen facing the silent television screen.

He stopped. "Rachel," he said softly. "Rachel?"

She raised her head and turned to look at him. He went to her and put his arms around her from behind. "What?" he asked. "What's happening, Sis?"

And she told him.

"That's insane." He was indignant at once. "That's totally insane. I barely know the woman and I know that much. Have you talked to anyone? What's going on? Who has she gone up against? There has to be something else going on here, Rachel. You do see how stupid this is, don't you?" He looked at her face and she nodded, agreeing with him.

Rachel knew that Richard's loyalty to his friends had never been blind — he always had an excellent sense of reality, always knew an individual's limitations without asking. If he thought Susan capable of selling drugs, and if he knew that Rachel loved her, he would have been a friend to Rachel anyway, without deluding himself about Susan's guilt or innocence. "It's a mistake, isn't it?" she asked, energy returning. "I knew it in my head, you know, but I couldn't make my body know it."

Richard nodded yes and was about to speak when the phone rang and it was Debora, Susan's lawyer and friend, with a message for Rachel from Susan. "She didn't call you because she assumed she could come and tell you about it herself." Debora's voice sounded weary and far away. "Neither of us expected this."

"Expected that she would be arrested?" Rachel was confused.

There was a long silence before Debora continued. "No. They executed a search warrant while she was at work this afternoon." Bitterness overtook the fatigue in Debora's voice. "I'm sure they'll say they tried several times earlier this weekend, earlier in the day. Anyway . . ." There was a long sigh.

"Anyway what?" Rachel had no patience.

"They found a kilo of cocaine in her house. I've been dealing with the fallout from that. And arranging bail. And fighting with the local police chief. And —"

"Tell me what I can do," Rachel interrupted the litany. And then she listened.

"Debora's putting together a committee," she told Richard a half-hour later as she hung up. "A few people have already called to tell her they want to help with the bail. Debora went to Susan's house after court — that's why she didn't call here sooner — and said it was a mess after the search. They broke the lock getting in." While she was speaking, Rachel sat down at the table and picked up a forkful of omelet from the plate Richard had placed in front of her. She looked at it with surprise as she was about to put it in her mouth. "Thank you, Richard."

He nodded. "So what's on the agenda? What do we have to do next?"

"Debora's arranged for someone to go over and straighten up her apartment. I can't believe they broke the lock on her door. Can they do that?" She thought Richard was looking at her with amusement.

"They're the police. In this town they do almost anything they want. I had a client picked up for vagrancy. She went out for cigarettes one night and forgot her I.D. By the time a lawyer got her out the next morning, her apartment had been searched. Not legally, of course. But they'd had her keys overnight and must have decided to see what else they could get."

Rachel stared at him. Okay, so she was naive. No, she shook her head to clear it. She knew this stuff, she just didn't want to know it.

"I'm going to meet Debora downtown in about an hour and sign some papers to get the bail process going. Debora's scheduling a meeting at her office first thing in the morning. With some people who know the political scene here. She says she can handle the legal things, but she'll need help figuring out the political angle." She paused for another bite.

"She really doesn't know what's going on then?"

Rachel shrugged wordlessly, and he went on. "It's not like the kind of entrapment where they had hidden cameras and she did something foolish in front of them, right? She had to have been set up. Somebody planted the stuff there in her house, probably while you two were away." Rachel nodded, still eating. "So the only question is who. Want my guess?" he asked, his voice teasing.

"I know, I know. You think it's the police — or the feds. But Debora doesn't see it that way. If she did, it would be simpler for her. But she says they have nothing to gain by this. It isn't like Susan's been a troublemaker these last few years. It just doesn't make sense, Richard, none of it." Her shoulders slumped down again.

"Not yet. But it will, Rach, it will."

"Yeah," she said, "sooner rather than later if I have anything to do with it."

Late that night, alone in her room after everything she could think of to do had been done, Rachel sat in the silence.

She saw an image of herself, sitting on the stone porch steps. It was July, the night before her ninth birthday. Behind her in the porch swing was her father, jovial, outgoing, filled with goodwill, his large solid body swelled with satisfaction as he surveyed his daughter, eager to please, his wife, quiet and compliant at his side, a small smile of surprise around her eyes. They knew him like this once or twice a year. Then he was the father Rachel wanted, the father who noticed her, who played with her, talked with her. That night he told Rachel he would be bringing home something special for her birthday. Eagerly she had gone to bed and waited through a sleepless night. Waited through the next morning and afternoon of her birthday, sitting on the porch swing where he had made the promise, pushing herself back and forth, back and forth, as the scent of drying, newly mown grass steamed around her. All day her mother never came out of her room. Her father didn't come home that night or the next. Not unusual. Business often kept him away for days. The grass dried and the scent began to fade as Rachel sat on the porch swing. When he did come home, he had forgotten it all — the promise, the birthday, her.

If it had only happened once, she could have put it behind her easily, but disappointments were something she'd become accustomed to as a child.

She wandered around the bedroom, dropping her clothes on the rocking chair in a corner by the window. In the bathroom she looked at her face in the mirror. Should I trust her, she asked her reflection, or is Susan on another journey? One that doesn't include me. Because she could not deny the possibility that what had happened to Susan this afternoon might be the most important thing she would ever have to face. Her fear, she realized, was that Susan might have other things to occupy her, more important things than loving Rachel.

She took a deep breath. There was no scent of newly mown grass hovering around her tonight. She would let herself believe in the future. At least until tomorrow.

Susan, sitting on the edge of a hard cot in a single holding cell, was sure during most of the night that morning would never come. And if it did, she wasn't sure she wanted to see it. For the first time in her life she was experiencing pain she had not deliberately courted.

She could never remember exactly when or how she realized her parents were arranging their lives in order to avoid pain, but it was early. Her mother had deliberately separated herself from a drunk and abusive father — and a mother who believed she deserved what God had sent her. No pain, no gain was a saying her mother had never heard. To her, pain was real, a fist in the face. Pain was failure, not being good enough to placate the angry spirit of her father when he drank. And all during her growing up years, Susan's mother had heard from her own mother that God had willed it this way. So she had listened and made sure she arranged her life differently.

When Susan was a child, voices in her parents' house were never raised. Her mother was refined, not too intellectual but nonetheless genteel. And she married wisely enough for what she needed. David, Susan's father, was another only child and a Jew from Boston who was trying desperately to assimilate. He seemed to want exactly what Susan's mother wanted — a calm life, a pain-free life. But he could never walk away from his family the way his wife had. And so Susan's mother got David and she got his mother, Yetta, who was omnipresent, living only three blocks away. Yetta was different and she became Susan's role model all her growing up years.

Not that Yetta had been a rebel in the way that Susan had. But she refused the niceties and refinements of her adopted country. With her thick accent, broad peasant face, love of strong fish and garlic-flavored anything, Yetta was large, noisy and messy. An embarrassment to her son, who loved her in spite of himself and cringed in her presence.

Susan had chosen excitement — drugs and sexual rebellion — as a way of pushing away from her parents. She'd known that for a long time. But tonight, sitting on the narrow jail cell cot, crossing her legs, one over the other, then back, never finding a way to get comfortable, she was finding it hard to justify the old "no pain no gain" shit. Her life had been pretty good recently, she couldn't deny that. She felt relaxed and confident at work. Her relationship with Jacob, her son, had evened out. She liked the man he was becoming and the woman he married. And while she never wanted to be a grandmother, she had two granddaughters of her own, the oldest of whom, Megan, had at age three started to recognize her voice on the phone and giggle into the receiver.

Susan had even begun to think she might deserve Rachel.

Remembering Rachel derailed her other reflections, shoved open the mental door she'd been leaning against earlier in the evening in order to keep thoughts of Rachel away. Images poured in like the water rushing down the Ausable. For a moment Susan felt as if she were the river, being driven by forces she didn't understand, rushing past any known landmark on her way downstream. She imagined Rachel upstream, her hand stretched out, mouth open in surprise, at the speed and ferocity of Susan's journey. Hadn't they just been standing together on the bank? She leapt to her feet in the narrow cell, pacing three strides across, three back, back and forth until dawn.

CHAPTER SIX

Susan accompanied a matron out to the holding area of the county jail at eight o'clock the next morning. Through a double thick glass window, she could see Debora when she came in and greeted the matron. Debora gave Susan a discreet wave, then sat to wait for Susan to be processed out. With a picture but no sound, Susan could only watch helplessly as the matron ignored the lawyer's presence. Clearly, she hadn't had her second cup of coffee yet and nothing was going to get started until she'd personally filled the coffee maker, dug around in the small employees' refrigerator for the coffee, laboriously measured the four tablespoons into the filter, and switched it on. Then she sat down at her desk and began the paperwork.

Susan watched Debora calculate whether to speak or not. Finally she stood up, said something brief to the matron, signaled to Susan that she'd be outside and walked out. An hour later, Susan joined her on the wide old brick stairs.

"I knew if I watched that performance any longer, I'd scream at the woman and then it would be noon before you were processed out."

"Got to you, huh?" Susan gave Debora a careful look.

"Idiots," she snarled. Then looked at Susan apologetically. "I'm a little out of sorts this morning."

"I'm not surprised," Susan agreed. "I am surprised you got me out of there so fast. How the hell did you raise that kind of bail overnight?"

"Susan, in case you hadn't noticed, you have friends in this town. Do you have any idea how many people you've done favors for, helped along the way? What? Did you think you were going to sit there more than the one night it took to get this organized?"

Debora's indignant tone comforted Susan, in an odd way. This was the woman she knew, not the quiet, tentative Debora of yesterday in the court-house.

"Sorry," she placated Debora, although she was not sure what the tirade had been about. "I've been in before." She paused, the admission difficult. "I guess I expected to be there a while."

Debora turned to face Susan in the narrow front

seat. Her thin face was worried and her red curls looked as though she had probably not even run a comb through them for twenty-four hours. There were dark circles under her eyes, and Susan knew she wasn't the only one who hadn't slept the night before.

She said in a soft voice, "Susan, we believe in you. No one who knows you thinks you did this. Okay? You need to hear me and hear me well. No martyr stuff. You aren't in this alone."

Susan nodded mutely. No one, she thought. Did no one include Rachel? But she couldn't ask.

"We're going to a strategy session at my office. We've formed a committee for your defense and for whatever else we may need in the next few weeks. As soon as we get a couple of things straightened out, we think you might want to go to work. Today." Susan looked up, alarmed. "Martin and Jimmy went to your house and cleaned up after the search. They put a new lock on your door —" She nodded as Susan gasped. "And they brought you a change of clothes." She paused for a moment, as if she didn't quite know how to say something. "I called Rachel last night as soon as I got free, but she had already heard the news on television. I'm sorry."

"What are you telling me? She never wants to see me again, right? It was all a terrible mistake, and thanks, but no thanks?" She slumped in her seat, the anger gone out of her.

"Susan," Debora's sharp voice forced its way past her self-pity. "I told you that no one thinks you're guilty. No one. So don't do this victim stuff." She paused, then said more softly, "I'm just telling you I'm sorry I didn't get to tell her myself first. She was upset. She didn't even know my last name, so she couldn't call me herself." Now a smile was pulling at her lips. "I thought you two were practicing intimacy. How could she not know your best friend's last name?"

"It's practically the only thing she doesn't know about you," Susan retaliated. If Debora was joking, it couldn't be all that bad. "So are you going to tell me where I stand with her, or what?"

Debora ignored the question. "Hmm. She did seem to know me pretty well." Then she laughed and started the car. "She's waiting for you at my office."

They pulled into the small parking place in front of Debora's office. Rachel was standing on the porch, looking off across the lawn toward the state capitol. As Susan got out of the car, Rachel turned and began walking toward her. They stood for a moment looking into each other's eyes, then embraced. Susan realized fleetingly that she was hugging a woman on the front lawn of the most radical law partnership in Albany, practically in the whole state, only a hundred paces from the state capitol where state workers were scurrying by on various errands. Still, she hugged her gladly, for a long moment, burying her face in Rachel's familiar smell, wishing she herself did not reek of jailhouse.

"I thought our honeymoon period might last a little longer than three days," Susan admitted ruefully when they pulled apart.

"Right, but it's not as if we're accustomed to smooth rides." She looked into Susan's eyes as if seeking confirmation.

"Not even once? I thought maybe my time had come around." Susan couldn't help the quaver in her voice and cringed at the sound of it. Her mind skipped from thought to thought. She saw a squirrel race down the trunk of a tree and cross the park lawn on a narrow hand railing. She wondered how they could be so fearless and balanced. She thought she should be going up to Debora's office for the meeting she was the subject of. But mostly she wondered if she couldn't just wander off down the hill with Rachel's arm still in hers and take a walk along the river.

"You need to go up to that meeting . . .," Rachel began, as though she could mind-read.

"Aren't you coming?" The fear in Susan's heart began pounding again.

Rachel shook her head no. "I don't know this town or these politics. I couldn't be helpful. But . . ." Susan waited through the pause, curious about what was coming. "But I thought you might want someone to go home with you tonight. After the police search and everything. I thought it might seem strange." She paused again, regrouped. "I didn't mean someone. I meant me. Can I go home with you tonight, Susan?"

"Yes, please," Susan took a deep breath as the squirrel leapt off the railing and raced back up the tree. "I'd really like that. I would really like that."

"Call me when you're ready to leave the office, then." Rachel leaned forward and kissed her. "I'll be home whenever you need me."

Slowly Susan climbed the steps to Debora's office and realized she was relieved to be going into a familiar setting. She was at her best in business meetings. It was one of the management skills she'd developed early in her career, part study, but mostly natural inclination. She felt she did some of her most creative work in meetings. But when she pushed open the door to Feldman, O'Grady, and Clark and saw all of those familiar faces looking at her, she suddenly felt shy.

Debora was at the head of the table, talking intently to her law partner, Amanda Clark. Amanda had joined the partnership after a stint at the ACLU in New York City. On her left were other friends, professional acquaintances really. Mattie, the director of Planned Parenthood. Bill, a professor from the university. Guadalupe, a doctor from the community hospital. Next to them were Martin and his lover Jimmy Bonito, a legislative assistant to a conservative Democratic senator from Syracuse. He'd gotten the post through family connections — his mother had worked for the party machine for decades — but Jimmy was a natural, and Susan expected him to try for the legislature himself in a few years.

She sat down next to Jimmy and looked around the table, acknowledging a couple of greetings. An older man leaned around a tall, square woman who was talking rapidly at him and gave Susan a wink. She couldn't help but grin. Charlie Leitman. Started with bagels and now owned most of the fast food businesses in the upstate area. Could probably buy most of Albany if he wanted it. Large, sloppy dresser, wild-haired and sixty. Susan loved him. Fifteen years ago she had no idea who he was, but he took her aside at her first AA meeting and started talking about how he, as an atheist and a Jew, managed to deal with all the God talk and underlying Christianity of the program. He became her sponsor and later her friend. She'd known him for two years before anyone told her he was wealthy. Which was why Glenda Mathis was sitting next to him, talking so earnestly. Trust Glenda, Susan thought, smiling to herself. Years ago Glenda had been a housewife and mother. Susan had worked briefly for Glenda's husband in Boston until drugs helped her drown in that job, like so many others. Susan had run into her in Albany several years ago and discovered that Glenda was divorced and had a woman lover hidden somewhere in another state. Glenda was a go-getter, energetic, no nonsense when it came to work. She wore a carefully applied layer of makeup and her hair was always freshly permed. She was as hidden in the closet as Susan, but nothing hid her ambition. She owned and ran a very successful financial consulting business and would have loved Charlie Leitman as a client.

Debora broke away from her private conversation as soon as she finished her last instruction to Amanda. Introductions were unnecessary. "The fifth person named in the indictment was arrested last night as she returned to the U.S. from the Bahamas."

Debora ignored Martin's muttered, "What a welcome."

"Jean Currie." She consulted her notes. "Worked in the Commissioner's office. With Eduardo, Susan?"

"Yes. I know her, but not well. Eduardo is the Commissioner's liaison to the education division." She shrugged, indicating to the group at large that she didn't know what to make of the charges against Jean. "I know Eduardo. I can't believe he's involved. But I don't know about her."

"The search warrant for Susan's house," Debora

plowed on with the update, "was issued legally on information supplied by an informer. We don't know who that was at this time."

"Where did they find it?" Susan finally thought to ask. She'd been acting as if it weren't her home they were talking about; the entire scenario seemed unreal.

"Under the radiator cover in your bedroom." Amanda, the civil rights expert, consulted her notes, then nodded confirmation. "You know, under the old wood and tin thing that lifts off. You had some rocks there, they said, but the cover could be lifted off easily without disturbing the rocks."

Rocks. Susan wasn't going to explain that. Not here. She had arranged a small circle of stones in the east window of her bedroom, arranged them by color and texture on the shelf of the radiator. She felt a fury rising in her chest. The violation was beginning to feel real.

"Was there any indication of how long the coke had been there?" This was Jimmy, quietly making notes on a legal pad.

Amanda answered. "I'm checking that too. If it had been there for weeks, heat might have damaged the plastic wrapper. We'd love to prove it was put there after Susan left for the Adirondacks on Thursday."

"That's nonsense," Glenda Mathis waved the thought away with a large hand. "Those old radiators don't always get that hot. Some of them barely warm up." She looked over at Amanda's frown and started to waver. "I'm just saying we'll have to do better than that, don't you think?"

"Debora," Jimmy Bonito asked, "what are the

chances of a police plant? I hate to bring it up, but we all know it's happened before. This looks to be the biggest drug case in years, even if they can't implicate the Commissioner. This thing is still real political. How far do you think they'd go? Can you talk about that here?"

Debora looked around the room. Everyone there had business with or worked for the state at different times. Susan could almost see her assessing the risk of saying aloud what she wanted to say. Debora's law firm performed miracles for people in trouble, but they were always out there on the edge. The last thing they needed was a slander suit.

"I don't have to tell any of you how difficult an issue that is," she began slowly. "I would be the last one to say it couldn't have happened. But I don't see, in this first analysis, that it's too likely. You're right, Jimmy. This is probably the biggest thing the local police have pulled off in years. It's good for them and the D.E.A. And I'm betting they kept it very, very clean. Scorzo," she named the new police chief, "has political ambitions. He wants these indictments to stick. He's not going to mess with evidence. After all, they didn't need to implicate Susan to make it big."

Martin was frowning, Jimmy scribbling madly on his pad. And Susan sat still in her chair, shocked. She hadn't realized how much she'd been counting on Debora and Amanda having some simple answer for all of this, an answer that would just fix it.

Debora was silent for a moment, then she began to speak slowly, reflectively, almost as though she were talking to herself. "What we're up against here is tough. After last night we're not just talking some vague conspiracy-with-intent charge. We're going up against a piece of physical evidence that says Susan possessed drugs with the intent to sell. We could discount, maybe, a witness who said he bought coke from her. We could bring out our character witnesses, and we all know Susan's character and know the kind of case we could mount. We'd scarcely be worried. But I have to tell you, this morning I am worried. Very worried. Even with all the help in this room, we have limited resources. I don't know where that coke came from and it's going to be tough to prove Susan didn't put it there." She shuffled her notes briefly. "We'll look at the lab analysis and look for technicalities, but beyond that . . ."

Debora paused again and looked at Susan, waiting, asking permission. The time for denials was over. Susan nodded at her, her shoulders hunched forward over the table, a protective stance, but her nod said, "Go ahead, do whatever it takes."

"We'll need the usual organizing committees — fundraising, publicity. This is no different than a dozen other projects you've all been involved in. But we need more. We need information. Political information. We need to all be listening, to find out what is really happening, not just what is being reported in the press."

As Susan listened quietly, she realized her whole life, the professional life she loved, was at risk. It was the thing that made her who she was, and she knew she might be about to lose it.

CHAPTER SEVEN

After the early-morning meeting in Debora's office, Susan changed her clothes, gave Debora a quick hug and headed outside. Her office was only three blocks away, across the park and down the hill a bit, but as she contemplated the distance, Susan saw other state workers rushing past Debora's front steps with a purpose and direction that Susan could only envy. Climbing a mountain seemed easy compared to stepping off her safe perch back into the everyday world.

Clutching her briefcase, leaning into a nonexistent

strong wind, Susan made it to the building that housed DASA, then up the elevator to the tenth floor and down the hall to her division. That she'd traveled these halls nearly every workday for ten years only made it harder now. Ten o'clock in the morning. The sun, cutting through a large staircase window, cast her shadow in bold relief and she felt it following her like a visible manifestation of the shame and self-doubt she carried inside. Knowing she had done nothing wrong didn't help. The past was too close today, too raw.

Susan walked past the secretaries in the reception area, nodded at them briskly and wished them a good morning, her heart thudding wildly, but secretly, in her chest. They took her cue, willing to pretend nothing had changed, and wished her a good day. She walked past the open doors of several of her staff, nodding blithely, then on to her own office where Martin sat at his desk in the outer room — having left the meeting at Debora's before her — waiting for her to decide how they were going to behave. Was it going to be business as usual? Susan knew it was up to her, and her personal desire pushed her toward pretending nothing had changed, trying to stay firm and go on with the day's schedule and somehow keep all of the education projects on schedule and up to date. It was what her mother would have done, Susan thought grimly. And Yetta? Would she have pretended everything was normal when her house was on fire? Not likely. In fact, it was not even a possibility.

"Martin." She called him into her office. "Call a full staff meeting for eleven o'clock. Everyone. No exceptions and no excuses. Phones off. In the main conference room." She was interested to see that he looked relieved rather than worried.

"We aren't going to pretend," she opened the meeting, "that nothing is wrong and nothing has happened. But we are going to go on doing the work that is here to be done."

She told them about the meeting at Debora's office, stressing the difficulty she faced because of the cocaine planted in her house. "I want each of you to know that I have not used or sold cocaine. Never." There was some irony in that, she thought. If cocaine had been around during her drugging days, she probably wouldn't be able to make that absolute a statement. "I have a history of drug and alcohol abuse. It's a matter of public record today, and it's nothing I've made a secret of. Like many of you, I came to work at DASA *because* I'd been down the road and back again with drugs. I know I'm not the only one who's going to be feeling it personally. We *all* need to remember that when the accusations start flying. A history with drugs and alcohol can be a job qualification here, not a disqualification." Half of her staff, Susan knew, were former addicts and alcoholics.

"Until they start using again," muttered Josie, one of the secretaries, in an angry undertone.

"That's right," Susan agreed.

Josie was the secretary and assistant to Tom Brady, her co-worker who had also been indicted. Susan guessed Josie had felt the weight of Tom's disorientation in the last few months.

Susan took a deep breath and confronted the obvious. "Tom isn't in today. Has anyone heard from him?" How to draw distinctions, she wondered, without saying he was guilty before proven so? How to separate her position from his? She needn't have worried. There was Martin, source of all information.

"I talked to his wife just a few minutes ago," he said. "Tom has decided to plead guilty to the charges. He entered rehab last night right after the arraignment."

The room was silent for a moment as they absorbed that news. Susan's first thought was that too many people must have seen Tom down at the pit for him to think he could beat this. And then she wondered if he offered to testify and if so, what would he say? She and Tom were not easy co-workers. He resented her authority and believed he deserved to be head of the education division; he'd said so, bitterly, to most of the staff at one time or another. His degree was in education, while Susan's was only in social work. But she knew his real complaint. Hidden beneath a veneer of liberal values which he could espouse glibly was his hatred of working for a woman, especially a lesbian. Susan had no doubt he'd ferreted that out about her too, no matter how discrete she tried to be in her professional world.

"Josie, Mark, I'll need to talk with you both after this meeting about some project reassignments, then." Best not to make any other comment about Tom for the moment, she thought.

Susan answered her staff's questions for another fifteen minutes — at least those she knew the answers to. Nineteen state workers had been picked up on possession charges, in addition to the five named in the indictment for conspiracy, possession and intent to distribute, and so rumors, speculation and downright vicious gossip were rampant. Susan let some of it air itself and disperse, but when it came around to whether the Commissioner was involved and the political innuendo about his feud with the Governor, she decided it was time to end the meeting. There would be plenty of gossip at every level of DASA today, and she didn't need to add to the churning, swirling stream.

Back at her own desk, Josie and Mark seated across from her, Susan began to review Tom's work load. Mark was eager, Josie hostile.

"The first thing I have to know," Josie demanded, her voice tight with anger, "is whether he's ever coming back into this department. Because if he is, I want to continue processing my application for a transfer."

"I didn't know you were thinking of that, Josie." Susan frowned. She didn't like being out of touch with her staff.

"You haven't known much about our unit for a while," Josie accused, not willing to back down. She shifted in her chair, crossed one slender ankle over the other and leaned forward, her dark face watching Susan's intently.

"No," Susan agreed slowly. "Tom was working fairly independently on a couple of projects. That was about to change. Next week, in fact, Eduardo would have taken over the AIDS and substance abuse training contracts. Now . . ." Her voice faltered. Now indeed. Eduardo was indicted himself. "I think we'll let that one rest until the Commissioner makes a determination on it. My concern is that you two be able to take over the unit together and run the rest of your programs. Will that be a problem?"

"Is he coming back?" Josie demanded again.

"I don't know, Josie," Susan said firmly. "If he does, I'll support your request for transfer myself." If I have a job here, she added silently.

Josie nodded, satisfied, and they began reviewing the tasks Tom had left unfinished in the unit.

Mark and Josie dealt with for the moment, Susan felt more at ease. The punishingly familiar weight of shame had begun to lift as she forced herself to deal with her daily routine. It was funny, like the familiar line of an old lover's cheek could bring back a rush of unwanted tenderness, so being accused of drugging — and all that went with it, the lying, stealing, selling — had brought the rush of guilt and fury at being trapped. It was like the paddleball game someone had made of velcro, she thought. Toss one of those accusations anywhere near her and it latched on with a death grip. Well, not quite death. Not now. Not anymore.

By three o'clock she'd had it. She called Rachel. "Come and get me," was Rachel's easy response. Susan walked the short block down the hill, exhausted but more relaxed than she had been a few hours earlier.

At Susan's house, Susan and Rachel acted as if this were a casual, everyday coming home. Susan took her mail out of the box, unlocked her door with the new key, and they went into the sparsely furnished living room.

"It looks about the same," Susan ventured after a short inspection. Martin and Jimmy had straightened up and put clothes back in the closet and drawers, but "about the same" didn't mean the same.

Together they walked over to the bedroom window and looked down at the stones on the radiator shelf under the window. Susan picked up a piece of rose quartz and rubbed it with her thumb, then handed it, already warm from her touch, to Rachel.

"You can make them yours again," Rachel whispered, kissing Susan's ear as she spoke.

Susan nodded. "I know. But for now, I'd like to put them away."

They gathered the stones into an empty running-shoe box and Susan put it into the back of her closet. Then she and Rachel lifted the radiator cover off to see what was there. Dust. In the center of the radiator was one clean spot where the plastic bag must have lain. About eight inches of empty space separated the top of the radiator and the shelf.

"Not a bad hiding place," Susan observed wryly, "if I'd had anything to hide."

"But not good enough. They never are."

Susan had unplugged her phone. "Anyone who needs to talk to me can do it later." She began to fix dinner. Normalcy was what she needed now, calm and routine.

They undressed for bed quietly, like lovers who had been together for years, across the room from one another, casual about the disrobing, crawling under the covers on opposite sides of the bed. For Susan, there was comfort in the lack of eroticism in their movements, their coming together for a comforting hug at the center of the bed before sleeping.

Before dawn Susan awoke drenched in sweat, looking for light, any light, filtering into the room. She had been alone in a dark cell in her dream, a cell as dark and narrow as death. Before she was fully awake she was out of bed and standing at her window, looking out at the sliver of new moon hanging just above the horizon. It wasn't much light, but it was enough to calm her, to let her know she wasn't in prison — yet.

Shaken by the intensity of her dream, she turned toward the bed to make sure Rachel was still there. Yes. Her eyes had adjusted to the moonlight. Yes, Rachel was there. She wasn't alone.

"Stop me if you're not ready to wake up like this," she murmured in Rachel's ear, as she pulled the covers away from Rachel's warm body.

Rachel murmured a soft acquiescence, but didn't open her eyes. Susan moved her hands from Rachel's shoulders to her breasts. She felt Rachel's warmth, breathed in her odor, tasted her skin. She, Susan, was alive. All of her senses told her so. She felt Rachel's sleepy passivity and began to play with it, enjoying the power of changing Rachel's breathing, knowing she could pull Rachel out of her sleep at any time, but preferring to move slowly, gradually at first. Her tongue sang a circle around Rachel's ear, then around her nipple, her soft round belly. She pulled herself to her knees, not wanting to touch Rachel except with her hands, her mouth, deliberately.

Susan smiled, then, in the dark. She was ready. Rachel had better be. She lowered herself the length of Rachel's body. Such complete body contact was a rush, but Susan didn't let herself stay with that rush for very long. She began to move, slowly, then harder, her hips pushing into Rachel's, pushing, swelling, stronger, stronger. She heard Rachel begin to pant beneath her and her own heart was racing. She held back, not wanting to come before Rachel, waiting for Rachel to give her the cue. And she did, with a long shuddering moan, a thrust of her hips grinding up into Susan's. Susan let it happen then, let herself meet Rachel in several strong sharp thrusts until the climax washed over her, receding in waves of sensation from belly to toes.

CHAPTER EIGHT

Rachel looked out of her study window at the steady drizzle graying everything it touched. October could be hard in the Northeast. About three days out of thirty the sun made more than a token appearance. She sighed, longing to be back in the sun-drenched autumn days of late September. The light, the leaves turning gold, beginning to love Susan . . .

No, she shouldn't put the latter in with the things she had lost, because her love for Susan was growing, not fading like the light toward winter solstice. It was just that, well, the first glow, the easy time — which Rachel had fully expected to last at least six months — had disappeared after the indictment. They were passionately in love, that was becoming clear to both of them in these overwhelming days since Susan's release from jail. Equally as clear was the recognition that maintaining this love, and the passion, was going to take conscious, careful work in the months ahead as they figured out what was happening and what they could do about it. She had to believe that it could be resolved, that it could turn out in Susan's favor. She had fought too long to view the world as a positive place. It did not come naturally or easily to her, this optimism. She knew she had the capacity to see human nature in all of its complexity; she now could expect astonishing kindness and generosity from people, but she still also knew the human ability for terrible, heart-rending cruelty.

Rachel began straightening her desk, sorting through unanswered mail for the "must deal with" pieces, tossing others into subcategories. But she couldn't stop thinking about Susan and the few hectic, fearful days at the beginning of the week.

She was finally going to Boston. Carmen had been understanding about the delay, but insisted that Rachel needed some perspective, some time away, if only a day. Rachel wanted that for herself too. She felt drowned by the events of the last couple of days, not just by the incessant rain but by the intensity of life with Susan under indictment. She needed space, a chance to refocus herself on her own life and work. The real reason she needed to talk with Carmen was her book, the book she had been gathering notes toward for three years. She didn't know if she could write it. She could hardly remember the initial impulse for the book. For three years she had been making notes about the lives and journeys of twelve women she admired. Women living today. Women working in the world in twelve different ways. None of them was outwardly connected to a religious life, though some maintained their connections to a spiritual tradition. The purpose of the book was to redefine spirituality for today.

Rachel and Carmen had talked long hours into the night about the bankruptcy of modern churches, the empty longing that led youngsters into the mob scene of a rock concert, the isolated loneliness of older people who made up the audience for television evangelists. The women Rachel wanted to write about were recognizing the vast alienation around them and working against it. It should be a wonderful book, an important book, but in the last few weeks Rachel couldn't think of a thing to say about anything. Whenever she sat with her pen in her hand to add to her notes, the only words in her brain were clichés about love and duty. She was exhausted by dutiful love, more exhausted than she imagined when she asked for the leave of absence, as if she had held her exhaustion and rage at the futility of trying to make enormous changes at bay with her busy schedule.

She flipped through her notes one more time, then closed the folder in disgust. She grabbed her backpack out of her bedroom, and went downstairs. Maybe a three-hour drive through the mountains in pouring rain would help her focus. Nothing else seemed to have worked.

Five hours later, lunch was over, and Carmen was

caught up on as many of the intimate details of Susan's case and Rachel's sex life as could possibly be pried out of her.

"So what's wrong?" Carmen leaned forward over her coffee cup and peered into Rachel's face. "You tell me you're in love, that you have faith that this indictment thing will work itself out, but something big is bothering you. What is it?"

"This book," Rachel admitted with a shrug. "I'm not sure I can write it. In fact, I feel like it's the wrong thing for me to be doing now."

"Is it the subject? Or the writing?"

"I'm not sure. Ministers — especially those of us who preach or give homilies or lectures or whatever you want to call it —"

"I call it preaching, honey," Carmen said, reminding Rachel she wasn't getting to the point.

"Well, then, preachers write books all the time. It's just that I've never written a book like this. The other two were put together from sermons."

Carmen raised an eyebrow at this description. "You know what I mean." Rachel's first book *had* been a collection of sermons from a feminist perspective. But the second had taken a series of the hardest moral problems Rachel could imagine — taken them, described them and then restated them from the perspective of the person bearing the weight of the problem. *Dialogues From Within Oppression.* That had been Rachel's working title as she wrote, and the book had created a sensation in a small circle of theologians and feminist theoreticians. "This one, it needs to be all one long argument. The women I'm writing about are examples. I don't want to simply tell their stories. That's surely part of why it's so hard." Rachel took a deep breath, "And I've spent months convincing myself that I can write this one."

"Of course you can. *If* you want to," Carmen said. "This isn't just any book. This is about where you, Rachel Smythe, *live,* isn't it?" Carmen was looking at her, but kept staring down at her coffee cup. "Am I right?"

"Yes." She didn't meet Carmen's eyes right away but watched the cream she had just poured swirl through her coffee. "Yes, basically, you're right, Car. That's what I tell myself." There was an emptiness in the pit of her stomach. "And you know what?" She looked at Carmen. "I am bored to death with the whole project. Maybe I don't want to live in that place anymore."

Carmen was looking at her, nodding a little, and she didn't seem terribly surprised by what Rachel was saying. "Do you remember why you asked for this leave of absence?"

Surprised, Rachel answered automatically, "Sure. Exhaustion, burnout."

"From what?"

With a sigh, Rachel repeated the familiar litany. "From doing more than my share, from taking care of others before I take care of myself, from not being taken seriously when I say what needs to be done . . ."

"And that's how I hear you describing this book, Rachel." Carmen emphasized her words by tapping her coffee spoon on the white table cloth. "You're writing about women who do what you've been doing and have the energy somehow to keep doing it. You've got a good idea at the core of this book, but maybe you've got to think about how you're focusing it. Maybe these women aren't the ones you want to write about." She laid her spoon on her folded napkin. "Maybe you need to be writing about yourself."

"God, Carmen, that's a depressing thought," Rachel said angrily. "Just what the world needs, another interior monologue about how I got to be better than everybody else. Or another book whining about —" She stopped herself. "I'm sorry. I don't know what's wrong with me, Carmen. It's that —" She sighed again. "So tell me. Why in the world should I be writing about myself?"

An ironic smile played across Carmen's face. Then she shook her head, her eyes full of mock pity. "You're taking something for yourself when you let Susan love you. You're filling some of your own needs for a change. No wonder a book about self-sacrifice isn't grabbing you right now."

"Okay, I can see that," Rachel said slowly. "But why write about me?"

"What is it you think you've just embarked upon, woman? You going to love this Susan with your body and not your whole heart and mind and spirit? When better should you write this book? Keep notes." She was on a roll now, tapping her coffee spoon vigorously. "You're going to learn something new every day. Count on it. You can write this book. But it isn't going to be only about other women."

Rachel was still not sure she understood what Carmen was saying. How could her loving Susan be a part of a book that redefined spiritual journeys? And just as quickly came the answer: how could it not?

Being with Susan was like walking through a familiar house and discovering new cubbyholes,

76

sometimes entire small rooms filled with unexpected delights, and, sometimes, with challenges. Just the difficulty of remembering that Susan saw the world as a Jew had surprised Rachel. She hadn't thought it would be hard.

She nodded, beginning to understand what Carmen was saying. "Sometimes," she began hesitantly, "when we're making love, I feel like I've been taken to a new place. It may sound weird, but it reminds me of some of those early women's liturgies you and I worked on in the seventies."

"Yes," Carmen smiled, "I know what you mean. Those were special times. We knew we were powerful, empowered."

"That's it. That's what I feel like with her. And you know what?" The confession suddenly seemed easier. "It scares me to death at the same time it exhilarates me."

"It scared us then, too," Carmen reminded her, "and we lived through it. We lived long enough to wish we could be that scared again, didn't we?" She was laughing, but there was a seriousness in her words. "We've learned what we do well, and we do it and we do it and we do it . . ."

"And we get bored with it," Rachel finished for her.

"That's right. So you've opened yourself to a new challenge. Write about how you became willing to do that. Then tell us what it's like to live back in that place where you're on the edge. We need to be reminded." Carmen reached across the table and put her hand over Rachel's.

"It'll be a different book than I'd imagined."

"It will be a book you can write. The best books

are those that no one else could have written. Yours will be like that." Carmen's satisfaction with her own insight was contagious, allowing Rachel to begin believing in herself again.

They split the check, paid the bill, but still lingered, reluctant to separate. Carmen was right, Rachel thought. She was about to embark on a journey. Their friendship was long-lasting, but it might be weeks or months before they spent time together like this again. Finally, Rachel drew herself away from Carmen's hug.

"Travel well." Carmen's whisper stayed with her as she slogged through the rain to her car. Travel well. It *was* a journey, she thought, and she had no idea where it would take her.

She drove back to Albany more calmly than she'd driven out, following a spectacular sunset into the Berkshire Mountains and west across the summit. At a rest area just over the highest point on the highway, she parked and got out of the car to admire the end of the fading sunset. Streaks of dark purple held up the magenta clouds lying over the valley in front of her. The wind was still, but the blown leaves and torn limbs littering the parking area told her how fierce the storm had been last night and earlier that day. Rachel watched the clouds undulating like waves on the ocean and she realized she was lonely for the familiar seascape she'd left behind.

As she drove out of the mountains, the relief of her conversation with Carmen began to penetrate and she could feel her shoulders relax, and the heaviness between her eyes lifted a bit. She knew Carmen was right about the book and about Susan, but she couldn't figure out how Carmen knew those things about her life. Years ago, it had irritated her, this habit of Carmen's, of dropping observations about Rachel's life as though they ought to have been perfectly obvious to her. "You act as if that had been written on some stone tablet I was just too dumb to read," she'd accused Carmen once. It was an argument that had gone nowhere.

What Rachel carried back across the mountains with her was a sense that she was loving Susan differently than she'd loved any woman before, and that terrified her at the same time it thrilled her. Before, she'd practiced caution without necessarily wanting to. It was a way of keeping her safe and it saved her by keeping her from the deepest of intimacies. Rachel knew that she had never lived with a lover, never connected her life and her future to another person. Carmen was right. If Rachel let this keep happening, and it was a big if, she would learn, she would go tumbling across new horizons without control, horizons she had probably never dreamed of. If. If Susan let her. If Susan was free to choose. If.

CHAPTER NINE

Susan stood at the entrance to the backyard of a rundown tenement house and stared down at the pit. Some tired brown grass straggled up over the edges of the pit, but in the center was mud, hard packed in some places, slime in others. A few pieces of broken board were scattered on the path leading down to the center, a futile attempt to circumvent the mud. Several men stood there, apparently oblivious to the light, cold drizzle of rain falling. Idle, chatting with one another, they ignored her as she looked down at them. This was where you came to get drugs when you had to have them and couldn't take a chance on not getting what you needed. Here anything was for sale, anything. This afternoon it looked quiet and neutral, but Susan knew it was a façade.

"Are you sure you want to go down there?" Darryl asked Susan.

Only 100 feet separated Susan from the men in front of her, 100 feet and a lifetime of difference. She knew too well what must have driven Tom down here to beg for the drugs he needed. She remembered what it was like to sweat on a cold day, shake on a hot one because she needed a fix. She didn't know exactly why she was here, but she wasn't ready to turn back.

"Yeah," she said, looking at her friend. "Are you okay with that?"

"Me?" He smiled without humor. "Susan, it isn't me who's out on bail. Cops come through here, I'm just a brother trying to help a brother. I got nothing on me and I got the agency behind me. Shit, I'll just pull out a handful of jimmy caps and offer them some. Here, officer, I'm distributing condoms, compliments of the AIDS Help Group. But how am I going to explain you? That's what I'd like to know?"

"I'll explain me," she said. "Do you know these guys?"

"Of course. The man in charge is the one on the left with the dreds. Mikey. The short weightlifter is his man, Jones. The others," Darryl shrugged, "they just hangin'."

Susan nodded. The biceps on the shorter man were larger than her thighs and he wasn't heavyset either. She knew they were being ignored, but they weren't unnoticed. The checking out time went both ways and it was customary, Darryl had told her, to pause and let people see you. It wasn't a place you wanted to go barging into unannounced. "Can we go down now?"

"Now or never," Darryl agreed and preceded her down the muddy path.

The men all knew Darryl and greeted him. He wandered around saying hello to several of them, without apparent intention, and Susan followed him quietly. When he got to Mikey, they all turned away and started other conversations. All except Jones, who stood, arms crossed, about three feet away, apparently studying something fascinating in the gray afternoon sky.

"Darryl." Mikey acknowledged him, then he looked at Susan and waited.

"Mikey, this is my friend Susan Myers. She came down here to talk with you for a minute, if you have the time. We don't mean to be in your way, if you've got some other appointments, you know what I mean?"

Mikey did. He apparently heard the diffidence in Darryl's voice and grammar and knew he was being asked for a favor, maybe a big favor. "Hmmmpff. Wellll . . ." He drew the phrase out as he considered. "You never got in my way, Darryl. And this Miss . . ."

"Susan Myers," she interjected, looking him in the eye. "Susan, please."

He was silent again, looking at her. Finally he decided. "Yes, I know you. We know who you are. You got trouble."

Susan was surprised but realized she shouldn't have been. Mikey survived by knowing more than anyone around him. She'd hoped he would know more than the police. "That's me. Trouble. I was hoping," she drew a deep breath, and took the plunge, "you might know more about my trouble than I know. Will you talk with me about it for a minute?" She couldn't think why he should take the risk and held her breath against his answer.

"I think I could do that." Mikey clearly liked his authority acknowledged. "Why don't you and Darryl step over here for a minute," he said and gestured toward the rim of the pit as graciously as if he'd been inviting them into his office.

A half-hour later, Darryl and Susan threaded their way back up the path, around the corner of the building and out to the street.

"So what do you think?" Darryl asked.

"Wow," Susan breathed in the city air, calming herself as best she could. "I'm glad the cops didn't decide to wander down this afternoon."

"They almost never do, but don't think they won't know you've been down. They don't need to raid it because they always know what's happening down here. Druggies need money and don't care who they sell. Mikey knows that. He factors it in when he does business."

"I know. It doesn't matter. I just didn't want to face another bust. Debora's patience might not stretch that far." She was finally relaxed enough to joke a bit.

Tom had been a regular for the last three months, Mikey had implied, never admitting he'd sold to Tom but letting them know how often he'd seen him, for how long. He'd been dealing for at least that long but something had knocked out his supply line for a while, about the time he'd started visiting Mikey. He wanted Mikey to set him up again as a dealer, but Mikey could see he was using heavily and didn't want to take a chance on him. Yes, there'd been another white man with Tom on occasion, especially most recently, and no, he'd never come down with a woman, not a short blonde woman — Jean Currie from the Commissioner's office — and certainly not a woman who resembled Susan in any way. Mikey didn't know what the purpose of the bust at DASA was, but Susan could tell he was flattered they asked. He did, after all, understand politics, although not necessarily the kind of politics the Governor and Commissioner practiced.

"I guess I just needed to check it out," she admitted.

"Find out if you have a double running around town?"

"Yeah. This whole thing makes so little sense to me, I couldn't really think of anything else to suggest, even to myself." Her depression was descending again, after the adrenalin rush of visiting the pit. "I don't know where else to even ask around."

"You know what I'd be curious about if I was you?"

"No, what?" Susan looked up sharply, immediately alert. He was nobody's fool, nobody's.

"I'd want to know where those nineteen people who were picked up for using bought their stuff. If they all bought it from Tom or John, then why are they arresting you?"

"That's information Debora should get from the discovery," Susan began. "But you're right. A couple were from my agency. They're not all from DASA. They're spread around town. But the names were in the paper, weren't they?" She was thinking fast now, seeing some possibilities where there had been none before. "I could talk to a couple of them, couldn't I?"

"Actually, I'm not sure Debora would think that was a good idea. Maybe you'd better check with her first." Darryl was retreating. He knew Debora fairly well and wanted to keep knowing her. "You better let her deal with it, like you say."

"Yeah, thanks, Darryl. Thanks for your help this afternoon. I couldn't have gone down there without you." Susan was anxious to be on her own. She had something to check out.

Later that night Susan called Rachel. She was tamping down hysteria, but couldn't keep the edge out of her voice. "I talked to one of the people arrested for possession tonight. Jocelyn Wilder. A dyke. One of the younger ones. Works down at CSEA. I thought she might tell me where she got her drugs, you know, so I could figure out who's implicating me in this." She paused for breath.

"I'm not sure that's a good idea, Susan. Did you talk to Debora about it? Are you all right What's happening?"

"I'm trying to tell you. No, I didn't ask Debora's permission. It's killing me, not knowing how this happened. So I found out where she lives and went out there. In Guilderland," she said, naming one of the western suburbs of the city. "You know what she said?"

Rachel was silent.

"She said, 'What do you mean, who did I buy it from? I thought I was buying it from you.'" There was more silence as Susan let Rachel absorb the full impact of this.

"Why did she think that?"

"She left orders and money in a drop in my backyard. She picked her drugs up there. From the flower box by the back of the garage. My garage. My yard. My house." Susan was nearly hysterical. The information was still overwhelming. "God, Rachel. What's happening?"

It was clearly not a question Rachel could answer, and Susan hung up after a few minutes, the adrenalin rushing through her body not in any way stanched by the brief conversation with Rachel. It was midnight and she felt it might as well have been high noon. She pushed away a vague dissatisfaction still niggling at her after talking with Rachel — or rather failing to talk with Rachel, for it was clear Rachel could not enter into Susan's high-speed mood. Susan flashed for a moment on the river, not the Ausable as she and Rachel had stood by it, but the one she had seen in her dreams that night in prison, the fast coursing river she was rushing down as Rachel stood on the banks, a puzzled look on her face.

She made a cup of coffee, opened a new notebook, laid out three different colored pens and sat hunched over the kitchen table staring at nothing. When she shook her head and brought herself back, she felt a little lonely. She found it odd to be focusing on something other than Rachel, she realized. The energy she once reserved almost exclusively for her work had been redirected these last few months. She thought she'd been pretty balanced — that was what she told herself, anyway. Passion in her relationship, focus and intensity in her work, a continued intimacy with Debora and one or two other friends. Why not? She sighed ruefully as she stared at the blank page in the notebook. The pieces of her life weren't well balanced. They were scattered like a jigsaw puzzle that some angry kid shoved off the table.

She wrote the name JOCELYN WILDER at the top of the blank page. She'd gone to Jocelyn first because she was the name on the list of those arrested on lesser charges that Susan was most familiar with. She didn't know her, really, but had seen her around in the lesbian community as well as in the state government crowd. She seemed ambitious, young and undereducated for what she wanted to achieve, but Susan thought she showed promise. Someone had taken her aside in the last year and taught her how to dress and tone down the makeup — told her she wasn't going to go anywhere looking like Madonna masquerading as a coed. But whoever her mentor was must have neglected to tell her she wasn't going far with a cocaine habit.

When Susan found her, Jocelyn's choices had been severely circumscribed by the plea bargain the D.A. offered her. No jail time, but she was going to have to plead guilty, cooperate and testify in court. Her attorney was trying to negotiate the plea down from a felony to a misdemeanor, and since this was her first offense, she'd been told she had a pretty good chance.

Susan had found Jocelyn's address and gone without calling ahead. When Jocelyn opened the door, she knew right away who Susan was and hadn't wanted to let her in. She did so reluctantly, when Susan insisted they had to talk. Her reluctance was there at each turn, but she was easily influenced, a trait Susan noted. In the same position, many of the younger lesbians she knew would have taken a "fuck you" stance toward the world.

Jocelyn hadn't wanted to implicate the person who first told her about the drop at Susan's house, told her where to leave the note and cash and how much.

"Maybe I should talk to my lawyer first." She looked up at Susan from under her eyelashes, assessing the possibilities. "Then I could get back to you tomorrow," she offered hopefully.

"Look," Susan insisted, "that's really not necessary. Your plea bargain calls for cooperation. You're going to have to give that name eventually. I need it now." She felt unyielding until Jocelyn began to sob loudly. That she sat calmly in the chair opposite instead of running out the front door was a good measure of her desperation.

"It was Astrid." She sniffed and wiped her running mascara.

"Astrid?" Susan was incredulous. Ignoring Jocelyn's stifled sobs became easy. "Astrid?"

Jocelyn nodded, not noticing the sarcasm in Susan's voice.

"Right. Astrid. How did you know her?" But every lesbian in the city knew Astrid. She was the one who produced the concerts and the radical dyke newsletter, who knew everything and mocked it all because she was too cool to be politically correct.

"We were lovers. Last year. For about a month."

Jocelyn's phrases were punctuated by deeply drawn breaths. A month was a long time in some parts of the dyke world.

Susan leaned back in her chair and tried to take this loyalty seriously. "Did Astrid tell you it was me selling the drugs?"

"She said it was your backyard." Her tone accused Susan of being unfair to quibble over words at a time like this.

"But she didn't say it was me?"

"No. I don't think so. I don't remember."

"Did Astrid tell you who told her about the drop?"

"You know Astrid," Jocelyn said impatiently. "She was born knowing things. Nobody ever had to tell her."

She got that right, Susan thought to herself, glad to see at least a small breach in her loyalty. She pushed Jocelyn a little longer, but there was nothing else to learn. Susan drove home, still stunned by having someone look her in the eye and announce, "Who was I buying my drugs from? Are you nuts? I was buying them from you."

Sitting at her kitchen table, as one o'clock came and went, Susan kept doodling in her notebook. A line with an arrow led from Astrid to Jocelyn. Big deal. She started making circles, trying to think of all the parts of the communities they'd been connected to. Jocelyn had come through some kind of internship program. She had some vague recollection of her connected to one of the Women's Business Seminars the Governor's office ran. That put her in about six other circles, including those of Debora's law partner, Amanda Clark, and Susan's own business associate

Glenda Mathis, both of whom had been mentors to interns at one time or another.

She sighed and closed the notebook. Nowhere. This was getting her nowhere closer to understanding the one crucial piece of the puzzle, the keystone that held it all together. Who had put cocaine under her radiator cover? And why?

CHAPTER TEN

Susan called Debora from work the next morning. "Susan, are you nuts or what?" Darryl had been right. Debora was not pleased with her late-night investigations. But she only grinned at the tough tone in Debora's voice. They'd been best friends for fourteen years, since day one in grad school where they found themselves in the same M.S.W. class. For about three weeks — until Debora quit cold. She'd known right away she would never be a social worker. Susan was amazed. Newly sober, she couldn't imagine that anyone could make a decision that quickly and firmly. "I need more power," Debora insisted. "Bureaucracy will always be with us, but I don't need to be trapped inside it. I want to be able to fight with it." And fight she had. Whatever else happened, Susan knew Debora would fight for her.

"Debora, I had to ask," she began, her voice patient, a counter to Debora's anger.

"No. You didn't have to ask," Debora exploded back at her, knocking her confidence into a small corner of the room. "Do I *need* to tell you about intimidating witnesses, contaminating the evidence and all of that? This is your life we are talking about here, in case you hadn't noticed. Whether you want to spend it in prison or here in the world. That's what we're talking about."

The anger Susan was so accustomed to hearing directed at others was suddenly coming at her. About to make a joke, she stumbled, unsure how to respond. "I know it's my life," she said finally, depression stalking her voice. "Believe me, I know."

Susan could hear Debora take a deep breath. When she spoke next, her voice was under control. "So Jocelyn Wilder thinks she was buying drugs from you. Tell me about it, Susie."

"I don't know much more than that. She said Astrid told her about the drop."

"Were both of them getting stuff from someone else who used your backyard as a drop? Or was Astrid just covering her ass? Was she selling, do you think?"

"Maybe." Some of the tension had eased, but there was a residue of discomfort or Susan would have made a joke or a wisecrack about Astrid, Ms. Radical-Political-Dyke. She couldn't even muster sarcasm. "But I don't see how someone got into my house and hid stuff under my radiator cover. Or why."

"Hmmm." Debora was agreeing, and Susan could imagine her squinting in concentration. "Let's take one thing at a time. Someone was using your backyard because it was private and convenient. Let's focus on that for a minute."

"Like someone who lived close by?"

"Why not? Someone who wouldn't be noticed walking down the block regularly. Let's see. It's a neighborhood. Six blocks, about a hundred and twenty houses. About five hundred people. But most of them don't walk past your house on a regular basis."

"That would cause comment," Susan said flippantly. She wasn't sure where Debora was going with this.

"Think about it. Can you talk to the neighbors on either side, casually, and see if they think of anyone?"

Susan smiled, feeling a little smug. Debora was going to let her keep asking questions. She played it low key. "Sure. And I'll find out where Astrid lives. But I've never seen her around my neighborhood, that's for certain. She's not someone I'd miss. Or forget."

Debora was still thinking. "People walk dogs in your neighborhood?"

Susan pulled the phone away from her ear, looked at it and shook her head. It really was a question. "Yes, Debora," she answered politely, "people do walk dogs in my neighborhood. What's the point?"

"It gives you a reason to be walking, right? And

about the same time and place everyday. And if someone saw you coming out of the backyard, well, the dog made me do it. If you see what I mean."

Susan did, actually, and stopped laughing. It made perfect sense. Until she tried to put it into her neighborhood — Mike, the drunk three houses down with the decrepit old black lab? The lady across the street with the two yappy terriers? "I don't know. It sounds possible but . . ."

They gave it up after a few more minutes of speculation. Susan tried to turn her attention to work. Her desk was covered with memos to respond to, RFPs from federal funding sources she needed to make decisions about, not to mention the work of her own division. But her mind kept turning back to dog walkers. Dog walkers were one thing, but people going in and out of her backyard were another. Of course she would talk to the neighbors when she got home. And then she realized that of course this couldn't have been happening while she was home. She pulled her jacket around her shoulders, chilled at the thought. Someone knew when she was home sleeping in her own bed and when she was not.

She called Martin on the intercom. He closed the door behind him and waited for her question, eyebrows raised.

"Martin, who in this office knows my travel schedule?"

He shrugged. "Practically the whole office. We have to schedule things around it. Why?"

She slumped in her chair, disappointed. But of course. She'd already known the answer.

As she explained what she'd learned from Jocelyn, what she and Debora had been theorizing, Martin looked glum. "You think it's someone in this office, then," he said finally. It wasn't a question, and he didn't have to say Tom's name. "He doesn't live that far from you. Just the other side of the boulevard, right?"

Susan nodded. Right. A lot closer than Astrid, if the directory listing for her was to be believed. "Of course he works during the day, but he always knew when I'd be traveling on business?"

"Yup. He had to." Then shifting to another foot, still leaning with his back against the door as if to keep out intruders, Martin asked, "So did Jocelyn tell you when she bought stuff? Was it only during the week? When you were off on business?"

"No. She didn't. But my house is right on her way to the throughway. She'd go by every day coming and going to work. And it's not like I've been at home every weekend, either." Susan couldn't keep a defensive tone out of her voice.

"But people in this office didn't have any information about that," Martin reminded her patiently. He was about to add something when the phone on Susan's desk rang and they both saw the light indicating it was the Commissioner's private line.

"This is Susan Meyers."

"Susan." His voice sounded strained to her. "Could you stop up this morning at eleven. I want to talk with you about how that project with the health department is coming."

"Of course, Commissioner. I'll see you at eleven." Susan replaced the receiver thoughtfully. J. Lawrence didn't like communicating on the phone and preferred his staff to keep those conversations to a minimum. She would, of course, take all of her report notes on the AIDS and Substance Abuse education project upstairs with her at eleven, but judging by the tone of his voice, she doubted that was what he wanted to discuss. She hadn't had a private conversation with him since her first hour back at work after the indictment, when he'd expressed all of the right sentiments and assured her that her job was secure until, as he put it, "all of this is cleared up." He'd also reminded her that he expected her complete attention to all of the projects she was directing. "I know a situation like this can be difficult," he'd said delicately, "and there is a temptation to let it take over and run one's life. If you need time off, Susan, I hope you'll take it and not let the division suffer."

He knew she would. She owed him that. They'd worked together for eleven years, the entire time Susan had been with DASA. When the Alcohol and Substance Abuse departments were joined into one division, J. Lawrence had been the competent, forty-year-old, assistant director of Substance. His director was retiring, which made it possible for the merger to take place, really. But the director of Alcohol, who took over as the new Commissioner, was never able to get over the turf wars that had hindered the work of the two departments, and J. Lawrence had to fight continually being shuffled aside.

Susan had come in as an outsider, but it wasn't hard to see who was getting the work done. She sided with J. Lawrence every time, gave him information and logistical assistance whenever she could. Finally there was a new Governor who could force the leftover Commissioner into retirement and J. Lawrence Godwin became the first black Commissioner in the new administration. And the only, to date.

Susan chatted a minute with Anna Hughes, the Commissioner's secretary, shifting her files from one arm to the other as she heard about Anna's new grandson, until J. Lawrence was free.

"Susan," J. Lawrence reached over to shake her hand and Susan was glad to hear less strain in his voice. "Let me come right to the point." Then he paused, as though he couldn't.

Susan had been right, it wasn't about the health department.

"Umm. How is the case coming? Is Debora going to be able to get a dismissal?"

Susan shrugged nonchalantly and tried to project confidence. "That's certainly our expectation.

He nodded, not concerned about the details. "I wanted to let you know that Eduardo Villa is being dismissed from the indictment by the D.A. today. His lawyer called me at home last night to let me know. Apparently they were able to check out some of the misinformation given by the informant . . ."

Susan's attention was riveted and her brain went into overdrive. Who was the informer? Did Eduardo know? Would he tell her? Or Debora? Good for Eduardo. Maybe Debora would get the same call today. But then she realized that she couldn't simply disprove an informant's misinformation. There was that bag of cocaine.

She had been nodding, saying the right things about Eduardo, but J. Lawrence wasn't through. He was fiddling with something on his desk as if trying to decide what to say.

"All right." He'd decided. "This came to my office this morning by special messenger. I don't know who sent it or why they thought it would interest me. I was going to throw it away, but I realized you and Debora needed to know." He handed Susan a nine-by-twelve manila envelope with a typed address indicating it was for the Commissioner's eyes only. Susan pulled out two pieces of paper. On one, scrawled in large crayoned letters were the words: *Susan Myers, addict, queer, AIDS carrier?* The second, in the same hand, told the Commissioner to get Susan Meyers out of his division before copies of these photographs were sent to the local papers.

Stunned, she reached into the envelope and pulled out three small snapshots. She recognized them immediately. They'd been taken at the Cape two or three summers ago. In one she was asleep on a beach blanket, topless, lying on her back. The second and third were still topless, and Deputy Commissioner Susan Meyers was in various stages of public indiscretion with a woman she'd been seeing in those days who lived in Boston.

Susan couldn't stop staring at the photographs. If she looked up, she'd have to meet the Commissioner's eyes. She had no idea who might have taken the pictures. The gay beach at Provincetown was supposed to be safe, somehow. Protected. The one place lesbians could be out and playful.

Heart racing, her mouth dry, Susan tried to imagine what J. Lawrence must have thought when he saw them. In their eleven years of working together, she had never come out to him, never talked about her private life at all. She had no idea how he felt about gay people, although she'd never heard any derogatory statements or stereotypes come out of his mouth. And he had, after all, said his first impulse had been to throw them away. Her hand was shaking when she put the photos back in the envelope. Finally she had to look up.

He seemed to be taking it personally, to some extent. "I cannot imagine who would think I would be influenced by this kind of campaign." The idea was fine, but the pompous delivery did not calm her pounding heart. She knew J. Lawrence, had seen him in enough tight spots to know he became pompous when he didn't know how to respond.

Susan cleared her throat, hoping her voice would work well enough to give him some direction. "This changes everything. Clearly, the drug charges are part of some scheme to discredit me, perhaps to discredit you. If Eduardo and I had been smeared, it would reflect on you, since we both report directly to you." She was amazed to hear how calm and firm she sounded.

"I've heard rumors to that effect," he said quietly. "That the governor is out to crush me and appoint a . . .appoint someone he is closer to ideologically." He looked at her. "Don't believe those rumors. They aren't based in fact."

She nodded, knew he could play it that way. "Then it's an effort to discredit me. But this becomes evidence, and I think we ought to call Debora — right now — and see what she thinks we ought to do with it." Her real impulse was to burn it, right there in his office, to scream and rage and stomp out of his office. But she kept her anguish in check. Those years of hiding, of staying closeted — that was supposed to have been her protection.

"I support you, of course," he was saying as Susan tuned back in, his tone no longer pompous. "But to be honest with you, I am concerned about the division's reputation."

"Do you mean the drug charges," she had to ask, "or the fact that I'm gay and someone thinks that's grounds for dismissal?"

"I fully support the affirmative action position of this Administration, Susan." There was no hesitation as he continued. "*And* we both know this city isn't exactly cosmopolitan when it comes to these issues. I don't want those photographs going to the press. That's all." He ended the conversation by picking up the telephone and handing it to Susan. She dialed.

Debora sounded tired and then shocked. "I can't imagine a local paper that would use photos like that," she said, "but I could be naive."

J. Lawrence nodded into the speaker phone, as if he thought she was.

"Bring the envelope down to my office, Susan. I'll need to look at it. Don't touch the contents again. I doubt if we can still lift any fingerprints off of it, but we might want to try."

When Susan stood up to leave, her knees still worked, but barely. She felt unsteady as she walked toward the elevator, so she ducked into the restroom on the top floor for a moment and sat gratefully in a closed stall until her hands stopped shaking.

Since Rachel had been a part of her life, she had imagined several possible scenarios for coming out at work. She knew it had to happen. But the scenario had always been something benign, like taking Rachel to an office Christmas party and introducing her casually as "my partner," allowing her hand to rest on Rachel's arm. Nothing in that fantasy had prepared Susan to be handed photographs of herself — nude and queer, decidedly queer — by Commissioner J. Lawrence Godwin.

CHAPTER ELEVEN

Rachel woke up that morning about the time that Susan left the Commissioner's office, wandered down to the kitchen for coffee and was confronted by Richard's critical eye. He looked at her silently for a moment, one eyebrow slightly raised.

"I had a little insomnia," Rachel said defensively.

"I guess. When I didn't hear you moving around by eight, I checked to see if you were breathing." He stirred the honey into his herbal tea and for a moment the only sounds in the kitchen were the scrape of the spoon on the ceramic mug and the *glug*

glug of the coffee maker. "Want to tell me what happened?"

Rachel shrugged. But she did want to tell him. She had to tell someone, try to make some sense out of her jumble of feelings. "I think I panicked," she said. "All of a sudden, after Susan's call last night. I kept thinking, What have I done? What in the world am I doing? I realized," she was speaking to the far corner of the room, as if Richard weren't even there, "that if I went on loving Susan, my whole world was going to change, not just a little, but drastically. I was afraid." After a moment she added, "I thought I should call Susan back, tell her we needed to go slower, wait until after the indictment was cleared up, and then we could start over." She looked at Richard. "We couldn't, of course. But I wanted to act as if we could."

Panic — and the automatic response of digging her heels in with the full intention of staying exactly where she was — had once been Rachel's response to any change, even the more minor ones. After her parents died, when she sold their house in preparation for going off to seminary — that had taken major planning. She did it in stages, signing the document that irrevocably gave the house to someone else, then surviving the panic attack. Sending the tuition money to theology school in a money order rather than a check. Once the envelope was in the mailbox, she could let the panic happen. But she also knew she was her frugal father's daughter — she would go only if she couldn't get her money back.

She sighed. "Well, I know my world isn't going to crumble with small changes, or even large ones. I don't know why exactly my mother feared change so much, but I've spent a lot of time countering that inbred response." She was reciting the exact words she'd said to herself the night before as she lay paralyzed with fear.

"Susan," Richard said, "she's a change for you. But maybe it isn't all about her, do you think?"

Rachel stared at him. Wasn't Susan enough? And then she felt the waves of panic begin to rise in her again.

"Why am I always the last to know," she said finally, not really asking a question. Because of course the panic wasn't only about the possibility of a life with Susan. At some fundamental level, Rachel knew, deep down, she'd changed. There had been a shift, a large shift.

"You know it," he smiled at her. "You're just fighting this one more than most." Richard shifted in his chair, then admitted, "I followed Colin through this several times. Each time he decided he was finished with the church, in fact. He couldn't bring himself to make the break." He took a deep breath. "You never saw the hardest parts because he thought that if he admitted them — well, he always thought he'd be able to do it, make a clean break. Go off and be a teacher. Something like that. And he was going to tell you about it when it was done."

"I've only done it part way," Rachel said slowly. "I haven't left the church, just my role as minister to a congregation. I guess partly I'm wondering who am I without that? If I don't have a defined connection to people, won't I just drift away? No guy wires, no lifelines to anchor me."

Richard was looking at her, his head tilted. "Do you really think that will be a problem?"

Rachel looked back at him, long and hard. Did she? She wasn't sure.

They were both surprised when the doorbell rang. "For you?" Richard asked as he rose to answer it.

"I don't think so. I'm going up to Saratoga for lunch with an old friend. I don't have any appointments this morning."

But when he came back, he gave her a swift hug. "Yours," he said, taking his tea and disappearing into his study.

Rachel went to the front door reluctantly, unable to imagine who might want her — or even know where to find her. To her surprise, the figure leaning against the door frame was familiar, one of her Provincetown — what should she call her now? Not parishioner. Not client. "Angie," she said, letting her surprise show. Rachel could tell from her body language that Angie was going to need a lot of propping up.

"Hi." Her voice was lethargic, and she gave no indication that Rachel's surprise might be in any way warranted.

"Hi, Angie," Rachel tried again. "What a surprise. I didn't know you ever came over to Albany." There was no response. Looking closer, Rachel could see she was teary eyed. She paused, then tried again. "Is this a social visit, Angie? What's up?"

Rachel had seen Angie animated and she'd seen Angie furious, but this was new to her. The woman drooping on her front porch looked as though any remnant of spontaneity had died in her several lifetimes ago, but she did manage to heave a sigh and raise her head.

"I'm supposed to be doing some training for Glenda Mathis this week," she said with another profound sigh. "AIDS stuff, you know." Rachel nodded. She vaguely remembered hearing something about this from Susan. In fact, it was probably her fault Angie was here, since she'd mentioned her to Glenda a couple months ago at a party at Glenda's house. She'd told Glenda that Angie worked for the Boston Board of Education doing AIDS education in the schools. "She's good," she told Glenda. "I've seen her in public once or twice and heard enough about her to think she's very competent at the work she does."

Today Angie didn't look like she was capable of training anything, let alone producing the professional front that Glenda would require of her. A heavy woman who chose not to try and conceal her size, Angie could nevertheless look imposingly competent and professional when she chose to. Right now she looked more like a discarded rag doll.

"Can I talk to you?" she asked, her voice filled with pathos.

"Sure. I have another appointment at noon, Angie, but come in and tell me what's happening." Rachel was aware of her own amusement at herself. Hadn't she just been bemoaning her loss of a congregation who looked to her for support, the loss of a defined role in her community? Suppressing a sigh, Rachel stood aside and waved Angie through the door.

Rachel was simultaneously intrigued and irritated by Angie. She was a woman in her mid-twenties who could, on the one hand, be daring and outrageous, traits Rachel admired and, she sometimes admitted to herself, envied. But Angie was also a whiner — she hadn't learned how to take the consequences of her own daring.

Since meeting Angie two years before, Rachel found herself mentoring her through one misadventure after another. "You're the only one who could possibly understand this," was Angie's plea, and it was a hard one for Rachel to resist, though she was never quite sure how exactly she came by this reputation for tolerance with Angie. True, tolerance was an attitude she cultivated, but most of Angie's generation found Rachel's ethics and politics too forthright for their "issues." At times, however, Rachel once confided to Carmen, Angie's devotion was almost enough to make her reconsider tolerance.

But Rachel was fond of Angie. She understood their differences but didn't realize how much she was attracted to them. Angie came from a large extended Italian family in South Boston — five sisters and three brothers, all but one older than she, and dozens of nieces, nephews, cousins, aunts, uncles — all of those messy, difficult family ties that Rachel never had. Angie was sure of herself, sure she was right until proven otherwise, another trait that made Rachel furious and envious. She couldn't imagine what it would be like to hold an untested opinion.

Rachel took Angie upstairs to her study so they wouldn't bother Richard. She watched as Angie flung herself down on Colin's old worn couch and burst out crying. Between the hoarse sobs, Rachel could hear fragments of Angie's plaintive voice. "How could she . . . do this . . . to me? I never . . . all my trust . . . how can I ever? Why would she want . . . do this to me?"

Rachel waited a moment, then another. She knew better than to interrupt Angie too soon. But finally, it was time. "So, Angie." Her voice was challenging. "Maybe you better give me a rough outline before we run out of time here. Is this about Darlene? Or someone else?" She resisted the urge to shake Angie or rumple her hair.

"There will never be anyone else for me." Angie sobbed, her tears renewed. "How could she do this to me?"

"It's about Darlene, then?" Rachel's patience was fraying.

After a short silence, Angie seemed to collect herself, pulling in the bits and fragments she had scattered about her when she flopped on the couch. She tucked a soggy Kleenex into her pack and reached for a fresh one from her pocket.

"She wants a trial separation. She says she needs to take some space." Angie blurted this out, then went back to her Kleenex. "I wouldn't bother you about this, but you were so wonderful about our commitment ceremony and I feel you're part of . . ." Words seemed to fail her again. Rachel hoped she wouldn't find anything else for her to be a part of.

She stepped in quickly with her standard response. "Is Darlene saying the relationship is over?"

Angie shook her head, no. Rachel nodded. Good enough. Darlene was a tough little Texan who seemed to be able to cope with Angie. They may have looked like an odd couple — Darlene short, stocky and neat, with her Texas boots and a swagger; Angie was tall and large, always seeming to lap over the edges of most of the objects in her life — but Rachel rather liked them together.

"So maybe this is just a shakedown, not a meltdown, Angie. Maybe she *does* want space. I've heard you talk about how that's good for a relationship, no?"

"Rachel!" Angie's voice was indignant. "It's only been two months since our commitment ceremony. What are we talking about here, anyway, I want to ask you?"

Rachel hid her smile. This was the Angie she could deal with. Indignant. Opinionated. Energetic.

"We haven't even had time to figure out who's going to do the cooking, the dishes, the laundry. I mean, you have to spend time together to figure out how to live together, you know what I mean? You have to sort of be on top of each other. I mean —" She paused a moment, trying to hear how that sounded, checking to see if Rachel was hearing the sexual innuendo, but Rachel managed to keep her face in a pose that she hoped was blandly sympathetic. "I mean, underfoot or in each other's way. Oh, you know what I mean. We have to be able to fight and negotiate and figure out how it's going to be."

Rachel suspected that Darlene had heard this impassioned speech too and that she might be fleeing from it.

"You know, Angie, one of the things about figuring out a relationship is figuring out how we interact. We don't all process things the same way.

109

So while you have one way of getting at the important things by letting the friction just happen, someone else might not be able to do it that way."

Angie looked dumbfounded for a moment. It was a defense she used pretty well, to look at the speaker as though she were speaking a foreign language. Then the translation begins to penetrate. "Are you talking about class? You know, how she's middle class and I'm more working class? We've dealt with that in therapy." She waved the suggestion away with her hand, but her face said she was still thinking about it.

It took Rachel another half-hour to hear Angie out before she could ease her toward the door. "I've got a little preparation to do for this next appointment," she explained as Angie engulfed her in a grateful hug.

Rachel went back upstairs. She only had a few minutes to shower before she left to drive up North. She didn't have many friends left from her life as a child and young woman, but she had stayed in touch with Pel — or rather, Pel had stayed in touch with her — ever since they'd found one another as allies in third grade. Pauline Emily Lake. Pel to anyone who knew her well. Rachel had told Susan that she and Pel "had been lovers — sort of" as though that old relationship was all that existed between them. It was the part of her relationship to Pel that was most relevant to the conversation she and Susan were having. And yet Pel had stayed in her life in the more than twenty years since then, stayed most frequently during these last years when Rachel had been the head of her congregation in Provincetown. Pel had kept the connection by stopping by Rachel's office in the church annex. She would inquire how Rachel was doing, and linger with her hand on the doorknob until she had enough courage to ask whatever it was that was really on her mind — some question or issue that was puzzling her, usually of a personal nature. She and Rachel had never had a conversation sitting down, and over the years, Rachel had learned to wait and Pel had learned that she would.

They met for lunch in a small bar in Saratoga near the beauty parlor that Pel's lover of thirty years owned and operated. "This is different," Rachel quipped, "we haven't sat down to talk like this for years."

Pel nodded and looked around. They were in a scratched wood booth with a fake stained-glass lamp on the wall. The room was dark, dirty and comfortable. "Did I ever take you into that old dive here in the city? You know, that dyke bar where all the toughs hung out?"

"Remember? How could I ever forget? The Hudson, you mean? We played pool there, as I recall." Her words became drawn out with irony. "You'd just been reinstated, hadn't you? And you wanted to test it."

Reinstated. Pel rolled her eyes toward heaven and then gave a half-laugh, but Rachel couldn't really read her response. Reinstated after a six month ban for fighting with one of the other butches over a point at the pool table. That's what she'd told Rachel the night she'd taken her in there. But later, Rachel thought it was more likely a fight picked to show off for one of the women sitting at the bar.

"I'm thinking of opening my own place," Pel blurted out.

Rachel grinned and sat back in her booth. "Tell me about it. It sounds just right for you."

CHAPTER TWELVE

After lunch Rachel drove out toward the highway, thinking about Pel. She would never forget walking into the Hudson for the first time, into the dark and smoke. The beer smell seemed to seep out of the dirty wood floor and the red glow of light from the jukebox was about all the illumination in the place. She wasn't young that night, but she had been naive, and she'd stared at the women who looked like men milling around the pool table or flirting with women who looked like women — the whole range of women, from Barbie-doll slim and pretty to middle-aged housewives. Rachel had been appalled. And fascinated. Did she remember? Yes, she nodded again, alone in the car. She would always remember. She would especially remember how comfortable she came to be in that space, so much more comfortable than in her home. And — she laughed out loud in the car — she'd turned into a pretty decent pool player.

She wanted to talk with Susan. She wanted to tell her more about Pel, about how they'd made love over the downstairs room where her father lay dying. And how would they talk about Pel's way of being a lesbian? Could she say to Susan, Pel wouldn't let me make love to her when she made love to me. Could she say how comfortable she had been with that arrangement? How it let her relax and enjoy her own sexuality for the first time? Rachel knew that she'd learned things about herself from Pel, things she'd kept and cherished her entire adult life.

Habit drove her down the familiar roads. In her mind, she was back in the Hudson with Pel. And so she turned left on Broadway instead of going straight out to the interstate, only noticing her mistake as she was about to drive past the house she grew up in. She could have turned around, swung a U-turn right there in the broad, tree-lined avenue. But she didn't. Heart pounding, she kept on. The lawns in front of the old mansions got longer and longer, the houses larger and more ornate. The Smythe's home had been on the corner, a stone and wood monstrosity built by Rachel's great-grandfather at the turn of the century. Square stone inlay pillars supported a heavily beamed porch ceiling.

Rachel stopped across the street from the house and stared at her past. Nothing had changed, not the color, not the dark, shaded feeling of the house. The lawn was immaculate and unnaturally green for autumn, without a leaf on it, like a carefully tended golf course waiting to be teed off on. The whole house seemed to be waiting as it stared back at her through dark vacant window eyes.

Was it like that, she wondered, when she drove out of there sixteen years ago, expecting, with every muscle in her body straining toward optimism, to find a different life, a different Rachel at the end of her journey? She'd only been going to seminary, driving the five hundred miles to Virginia in her old Volvo station wagon, jammed to the roof with the treasures she wanted to keep. One carload. That was what she'd allowed herself out of the thousands of pounds of "treasure" in the family home. One carload. It had been enough. Memories don't weigh much, she told herself. Neither do those patterns of behavior we learn in our families. Shedding them took more than a right turn out of the driveway.

The porch swing was gone, she noticed.

Then she took a deep breath, made the U-turn and headed back down to Albany.

Susan looked up with surprise when she heard Rachel's car pull into the driveway. She had come home early after a difficult conference at Debora's office. If her old cat Toklas had been alive, she would have flopped on the couch and let the cat rub up against her chin and knead her paws in Susan's belly. But Toklas had died in the summer, her kidneys failing after fifteen years, and so Susan had wandered out to the kitchen to sit and read her mail. She'd thought about calling Rachel, but couldn't imagine quite how to tell her about the photographs. She was, at some level, ashamed to let Rachel know about them.

Susan walked quickly to the front door. "You look a little overwhelmed." She wondered if Rachel's lunch with Pel had been unexpectedly difficult. "Come on in." She regarded Rachel thoughtfully as she climbed the stairs to the front porch. "No, actually, you look stunned," she said, giving her a hug. "Was it that hard? What did Pel want?"

She shook her head. "No, Pel's great. Going to start her own business."

Mystified, Susan waited.

"I drove by my home," Rachel explained. "My parents' home, I guess I mean. The one I grew up in."

Susan was curious now rather than mystified. She wondered what it was that had affected her so? Being up at her mother's cabin hadn't upset her.

"Why does it still have that much power over me? I'm tired of this, tired of dealing with it." She looked at Susan for the first time since she'd come in the house. "I shouldn't have come," she sighed. "I'm sorry. I didn't mean to land this on you."

They headed into the kitchen. Rachel nodded when Susan gestured toward the tea kettle. "So that was my day. Yours?"

"Two newsworthy items," Susan began, trying to lighten their moods. But no matter how she told it, the envelope that had appeared on the Commissioner's desk wasn't amusing.

Rachel listened, astonished. "Do you know when the pictures were taken?"

"I know what year, which summer. I don't know when, or by whom. I know I'd never let someone take a picture of me with my hand on a woman's breast, no matter how silly or playful I felt." She knew she sounded defensive.

Rachel nodded, "Of course." They were quiet as Susan poured the tea. "What's the other item, then?"

Susan sighed. In some ways this had been harder for her than the photographs. "Debora has taken me totally off the case. She was upset that I went out and asked Jocelyn those questions, but someone complained that I was intimidating a witness. The prosecutor's office got a call this morning. Probably not too long after the Commissioner got the photos, as a matter of fact." She didn't need to tell Rachel all of it, that she and Debora had fought, seriously fought, for the first time in their relationship. They weren't doing too well with the change in roles, she told herself, but it worried her, it worried her a lot.

"What will happen then?" Rachel wanted to know. "You said on the phone this morning that she seemed okay with it, that she wanted you to ask some questions in the neighborhood. What about that?"

"She's got a new associate, some dyke who's new in town — Carol Whittier. She's supposed to ask the questions." Susan shrugged pretending it didn't matter, even though it did.

"What kind of questions? How could she talk to your neighbors? Imagine what they'd think!"

Susan couldn't even smile. "Actually, it might be

okay. She's trying to find out where Astrid is and how long she's been out of town. And whether any of the others indicted were under the illusion they were buying it from me. That kind of stuff. She's a lawyer. I guess it makes sense to use her." Susan was exhausted.

"I think I'd better go home tonight, sweetheart," Rachel said. "Let's both sleep. Come have breakfast with Richard and me. About eleven?"

"Thanks. I'll be in better shape by then." She let Rachel out and locked the door behind her. When did you know someone well enough to cry in front of them, she wondered. She had cried that afternoon in Debora's office. The tears had surprised her. She hadn't cried in jail when she was alone. She hadn't cried when she found Rachel waiting for her outside Debora's office. But after Carol Whittier left, after she and Debora had fought about whether Susan could be an active part of her own defense, after Debora had come out from behind her desk and put her arms around Susan, then she had cried.

She went back into the kitchen where she'd been sitting when she heard Rachel drive up. The half-opened mail was spread on the table. The room was dark. She sat down without turning on the light.

Fifteen years ago, her grandma Yetta had died. She'd died in her sleep on Thursday night, but her friend Gert didn't find her until nearly noon the next day. Her father had called the apartment in New York City where she'd been crashing and left a message, but she didn't learn of the death until Saturday afternoon. She made the funeral on Sunday morning with just a few minutes to spare, not knowing why she had come. Her father and her son Jake sat in the front of the small group in the synagogue, both wearing yarmulkes. She'd never seen Jake in one before and she'd never seen her father weep. He wept as the cantor chanted, he wept at the cemetery as they lowered the plain wooden coffin into the ground, and she had wept with him. Sitting quietly in the dark kitchen, she remembered sitting shiva with her father in their darkened living room. She had only stayed for three days and then fled, drained by the weight of her father's grief and her own experience of emptiness. Yetta had been her anchor. As long as Yetta was there, Susan could stray as far as she wanted. Now it was up to her.

Once again, Susan felt, it was up to her to figure out her direction.

Richard was conducting a Bach oratorio when Rachel came in, the music pouring out of the stereo in waves of intermingling grief and joy. He stopped long enough to say hello, then went back to his practice. Rachel sank into a chair and let the music wash over her, glad not to talk for a moment.

After a while the music stopped. When Rachel looked up, Richard was sitting in the chair across from her.

"Richard, you never talk about your childhood," she said suddenly. "Why? We always laughed about Colin and his mother, the baseball gloves and football gear she tried to get him interested in. All that stuff about finding him healthy male role models —

coaches, truck drivers — and he'd just fall in love with them. Why didn't we ever talk about you like that?"

Richard stayed silent long enough for Rachel to wonder if she shouldn't have asked.

"Was it just that we had more contemporary things to talk about?" She was willing to let him off the hook if he didn't want to answer.

"No." There was a pause. "It was because my childhood was hell and it didn't seem worth remembering."

Rachel waited, quiet.

"What's the point?" He shrugged as though he found it humorous. "That part of my life is about an inch on a foot-long ruler. Most of it's been a lot more fun to remember than the first inch. And I've only got about a quarter of an inch or so left." He moved his fingers as if he were holding an actual ruler. "Here's where I need to be."

Rachel crossed the room, sat down beside him and took his hand, moving her own along the invisible ruler. "Well, I went back to here today." She indicated the first inch. "Why does it still have power over me? Why does it make my hand shake? Why can't I be a grown-up and leave that behind?"

"If it still has power over you," he said slowly, "you must still want something from it." He put his hand over hers and took it away from the ruler. "That's what set me free, finally. I gave up on my past. I took it all — the fights, the fury, the wounds, the things it might have been if — and I made them into one big helium balloon." He shaped the balloon, just like he had the ruler. "And I took it out to the river on a windy day and said good-bye to it. Gave it a shove up in the air and let it go."

"You let it go?"

"Yeah. You know, the way they tell you to do in twelve-step programs. Let it go. But they never tell you how exactly to do that. I figured out the helium balloon all by myself. You're welcome to practice with it, if you need to." He was smiling now, a secret kind of smile, but he wasn't joking.

"Thanks, Richard." He hadn't told her anything about his past, really, but it was enough. Rachel felt calmer. "I may need to borrow that balloon."

But in her dreams that night, it wasn't the past that went up with the brightly colored balloon, it was Rachel, the adult Rachel, launched off the front porch step, dodging the rock pillars and arch as she rose, holding tight to the string of a multi-colored balloon. Terrified and exhilarated, she cleared the edge of the slate roof on the second floor and rose up toward the stone turret that stood sentinel watch over the green, green lawn. That turret had been her childhood escape, a hideaway, and she watched as it grew more and more distant. Was this what Richard meant by letting go? she asked in the dream. She was gripping tightly to the lifeline that connected her to the balloon. No. How could she ever let go? It was far too much for anyone to expect.

CHAPTER THIRTEEN

Thanksgiving

"Count on it," Carmen's voice boomed across the nearly empty room and bounced off the old beams of the renovated barn that was Glenda Mathis's home. "You've only seen the beginning. Menopause was unmentionable for years. Now it's a medical disorder. Hmmpf." She paused and surveyed the table she was setting. "Rachel, do you know any woman in her right mind who would take estrogen supplements for the rest of her natural life, just because she stopped bleeding?"

"Yeah, lots. The propaganda's intense. Your bones will start breaking, your blood pressure will climb off the scale, not to mention having hot flashes and getting wrinkles." Rachel was arranging flowers into three separate vases, one for each of the tables. Glenda had offered to have a Susan Myers Defense Committee Thanksgiving dinner at her home, an old renovated barn just beyond the city limits.

"Oh, wrinkles." Carmen hadn't given up on the menopause theme. "He must have forgotten to tell me about that. I'd have said yes in a minute to be saved from wrinkling in my old age." She put her hands on her hips and looked at Rachel. "What do they think our mothers did?"

"Suffer, I would imagine," Susan interjected. "Life today is supposed to be pain free. It's guaranteed in the Constitution, don't you remember?" She set up the folding chairs she was carrying and went back out to her car for more.

"Right," Carmen said to her retreating back, "that's the amendment they put in right after the one that freed the slaves."

"I'm waiting to see the day when science declares that testosterone alters normal male behavior and we have to medicate the entire sex to relieve them of their tendency toward hyperaggression and violence." Carol leaned across the table, setting glasses at each place.

Rachel raised an eyebrow at Carol. "Is that lawyer-speak?" Carol was the new hire in Debora's law office.

"Well, it *would* make life almost pain free for women," she insisted.

Glenda carried a dessert tray out, elbowed Susan out of the way, and put it on the sideboard.

"Uhh huh," Carmen looked at Carol speculatively. "And how long are you going to be waiting for this?"

"Yeah, Carol. Redefining normal. Now are you going to let the scientists do that or the psychologists?" Lindsey, Carol's lover, was putting Rachel's flowers on the tables. "Or the lawyers?"

"Not to worry," Rachel followed Lindsey around, checking the effect. "I'm sure the politicians will do any cultural redefining we might need."

Rachel was happy today, more relaxed than she'd been in the weeks since Susan's indictment, glad to have Carmen visiting for a couple of days. Nothing had changed, really, not in the legal situation, anyway. She knew that, but tomorrow they were going to the Adirondacks to hide in Rachel's cabin. Three days alone together. Rachel worried that it wouldn't be good for Susan to be away from the center of things for that long. And then she would remind herself, it was only three days and the rest of the world took this long weekend off, too. What could happen? She thought they both feared another smear attack, another letter to Susan's office or something worse. The threat of waking up to a full page photo spread of Susan in the local newspaper had diminished somewhat in its immediacy, but Rachel knew the possibility of it was always there, hovering at the edge of their pleasure in one another.

She saw Glenda standing in the center of the long dining room area, hands on hips, surveying the scene with apparent satisfaction. Her hair was newly permed, her lipstick and eyeliner penned in firm lines, and she was wearing a long floral hostess gown. "I planned this area to be able to entertain like this, but I never seem to have the time to actually do it." She was talking to Carmen, explaining that she'd wanted the entire lower level of the barn to flow from one open area into another — kitchen to dining area to living room and the large open fireplace. Carmen, dressed in her usual, comfortable African cloth pants and shirt, nodded, her round face bland.

"I'm glad I don't have to pay the heating bill," Susan murmured irreverently into Rachel's ear.

"Or haul the wood for that fireplace," Rachel agreed.

Just then the large barn door to the room was flung open dramatically and Angie came in with a rush. Behind her trailed Darlene, a small compact woman in cowboy boots carrying a huge salad bowl. "We came a little early," Angie explained. "What can we do to help? Where do you want the salad? All the dressings are in here." She waved a plastic bag in the air. "Hi, Rachel. Is this *her*?" She stood in front of Rachel and looked Susan up and down, as much of her as was visible.

"Hi Angie, hi Darlene." Rachel stood with her arms around Susan in the embrace they had been beginning when Angie flung open the door. She seemed at a loss for anything else to say, but didn't loosen her arms, holding Susan close.

"I'm Susan Myers," Susan laughed, brushing her dark curls off her forehead. "Does she hug a lot of women like this? Or did you suspect that I might be her new lover?"

"We guessed," Darlene said dryly. "Sweetie, leave these women alone and help me find a place to put this salad bowl down. You can do inspections later."

Obediently, like a large shaggy sheepdog following a feisty terrier, Angie followed Darlene across the room.

"That was Angie," Rachel said.

"Not to worry, Rach," Susan nibbled on her ear. "I'll be finding at least a dozen of my old friends who will want to check you out, make sure you've got all the right parts, you know."

"I expect they'll do it with a little more finesse than Angie, though," Rachel laughed.

The door began opening regularly then, as friends were arriving. Rachel wandered around the large dining area as Susan went to greet Charlie Leitman. He came in shaking the dampness off his tousled hair. Behind him were Martin and Jimmy, waving a bunch of yellow roses.

Carmen was holding forth in the living room with Glenda and a couple of her young interns as her willing, captive audience. "Have you got to this menopause thing yet?"

"Have I?" Glenda seemed glad to concur, and Rachel thought she enjoyed shocking her interns. "I bleed like a son of a bitch for two weeks, then nothing happens again for three months. I'm trying to counsel a client on the difference between investing in life insurance or the bond market and I turn beet red, my head tingles for a minute, and then sweat pours off me. Thank God for the tingle. Sometimes I get enough warning to escape to the bathroom." She was laughing, enjoying showing off, but she was keeping an eye on Charlie Leitman, too, making sure he wasn't at this end of the room yet.

"There you are. That's it," Carmen agreed. "How do you convince a client you aren't sweating because they're in such deep financial trouble? You should get it some Sunday when you're in the pulpit."

"I'll bet you get instant conversions, Carmen," Carol chimed in from the circle that had gathered behind Glenda and Carmen, "if your congregation thinks you're working that hard."

Carmen started to answer, but Glenda cut her off.

"I think the food line is open for business now," she announced. "You all better head over."

Rachel followed Glenda across the room to where Susan and Charlie stood talking. "I'm so glad you could come," she held her hand out to Charlie graciously, no longer the bawdy, raucous voiced comic.

"How have you been, Susan?" she turned to Susan, her voice seemed filled with concern. It made Rachel wonder — hadn't she and Susan been setting tables in the same room together for the last hour. "I hear you're still working. I think it's very brave of you, under the circumstances, to keep on like that when . . ."

"I told her it's the only thing to do," Charlie interrupted. "You can't give in at a time like this. It's not about what people will think," he held his hand up to stop Glenda's protest, "it's the only thing that will keep a person sane, doing what you're used to doing."

Glenda obviously disagreed but didn't want to contradict Charlie. "I see what you're saying," she said slowly, "but what about Susan? This must be a strain on her. Aren't you longing for a vacation?" she asked, changing her focus to Susan.

"Sometimes," Susan admitted. "But not usually when I'm at work, actually. And there's no vacation that is going to make all this go away and not be here when I get back."

"But the strain, the strain," Glenda was shaking her head, a worried look on her face. But when she saw the look of irritation cross Susan's face, she gave it up. "You and I," she turned to Charlie, "should have a chat someday. I have a couple of projects I think you might be interested in."

He nodded and allowed himself to be taken off to the buffet table by Glenda.

The dining room held three large round tables, each seating six or eight people. Susan pictured her own small table in the pantry nook of her kitchen. She and Glenda surely had different aspirations these days. It hadn't always been that way. When they'd known each other back in the late sixties in Boston, Glenda had been a housewife, staying at home to raise her two sons, while her husband went out to make it in the financial world. Susan had been a working mother, of sorts, when she could get out from under the drugs long enough. And there were some fairly long periods when she was nearly functional — she'd done a stint as an adjuster for an insurance company, worked in the front office of a law firm. Always the drugs found her, and the men in those high powered jobs seemed to be able to handle it better than she had.

"Hi," she put her hand on Rachel's shoulder. "You are saving that seat for me, aren't you?"

Rachel patted the empty seat next to her. "For no one else."

Conversation was low key, comfortable. Susan was starting to relax. She'd been afraid she might be the focus of people's attention, in spite of insisting this wasn't an "event" but a dinner. And basically, there was nothing new to tell anyone who asked about the case.

She caught Debora's eye at the next table and Debora winked at her, not daring to make any other, more flippant communication, wedged as she was between her law partner Amanda Clark's handsome Jamaican husband, Winston, and Glenda Mathis. At the third table, five younger women were arguing with Angie about AIDS education and its effect on the lesbian community.

"Trust me," a trim blonde twenty-five-year-old named Tyler was saying. She paused to swallow a mouthful of roast turkey, then waved her fork in the air for emphasis. "Most lesbians would rather talk about sex than have it. Don't you think that makes discussions of safe sex rather irrelevant?" Her tone was sarcastic and the tilt of her head as she looked at Angie was meant to be provoking. Tyler was Glenda's other trainer, working primarily with efficiency and time management sessions for low level managers in state government.

"You mean," Darlene interrupted, protective of Angie, "if a kid has one chance in a thousand of being struck by lightning if she's swimming in a pool during a thunderstorm, you shouldn't bother to warn her about the danger?"

"Lesbians aren't children," Tyler sneered, "we're perfectly capable . . ."

". . . of doing self destructive things and making fools of ourselves," Carol interrupted.

"I think women are just afraid to talk about sex, period. Not just lesbians. It makes doing AIDS education hard, isn't that right, Maria?" Lindsey tried to bring Maria Gomez into the discussion on her side, but Maria, the only woman of color at that table, just shrugged.

"You're all giving Tyler too much space. First, I don't agree we'd rather talk about it than do it. Second," Carol tapped her fork on the table for emphasis, "how do you separate talk from sex? Tell me talking isn't part of what you do sexually, Tyler?"

"Of course it is," Tyler said, dismissing the point. "What I'm talking about is the way lesbians want to be victims, too. What is it? We feel left out? Or what?"

Susan thought Angie might lunge across the table at that dig, but Darlene put a restraining hand on her shoulder.

"Tyler," Darlene drew herself as upright in the chair as her five foot frame would allow, "I know this might come as a surprise to you, but some people are victims in this world." She looked Tyler up and down scornfully. Her Texas drawl grew stronger. "Of course, someone with your background might never have seen someone like that. Have you ever thought . . ."

Tyler's lips were tightening and a flush was rising

to her cheeks when Carol leaned over and intervened. "Hey, you two, can't we just agree that some people are victims and some people are whiners? I mean, face it, okay, you're both right. You know, I heard on the news the other day that if you add up all the groups that consider themselves oppressed minorities, their number comes to 374 percent of the U.S. population."

"That just proves my point." Tyler was not appeased nor interested in reconciliation. Tyler's voice had risen a few decibels with each interchange.

Susan watched the interaction at the next table. "If this was the bar," Susan said softly, "I'd say we needed a little intervention here." Rachel nodded agreement. She stood and went over to the next table.

Susan was still watching Rachel when Carmen sat down beside her. "What are you seeing?" she asked.

"I'm supposed to be the human resources manager," Susan said slowly, "it's my training." The younger women at the next table were laughing raucously with Rachel now. "But I wouldn't have known what to do with that situation just now. I think I know her, that we're alike in so many ways, and then I realize she lives someplace totally different from me." She looked closely at Carmen to see what the question had really been about. The large face with the square jaw, framed with an Afro that was on the verge of losing control, seemed quite unreadable. "I don't want her to be the same as me. I don't need to change her. I love learning who she is."

"Not to worry," Carmen smiled, "you can't make Rachel be something she isn't. And right now she's pretty much focused on being with you in her life. I hope you've got room for that?"

"Without question," Susan said forcefully, then she hesitated, "assuming I have a life." Oh, fuck. She'd done what she said she wasn't going to do this weekend. She wanted to live as though this case was going to resolve itself, turn out to be a small glitch in the life she was planning.

Carmen was still smiling at her. "Listen. Sometimes the lessons we need to learn from the things that happen aren't always obvious while it's going on."

Susan felt herself start to flush. Was she that readable? Or was Carmen a good reader? Probably both. "I am the impatient type," she admitted. "If I didn't plan it, I want it to be over with and the lessons learned yesterday."

"Susan, did you plan Rachel?" Carmen asked gently.

Susan's head came up sharply. "No," she was defensive now, "but I did pursue her."

"Ummhmm. You don't have to think the way I think, but at some level, you pursued this indictment, too, don't you know? It didn't happen in a vacuum. You made choices along the way that have led you to this, even if you weren't aware of it."

"That's hard for me to hear. I think I understand what you're saying though. That if I'd done something differently ten years ago, like not working for the Alcohol and Substance Abuse Division, then this wouldn't be happening?" As she asked the question, Susan knew that wasn't what Carmen meant. "No. It's deeper than that, isn't it?"

Carmen just nodded. "You'll be fine, Susan. Put

132

some trust in your friends." She gave Susan another long, assessing look, and this time Susan could meet her eye. "Just be sure you know who your friends are."

As if on cue, Angie swooped into the chair next to Carmen, leaned across the table, and asked no one in particular, "Wasn't she wonderful? Did you see that? I *love* women who can take risks like that."

"Let me guess," Carmen played. "You're talking about Rachel?"

"Darlene," Angie breathed, undeterred. "What a woman. Did you hear her tell Tyler off? I can't believe I'm married to her. Isn't life amazing?"

"Weren't you and that Darlene having a bit of trouble last month?" Carmen asked. "Didn't we have a conversation about being couples or did I dream it?"

"We did." Angie drew herself up, dignified. "When two mature individuals confront their problems head-on, it doesn't take that long to work them out."

"I'm glad." Susan heard Carmen's irony, but Angie seemed not to notice.

Susan picked at her half-eaten piece of apple pie, then shoved it away. We can leave pretty soon, she thought.

Her conversation with Carmen was troubling her. Maybe Rachel and she could talk about it. Susan was sure Rachel would know what Carmen meant — that she had pursued this indictment. Every fiber of her being wanted to deny that.

Rachel was saying good-bye to Angie and Darlene. Darlene had her arm around Angie's waist and Angie's arm drooped possessively over her lover's shoulders.

"I want to know what you said to get them laughing so hard at the next table," Susan pulled Rachel away from the drafty front door. "I thought they were just about to achieve meltdown and you have them in stitches in a few seconds?"

Rachel shrugged. "Sex. It can be threatening and infuriating or it can be hilarious. I think I said something about seeing a dental dam for the first time in the dentist's office and starting to laugh." Susan smiled, remembering the occasion. It had happened just last week. Dental dams had not been a priority item in their early conversations, either. Not that they were going to let Angie know that. "Then I just reminded them there are such myths about lesbians as sexual people. On the one hand we get furious when people think that about us — that all we do is have sex, day in and day out, that sex is what defines us. On the other hand, we kind of like it, seeing ourselves as profoundly sexual. It's part of our rebellion as women. Women weren't supposed to enjoy sex for so many decades. We're the answer to Queen Victoria, don't you know?"

"Her prayers or her nightmares?" Debora asked, coming up behind Rachel.

"Probably both." Rachel waved to two of the younger women who were leaving and went over to say good-night.

"How'd I do?" Susan leaned comfortably into Debora's shoulder.

"You were a mensch, kiddo. Folks needed to see you here, see you being okay, you know, in order to keep on keeping on." Debora was twisting the small garnet ring on her wedding band finger, a gift from Sarah.

"Are you seeing her this weekend?" Susan asked, her hand on Debora's.

Debora looked up, confused, then realized what Susan meant. "Oh, yes. Tomorrow, I'm going down." She looked around the room, then lowered her voice and asked, "Is Glenda bidding on a contract for your office? I thought she did more financial management stuff?"

"She's branching out some, consulting on just about anything she can get paid to consult on. But I haven't heard anything about her and DASA. Why?"

Debora was frowning. "I think I heard her talking to Angie about it. Or Angie was asking her about it. They were in the kitchen. I wasn't meant to be listening."

Puzzled, Susan shook her head.

"What's gone out to bid at five million for three years of training?"

"The AIDS and Substance Abuse training for rehabs and state facilities," Susan replied.

"That's it." Debora was mulling something over.

"So give. What's the deal?"

Debora thought for a moment, checked to make sure they were still alone in their corner of the living room, then said, "I think I heard Glenda say you may not want her to get this contract. At least she's worried. That's what she told Angie."

Susan shook her head. "That's not a contract I have any jurisdiction over. The Commissioner and his staff will decide it. But I didn't think Glenda's firm was large enough to handle a contract of that size. Are you sure she's bidding on it?"

Debora nodded. "She told Angie she's developed some software programs that will cut the training

135

time in half. She's had interns working on it for over a year now."

"That's strange. The interns in our office from the Policy Studies Institute have been working on a computer based curriculum for training AIDS trainers. Some of them work for her, too. But she doesn't own that program. I don't think she does. She couldn't." She paused, a little less sure. That was the project Tom had been working on before his arrest. It was nominally under her jurisdiction, but it had grown too large — and too potentially revenue-producing — to stay in one department. J. Lawrence had intended for Eduardo to take it over for the division last month. And now that Eduardo had been dropped from the indictment, she assumed that would still happen.

"Didn't you know Glenda when you lived in Boston?" Debora couldn't seem to drop this, and Susan didn't know why.

"Sort of. I knew a lot of people then that I don't know now. That was before I got straight. Glenda was around. She was married then. Why?"

"Were you and she lovers?"

"Debora! Would I not have told you? If we were, I was in a total blackout," Susan said incredulously. "Can you really imagine it? Even when I was drugged to my earlobes, I wouldn't have been able to make love to a Glenda Mathis."

Debora grinned. "You're such a diplomat. I can see how you've gotten this far in bureaucracy with skills like yours. So how well did you know her then?"

"I worked for her husband for six months." Susan was impatient with the subject, wanted to push it away. Glenda's husband had been a daily pot smoker who brought his stuff to the office with him, insisting it wasn't a problem, just a helpful habit, like coffee. Susan shook her head, chasing away the memory. "I think Glenda and I talked a couple of times about having sons. She has two. It was just before my parents took Jake, and I was having a lot of trouble disciplining him, setting limits for him." Susan shrugged. She and Debora had covered this ground before.

"That's it, then?" Debora kept pushing, her green eyes a little sly.

Susan looked at her, perplexed. "She may have had a thing for me. Who knows. I wasn't paying much attention to anybody but myself in those days. I got the feeling she wanted to come out, but I stayed pretty far away from it. That was not an issue I wanted to explore with her. Let's drop this, okay?" She glanced over her shoulder. She was not happy talking about Glenda in her own living room, even if they were sure they couldn't be overheard. There might be more she needed to tell Debora about this, but not here, not now.

To her relief, Rachel spotted them and pulled herself away from Glenda, Martin, and Jimmy. She slumped into the sofa next to Susan. "We can go now?" she asked Debora.

"You can go now, *liebchens,*" Debora dismissed them benignly. "I'm outta here too."

They collected Carmen, thanked Glenda and were gone in about a minute. "Praise be," Rachel intoned, half laughing.

"You can say that again," Susan agreed.

"Praise be," Carmen obliged from the backseat.

"Why don't you two go on up to that cabin tonight? It's only eight o'clock and Richard and I can take care of ourselves, you know. It's not like we don't have things to catch up on."

"Sounds good to me," Susan smiled at Carmen in the rearview mirror. "Rachel?"

"Please. Yes, please."

CHAPTER FOURTEEN

As they drove up to the mountains, Rachel told Susan how she and Carmen first met Richard and Colin. "I went to visit Carmen in Birmingham where she had her first congregation. I'd no sooner gotten there than she told me the rumors she'd been hearing about this Episcopal priest up in the university town two hours north. When lightning struck the church steeple in a July thunderstorm, Colin started getting hate mail accusing him of offending God." She paused, apparently caught in a reflection. "I guess he'd thought he was being discrete, but his closet door had gotten pretty thin."

"I said we should go up and meet him, see what kind of help or support he might need," she continued. "It was 1981 and Carmen confessed Colin was only the second gay person she'd ever met. I was the first."

Susan nodded, so Rachel continued. "I think they would have tolerated him except that his lover in those days was black. Louie was a New Orleans queen and more than Alabama was ready for."

"What did Carmen make of it all?"

"I think she was surprised at how easy it was to like them. They were totally irreverent and nutty together. Richard sort of evened Colin out. Louis — well, he just stoked the fires. They were only together about a year, but it was enough to end Colin's career in the southern states." Susan was quiet. "What are you thinking?" Rachel asked.

"That I know what it feels like when a closet door gets thin." Another moment of silence as the car hummed on the snowpacked interstate.

"Did you never hide?" she asked. "Were you always so sure. How did you get that way? I feel so afraid sometimes. Then I feel like a coward or a fool." Her voice had grown bitter.

"Susan," Rachel said sharply, "I had nothing to lose, remember? Nothing. Sure, I wanted to prove myself, my work was important to me. But I always had the family money behind me if I took a wrong step. I had no kids to support. No kids who needed me to look normal so they could just live their lives and go to school." She stopped and took a deep breath. More quietly, she finished her thought. "For me, there were rewards in being out. I was part of a movement. Being out, being visible — that was what I could contribute. It's not simple. Don't punish yourself. Please."

She glanced sideways at Susan and put on her turn signal to exit the Northway. Keene Valley was only a few miles away now. She hoped they could both relax for a couple of days. They needed some time. They needed to be less desperate with each other.

They walked from the car toward the dark cabin. Rachel felt the distance between them as though they were strangers again and wished for a moment that she had walked out of Glenda's house and driven straight to her own. Alone. Was it only six weeks ago that they had come to this place together for the first time?

Rachel went out to the car for the bag of groceries and when she came back, Susan had lit the kerosene lantern and kindled a fire, leaving the stove doors open.

"Sit with me a minute," Rachel urged. She hated feeling Susan retreat.

Susan shrugged, clearly unwilling to give in and unwilling to start a real fight. Rachel pulled her down on the couch and put her arms around her, but she wouldn't relax.

"What was it?" Rachel asked, letting her arms fall away. "Can you tell me about it?"

"I don't know," Susan shrugged again. Then she sighed. "It was when you used that image, about the closet door being thin. Or transparent, even. Something hit me."

Rachel nodded, waited. At some level it was

impossible for her to imagine the terror of being exposed as a lesbian, to imagine how that could mean having the most important things in your life threatened. She could remember being somewhat afraid that her father would find out about Pel. She could imagine being disowned, even in the few months before he died. Letting him find out, or telling, would have been the ultimate rebellion, but Rachel had chosen not to let him know. The struggle between them had been more about who would control her life than whether or not she was a lesbian.

"I was terrified," Susan said. "I don't know why exactly. I had an image for a second of coming back from these three days away and seeing that photo of me and Monique in the newspaper."

Rachel listened.

"So then my whole life flashed in front of my eyes —" She laughed a little at Rachel's surprise. "No, your driving wasn't giving me a near-death experience."

"Oh, good." Rachel could feel the spring-tight tension in her gut begin to relax a little. If Susan could still crack a joke . . .

"I've hidden who I am for so long, the thought of being exposed as a lesbian seemed terrible. Worse than anything else that's happened. Why?" She turned to Rachel then. "This is nuts? Why do you think I feel like that when I know rationally that I won't lose my job now if people find out I'm a lesbian?"

"I'm not sure." Rachel wasn't ready to leap into

this discussion yet. "It seems to me that people use the closet as a way of keeping control. Information always gives you a kind of control. People who have more information about others can manipulate them, that kind of thing."

"That's right," Susan agreed. "I knew that even before I became a manager. Martin knows it. There's a protection in having information. I'm not sure he knows that part yet — he doesn't really know what to do with his information yet . . ."

Rachel waited for a moment, then suggested, "I think that some gay people have to hide, and some get into the habit of hiding. So even when there's no more reason for it, we keep doing the same thing." She searched Susan's face for a response but couldn't find one. "Just imagine if someone had found out you were a lesbian when you were doing all that work in the high schools a few years ago. Would Susan Myers be a Deputy Commissioner today?"

"No way." Susan was firm about that.

"So it wouldn't be stretching the point to say you might have a reaction to being exposed today. And let's face it, Godwin might not fire you over this, but your standing with him, your ability to get things done in your division, those things could be affected. This isn't all about the past, is it?"

"No. It isn't." And yet Rachel could see that there was something more to her fear.

"What else?"

"I've worked so hard to build my networks, to gain the respect of the people I work for, the people who work for me. It's not enough for me to be competent, I want to be respected and —" She paused, then said, "I want to be respected and liked."

Rachel nodded. She didn't think it odd. "If people really feel about gay people the way this culture tells them they ought to, then coming out means, well, it might mean people will cut you out of the network."

"Or despise me. Like Tom does. I hate being closeted, but I don't know if I have the guts to do anything else."

Rachel pulled away from Susan so that she could look at her more fully. Was it possible, she wondered, that Susan was talking about them, about their relationship? But she said nothing.

"This problem between Tom and Josie, for example," Susan explained. "I should have been more on top of it."

Rachel didn't see the connection to that and being closeted. "Why do you say that? You're not omniscient, Susan. Aren't you being a little hard on yourself?"

"Maybe. But I know I hesitated longer to confront Tom than I would have if it had been someone else on my staff. I think he knows I'm gay. He's kind of hinted at it a couple of times. Basically, I've been afraid of his anger. I know he carries a vicious homophobia around with him and I didn't want to get hit with it when he started swinging." She paused, then went on. "Because I know myself well enough to know I'd swing back. Big time. I don't like being angry at that level anymore." Then she laughed. "Besides, as a management technique, the slow burn is more useful — it lets me respond a little more appropriately."

Rachel nodded. She thought she was beginning to catch the drift of Susan's dilemma. "So, what would Josie do if she knew you were gay?"

"That's the question, isn't it? I don't know, I can't know. Maybe it couldn't be worse than it is now. She thinks I'm a coward for not confronting Tom more directly. And I've let her down, I know that. Would it have been worse if she knew? I don't know." Susan leaned back toward Rachel. "You see, usually in my work life, I know how to weigh a decision and make the right choice. I can size up an opportunity or a person in a moment. Part of it is skill and part intuition. I can make people see my point of view; often enough I can even get them to agree with me. When I deal with my staff, I don't have to supervise much. They usually want to do what I need them to do. I didn't get these skills overnight. I've worked damned hard for them." Her voice was defiant.

Rachel nodded, impressed in spite of a predisposition toward dismissing this sort of talk.

"I read. I pay attention to what I'm doing, to what's happening around me. What I value most is that the people I work with are as excited by and interested in their work as I am. I don't apologize for having a high regard for my work — women do that far too often, and we're as devalued by ourselves, sometimes, as we are by the men who hire and fire us." She looked at Rachel and laughed. "Enough lecture. It's just that I think I'm good at what I do. Very good. So it's hard for me to accept what happened with me and Tom and Josie? How did I let that get so out of control?"

They talked until midnight, until it was clear that

Susan's fears of losing her protection weren't about the past at all, but about her current situation, and a very real fear of losing the work that defined her.

The sun rose the next morning long before Susan and Rachel did. During the night the snow had continued and the sun was glaring off the fresh snow that covered every surface.

Determined not to let her mood of last night reassert itself, Susan leapt out of bed after only one cup of coffee and announced she was ready to make pancakes. Rachel watched pensively from a chair in the corner of the small kitchen, wishing it weren't so hard for her to switch moods, wishing she could trust this warmth and enthusiasm. When Susan asked where the spatulas might be, Rachel smiled and pointed silently at the drawer. Susan whipped open the drawer and pulled out a huge spatula, meant for turning — who knew what? — large omelets? She laughed and shoved it back, half-watching the pancakes on the stove that were bubbling and nearly ready to turn, and when she shoved a second time, it seemed as if the whole drawer collapsed.

"Damn," she muttered. Then, "Help me, Rach. I need it *now*."

Laughing, Rachel left her seat in the corner, handed Susan the smaller spatula and fiddled with the broken drawer. She pulled it out and, past what had appeared to be the drawer's original back piece, was a space. Finally she was able to lift the whole drawer out onto the kitchen counter. "My God, look at this, Susan." She was staring at a packet of envelopes that had been concealed behind the false back.

"What is it?" Susan asked, tending to the pancakes that needed turning.

Rachel held one of the pale blue envelopes up to the light for both of them to see. "It's my mother's handwriting. I can't see the date, but she wrote it before she was married. Look, it's from Enid Flint to Wallace Smythe. And here are a couple from him to her." Those were on a heavier white paper with a printed return address and the Harvard seal.

"Courting letters. How neat. I wonder why your mother put them there?"

Rachel wondered too, but breakfast was ready to eat and so she shrugged, tossed the dozen envelopes back in the drawer to deal with later. She didn't want her parents' voices intruding into this time with Susan. She couldn't imagine either of them approving of her life. The family roles, she'd told others frequently, were pretty standard fare — requiring that a woman remain subservient to her husband. As an adult, Rachel had been able to see that her mother had multiple reasons to acquiesce in such an arrangement. Enid Flint had married out of her class, way out of it, and Rachel thought because her mother had been an orphan and had no family of her own, that she felt — more than other women of her time, perhaps — that she didn't have a right to have a voice of her own.

"Aren't you going to read them?" Susan asked, mopping the last bit of syrup from her plate with a final bite of pancake.

"Later." Rachel had been quiet while they ate but Susan wasn't going to let go.

"So was it a romance? You've never said much about your mother — just that she had been an orphan. I've heard more about your father."

"I don't know, really. A romance? I think his parents didn't approve, but no one ever told me that. And they were both dead by the time I started school." She shrugged as though that were an end to it.

"Was she happy?" Susan asked quietly.

"Happy." Rachel fiddled with her coffee cup and then looked at Susan. "If she'd been happy, I don't think she would have had to drink herself into passivity."

Susan's eyebrows shot up, and Rachel guessed she'd sounded pretty bitter.

"It meant she was never present," she said. "By the time I was five I knew I didn't have a mother I could count on. She might focus on me for a minute, but then . . ." She shrugged. "I think she drank so that she could be what my father required of her without protesting. I thought I'd gotten over the resentment."

"That's a hard one to get over. Especially if no one else was there for you." Rachel thought Susan must have been remembering Yetta.

"I adored my father," Rachel said bluntly. "What else was I to do?" She looked at Susan, watched her watching. "This isn't what I wanted today to be about," she said softly. "Let's go out on the skis, what do you say?"

Rachel tried to shake off her ghosts as she stepped into the ski bindings and pushed out across the golf course hills to the forest trails beyond. But beneath her fierce concentration on the rhythm of her skis — push, glide, push, glide — was the memory of herself as a child, following her father around the grounds of their home as he gave directions to the gardener or groundskeeper. Following, waiting for him to notice her. Just as her mother sat on the porch or in the high-ceilinged sunroom, waiting to learn what was expected of her and then do it. She led the way out on the snow finding trails she'd skied most of her life. Susan followed, awkward at first, gradually getting her balance, until they skimmed over the snow like giant birds intent only on seeing what was over the next horizon.

CHAPTER FIFTEEN

Back at the cabin, they built a fire in the fireplace. Nursing cups of warmed-up coffee, they snuggled in close on the couch and for a moment Rachel thought they might be able to put the last evening and morning behind them. But within minutes, Susan started to nod and doze. Rachel held her in her arms and stroked her curly hair, ran a finger across the fine bones above her eyes and along her nose. Susan smiled with sleepy pleasure at first, but soon was sound asleep.

Left alone, Rachel couldn't help thinking about

her childhood and her family. As the only child, Rachel was the heir in spite of herself. Meant to be the dutiful daughter, for many years she tried hard to do what was expected of her. Until she realized it was killing her, just as it had killed her mother. Her escape hadn't been dramatic or simple, and it didn't happen all at once, but she refused to be squelched. Maybe, she thought, maybe her mother's example had acted like an antidote for her, not allowing young Rachel to acquiesce in her own oppression like her mother had.

After four years away at college, Rachel had come home to nurse her dying mother. It was expected of her. Her father nodded his approval. She would live at home until she married.

Rachel looked down at Susan, curled up asleep in her arms, half-lying on Rachel's lap. She had lived there for a while, through her mother's illness and death, well into her father's final series of strokes. She'd never openly rebelled, but always kept her mental reservations firmly in place.

Restless, she eased out from under the sleeping Susan and paced the living room, cup of coffee in hand. Finally she was standing once again in the kitchen in front of the drawer half-hanging out of the cupboard with the old letters shoved to the back. She set down her coffee and scooped up the letters, taking them back to the living room where she settled in the middle of the floor. She picked up the first faded blue envelope addressed in her mother's hand.

The flimsy blue envelopes were like a voice from the past, Rachel thought, a mute testimony of a woman who had no money or resources. Faded, plain, they were subtly acceptable but not outstanding. In contrast were the three envelopes penned in her father's heavier script on cream-colored envelopes embossed with the crimson Harvard seal. That message was unmistakable.

April 20, 1941, was the date, and the thin pen addressed her father as Wallace. Of course, she thought, he was never known by a nickname. She glanced through the one-page note that thanked Wallace for the walk along the Charles River during the regatta. There was scarcely a voice in the note, let alone a personality. Rachel had heard their story, repeated first by her grandparents when she was a small child, told with an aura of disapproval. Later, her father told their story as a ritual, the purpose of which she didn't understand. She knew her mother had been a shop clerk at Filene's, selling women's gloves, when Wallace first noticed her. He was buying a gift for his mother and was in a bad, bullying temper, which Enid had coaxed him out of. He'd never minded admitting that.

But never in Rachel's wildest dreams could she have imagined what followed in those letters — Wallace's proposal of marriage, Enid's refusal and her reason, his terms for making a marriage that would suit them both, if she would follow his directions to the last detail. Rachel's coffee grew cold at her side as she read letter after letter written during that fateful spring and summer of 1941, leading to her parents' marriage in a lavish ceremony a few days before Pearl Harbor. Her mother, she realized, had stored the letters in the cottage so that Wallace wouldn't destroy them. She had left them there for

Rachel to find. For the first time in her life, she had reason to believe that her mother had been thinking about her. She wanted to tell me, Rachel thought, tell me in spite of her fears.

"I cannot marry you," the young Enid Flint had written, "as I am not the woman you think you see." She had come to Boston from Akron, Ohio, not as an orphan, but as a pregnant, disgraced young woman sent away by her angry, violent father. She had worked in a grocery in South Boston until the birth of the child was imminent, and then had been taken in by the South Shore Home for Unwed Mothers. Her baby, a girl, was born on January 3rd, 1940, and given out for adoption immediately. Afraid to go home, she had found the job at Filene's only three months before Wallace discovered her.

Wallace's letter in return was illuminating. Rachel drew in a sharp breath when she read it and then looked at the date. It had not come at once; he must have pondered this, but she doubted he talked it over with his chums at Harvard. The women of his own class, he told Enid, did not attract him. Knowing her father's need to control every part of his life, this made sense to Rachel.

What drew him to Enid was made even stronger by her letter, he'd said. Not her honesty, Rachel thought, not her courage, but the fact that he now had a way to own her. His terms were simple and straightforward. She would say she was an orphan and cut all ties with her family in Akron. She would never tell anyone about the child — he said he didn't want to know anything about it or the man who had been Enid's lover before him. She would obey him in this and in all things during their marriage and their union would be satisfactory to both. That was his word. *Satisfactory.* No mention of love or passion.

Apparently it was a bargain Enid Flint could not refuse. Rachel tried to imagine her in 1940, sent away by her family, bruised by the loss of a lover and a child, living in a room in a noisy boarding house in South Boston, commuting to work on the trolley, trying to save a few pennies, for what? Did she send money to her mother? What was her family in Ohio like. My God, Rachel realized, I have cousins and aunts and uncles, maybe, that I've never known. And somewhere, lost in time, she had a sister, a half-sister, her mother's oldest daughter.

All of her life, Rachel had lived knowing she was alone. Her father's brief visits to the nursery only confirmed that. From as early as she could remember, Rachel envied those children with brothers and sisters. Any family, if she was truthful, with all of its noisy competitions and disagreements, made her envious.

She fingered her mother's letters, turning over the thought that her mother must have been a one-rebellion woman, and the consequences of that rebellion must have seemed so dire that she had accepted continual acquiescence. Almost.

There were two more letters in plain white envelopes that had been hidden in the drawer with the others. One was a copy of her letter to the adoption agency requesting that, if her daughter should ever ask, she be told her mother's name was Enid Flint, originally from Akron, Ohio, that she married Wallace Smythe of Saratoga Springs, New York, and that her daughter's father's name was

Brian Calhoun, originally from Dayton, Ohio. The second was a letter from the adoption agency saying they had no authorization to honor such a request. They were both dated in 1953. Rachel had been ten years old when Enid wrote her request. They, mother and daughter came to the cottage often during the summers between the time Rachel was ten and the time she began high school. Enid might have hidden the letters at any time. But when she wrote the letter in 1953, she could not have been sure that — if the agency had been able or willing to honor her request — Wallace would die before her daughter found her. She must have been willing to violate the terms of her contract with him. Years later, it seemed she did have another rebellion in her.

One of Rachel's first lessons had been that people were drawn to her because of her money. As a child and as a young woman, the temptation had been to use that to her advantage; it was only later, after many more hard lessons, that she had figured out that money weakened rather than strengthened her connections with people. After the death of her father one of the first things she had to deal with was what to do with his money. She thought she didn't want it. She thought she hated it, knew that it was a burden. At first she wanted to give it away. And she tried — she gave away large amounts, but it kept coming back, sprouting up in dividends and options and things she'd never heard of. But she soon realized that giving money away created almost as big an obligation and burden as having it.

Gradually she'd learned to live with her money, learned when and how to give it away. And she held on to one principal she was sure of — that she wanted her giving to be direct, from her to someone else, and she always preferred that what she gave wasn't only cash; she needed to be of use because of who she was, not because of what she had.

I learned how not to let money isolate me, Rachel realized. My mother never did.

Following an impulse, she left the letters lying in the living room and put on her boots and jacket. She walked down the driveway through a pine forest so deep it was dark in the bright snowy afternoon light. The road up to the cabin was silent. A raven screeched at her and she headed up the ridge to the golf course and looked out over the snow-covered hills that stretched toward Haystack Mountain, sharp and grim in the distance. She wondered at her calmness. Why wasn't she more upset at what she had discovered? Here was the family she'd longed for — hidden from her. Rachel had been looking for something her entire life, and hadn't she just found it in her kitchen drawer?

She shook her head at the raven. No, she'd lived in a house filled with hidden sadness, a sadness that lay just beneath the surface and covertly affected everything that happened. She may not have known what created the sadness, never known what questions to ask her mother or father to find the name of what she was feeling. But she *had* lived with it and knew it well.

Understanding, really understanding, what it meant that her mother had hidden those letters — and had intended for her to find them — might take a very long time indeed.

She looked back at the footprints she had made wandering through the snow. "My mother is dead,"

she said it aloud, "and I never felt her love for me."
She could almost feel her mother reaching through
the vast ocean of space and time, feel her in the
letters she had written as a young woman, in the
secret drawer she had fashioned — hidden, but not
too secret to be discovered. Standing absolutely still,
trapped between the sky and the snow, she imagined
her mother smoothing the letters, sliding the drawer
past the catch that would stop it from coming out far
enough to reveal the letters prematurely. She could
feel the sadness lift away from her mother's memory.
She looked up at the sky, tears in her eyes. The
raven drifted overhead, spun, laughed raucously and
flew into the sun. In so many ways, she was not
alone. Believe it, she whispered to herself. Begin to
believe it.

CHAPTER SIXTEEN

Susan sat on the floor reading the letters. It was an interesting experience, coming as she did from a family where she was the only secret, the only disgrace, the history the family wanted to hide from the neighbors. She couldn't imagine there being any other secrets in her family. Drug arrests. An illegitimate child. More drug arrests. And yet, however hidden they had kept her, however horrified they were at her life, however much they might have wanted her to go away or belong to some other family, they never sent her away. She shook her head thoughtfully and tried to imagine Rachel's mother as a young girl, probably not a conscious rebel, but a young woman who was trapped in a life she didn't understand and couldn't control. Sent away. Denied. Her only revenge had been to do the same to them. Deny them. Forever. As though she were dead. No, she corrected herself, as though *they* were dead.

Rachel came in while Susan was reading, nodded and went out to the kitchen. Susan finished and took her empty coffee cup into the kitchen for a refill. Rachel was staring at the utensil drawer as if she were waiting for it to speak to her.

"Rachel?" Her face was tear-streaked. She just shook her head. Not a "no" shake, but an "I don't understand" shake.

Susan led her back into the living room, back where the fire was playing on the already darkening shadows around the room. She sat down and pulled Rachel down next to her.

"You know how when people say they're in a fog?"

Susan nodded.

"Now I know what that means. It's not inside you. It's that there's something between you and the outside world. Inside," she brushed her hair off her face, "inside it's crystal clear." Her tone was bitter.

"What's clear, Rachel?"

"My childhood. My life. These scenes keep playing over and over. Like I lived it yesterday. And without —" she paused, looked at Susan, searching for the right word — "without the lies, the myths, the stories I made for myself so that I could go on."

Susan couldn't follow it all, but gradually Rachel showed her how it had worked. Sometimes, in her desire to be "like" her friends, she consciously constructed an image of her family that fit. These times, her father became a stern but loving patriarch rather than a bully who was pushed by his own fear of losing control. And her mother? An alcoholic, yes, but basically a passive woman. Rachel had always suspected that her mother had used the alcohol, and perhaps prescription drugs, to maintain her mask of calmness, of serenity. "But I never realized the depth of . . . of her pain, I guess. How could I have?"

"She didn't want you to know, not then, not while you were still growing up. She wanted to protect you, Rachel."

"That's not exactly a perspective I've had before today," Rachel said, her voice still bitter. "I thought she found me, well, uninteresting. I could never get behind the mask, to see who was there. I gave up trying after a while. She didn't want to be known and I thought she didn't want to know me either."

"That must have been hard for both of you."

Rachel nodded, quiet for a moment. She drew Susan's arms closer around her. "I tried the same mask, without the props of drugs and alcohol. I didn't know it wouldn't work for me until I got furious at my roommate when I was in college. I don't have any idea what the argument was about, now. All I remember is that feeling. I was astonished, sick, that I could feel like that."

"Like what?" Susan pulled back a little, watching Rachel as she spoke.

"Like I picked up the iron and threw it across the room at her. If I'd killed her, I wouldn't have minded right then. I wouldn't have minded until I came to my senses."

"You threw an iron at your roommate?" Susan knew she shouldn't laugh, but she couldn't help it.

Rachel seemed to snap out of it. She grinned at Susan's amusement. "So much for serenity."

"Rachel, it's normal to have emotional ups and downs."

"I learned that. Later. What I was feeling that day wasn't normal. It was a backlash. Before that, the only extreme emotion I'd ever felt was panic — fear that I'd done the wrong thing, or that I might do a wrong thing."

Susan nodded, beginning to understand that if she had chosen to hide herself in a closet, Rachel had hidden behind a mask.

"Is this making any sense at all?"

"Oh, yes," Susan roused herself from her silence. "Yes, but in a weird kind of way to me. The panic I used to feel wasn't that I might do something wrong, but that I'd end up doing exactly what everyone else was doing and no one would pay any attention to me. I did wrong things as often and as extremely as I knew how. Even now, I need to be noticed. I told you that. It's what drives me." She paused, then said, "It's funny, my impulses said don't conform, push off from everything that's the norm. Yours said to pretend to be like everybody else." She gave a half-laugh that caught in her throat.

Rachel looked uncomfortable. Then she shrugged,

as though the old images were clinging to her shoulders. "For my mother to have left those letters there, it must have been . . . She had to have thought about me, not just me as a child, but me today." She looked closely at Susan. "Even if I wasn't always perfect, I have to learn to believe that she loved me enough to take that risk for me."

She didn't need to tell Susan, not tonight, about the other ways her life had been shaped by not believing she had been loved. Tonight it was enough to sit there in the dying firelight with their legs touching, holding hands as they talked.

When they finally went into the bedroom, Susan thought they would sleep together like they had the night before, tangled in the center of the bed, arms and legs entwined. And they did undress slowly, separately, each in her own world. It was only when Susan had stretched out under the comforter that Rachel brought the candle over to where Susan lay, pulled the comforter back and moved the candlelight down the length of Susan's body from breasts to belly to the dark hair between Susan's legs. With one hand she moved Susan's legs apart, the candle throwing a trembling light.

"Everything seems like metaphor to me tonight. When you move the light, everything changes. Disappear. Reappear. What's real? Am I sounding like a theologian?" She was teasing and Susan was glad something of Rachel's spirit was returning.

"Put the candle down," Susan whispered. "I want you now. Is that real enough for you?"

Rachel nodded. She set the candle on the nightstand and turned to Susan.

"Make love to me, Rachel."

Susan liked the way Rachel's eyes darkened as she moved out of the candle light and into the shadow of their bed. She waited while her lover's fingers opened, probed. She resisted the temptation to pull Rachel's face down to hers, wanting to see where this night might take Rachel. When her cunt was very wet, Rachel took Susan's hands and brought them down, letting her feel her own wetness. And then Rachel's tongue was there with Susan's fingers and they were all moving, wet and slick, playing with her slippery hard clit, pushing against it, teasing it back until Susan felt Rachel's fingers inside her, felt her push deep inside and the orgasm pushed back at Rachel, following her rhythm in wave after wave.

They drove back down to the city the next day in the late afternoon sun, relaxed and easy. "You know, it's weird." Susan frowned. "When we drove up here the worst thing I could imagine was coming back and having those pictures be made public. Right now, well, it's just not that important anymore. Not that I want it to happen," she hastened to add, and Rachel grinned.

"Since we're on the subject," Rachel suggested, "tell me how it works, this partial closet of yours. Some people know, some don't. It's not just lesbians who know. Like Charlie knows about your life, and he's not gay."

"He's not gay, he's A.A." Susan laughed at the rhyme. "He had to know. The few people outside the lesbian gay community who know ... it's sort of on that basis." She paused, searching for examples. "I would only have lunch with people who were business associates, not with friends. I didn't want to be seen downtown with people who were known to be gay. It didn't seem a good idea. Debora's so out — she and I never met for lunch. We'd meet at the health club or have dinner at her house or mine." She thought some more. "When I didn't have a business lunch, I'd take my lunch, eat alone in my office." She laughed, but didn't feel amused. "You get a lot done like that."

"Sounds kind of lonely to me." Rachel gave her a sideways look.

"It's what I was used to, Rachel."

"Who in your business life does know you're gay?" Rachel asked thoughtfully. "Tom probably knew. Who else?"

"You mean among straight people?"

"I guess so. Do other gay people in that setting know one another?"

"Mostly. I think Martin knows everybody in state government who even had a same-sex wet dream. He makes it his business to know. It depends. Why?"

"I was thinking about the photos."

"Yeah?"

"It had to be somebody who knows you're gay and knows what effect that would have on you at work, right?"

"Somebody like Tom."

"Is that what you're thinking?"

"It would be an easy hit. Only one problem. Tom's never been on a gay beach in his life, so it's hard to figure where he would have found those photos."

There was silence for a moment. Susan was thinking about going back to work, going back to life under the shadow of this indictment, a shadow that seemed to grow darker and darker as the trial date in January grew closer and still there were no answers about how the cocaine had gotten into her apartment. Thanksgiving dinner seemed a lifetime ago and she was trying to recall her conversation with Debora. "Debora asked me something about Glenda Mathis, what my relationship with her was like back in Boston."

"You've known her that long?" Rachel sounded surprised.

"I worked for her husband. For a while. I don't remember a lot of that time. The blackouts were getting pretty grim. But Debora asked me if we'd been lovers. We weren't, but . . . I wasn't entirely up front about what happened."

Rachel looked over at her. "One of those not-proud moments?"

"Yeah. I guess I knew she was interested. I think I was pretty contemptuous. Clearer about that than I needed to be. Something along the lines of 'you've got to be kidding' or 'not if you were the last woman on earth.' Something charming and tactful like that."

"Uh huh. I see what you mean."

"After that night I didn't see her again until we both ended up in Albany. I recognized her right away and I'm sure she saw me. The second or third time we were in the same room together, we sort of nodded politely. After that," she shrugged, "I just assumed we both wanted to forget the past."

"But she's on your defense committee."

"Yeah. I think we're fine. We worked together on a couple of projects recently. She asked me to do the United Way volunteer training two years ago. I liked her work. She's competent. And ambitious. I respect that."

They were in the city and Rachel was concentrating on the traffic. She pulled into Susan's driveway.

"Rachel." Susan snuggled against Rachel's side, her tongue moist and warm on Rachel's ear.

"Mmmm?"

"Spend the night with me?" It wasn't the plan. Susan was supposed to be getting ready to go back to work the next day.

"I thought you'd never ask."

Susan's apartment was warm and welcoming. Rachel seemed relaxed. "I'll let Richard know we're back," she said, picking up the phone as Susan disappeared into the kitchen.

When she returned, Rachel was holding the phone tight against her chest. "Richard is in the hospital. Pneumonia — pneumocystis. He's in intensive care, not responding to medication yet."

Susan took the phone out of her hand and hung it up. "How did you find out?"

"John had stopped by to leave me a note. He said Richard wants to see me. He's allowed one visitor for ten minutes each hour."

"Go."

"I'll be back," Rachel said distractedly to Susan's worried look. She took her mother's letters out of her suitcase and shoved them in her go-everywhere backpack.

"I love you, Rachel," Susan caressed Rachel's face, ran her fingers through the soft gray hair, and then walked her to the door.

CHAPTER SEVENTEEN

Susan sat astride the machine, her legs stretched as far apart as they could reach without being dislocated from her hips. Slowly she pulled them together against the force of the weights, then let them fall open. Three sets of twelve. Then she readjusted the lever beside her and the weights shifted. Now she had to press against the weight as she tried to force her legs apart. She was sweating heavily, trying to remind herself about no pain, no gain, go with the burn. Yeah, yeah. It was barely working. This abductor/adductor machine was one of her least favorite in the whole Nautilus cycle. Because of that, she never skipped it. Frowning with concentration, she pushed her legs apart for the last time, wondering what in her personality made her torture herself like this.

She couldn't seem to force her mind into a pleasant fantasy. Yesterday morning, waking with Rachel up in the mountains, seemed a hundred years away. She had walked vaguely through work, knowing there were things she needed to focus on but unable to. After the conversation with Rachel about Glenda and their mutual past, Susan had found herself trying to ferret out some clue, some hint about what might still be going on between her and Glenda. But all she could come up with was the same innocuous conclusion she'd offered Rachel — it was over, Glenda was good at what she did, it wasn't an issue for either of them. And it really wasn't.

Nonetheless, she'd told Martin as she left for the gym, "Pull any files in our division," she told him, "that reference Glenda Mathis or her company. Not just off our main system, but check each unit too, will you?" He'd looked surprised, but nodded obediently.

Rachel had called twice from the hospital during the afternoon to say that Richard was stronger, beginning to respond to the pentamidine. It had taken longer this time than the last, a precursor of the future. At least this time he was responding.

It was then, connected to nothing, no cue, no subliminal message she could ever uncover, that she remembered the key, and her legs snapped back together with a force that surprised her and made the weights clang amateurishly. For weeks she had insisted that no one in the world had a key to her house; no former lover, no friend, not the plumber or electrician. It wasn't something she was comfortable with, she reminded Debora. She didn't *have* that kind of relationships. Giving girlfriends her key so they could drop in and surprise her was not Susan's idea of fun. "I've always wanted my privacy," she'd insisted, and Debora had nodded and not asked whether Susan had given Rachel a key yet, because she knew she had.

And now this. Clara. The dyke who lived on the corner of her block. The one who was always willing to do something for anyone she knew. Last year, when Susan had been traveling more frequently, Clara had been nearby and willing and loved cats and had come in once a day to feed and water her old cat, Toklas. When the cat died last summer, it had never occurred to Susan to ask for her key back. She'd forgotten Clara had it, in fact.

. She got up from the torture machine and moved over to the quad workout, resisting the impulse to rush out of the Y and go to Clara's and demand her key back. The proper course of action would be to call Debora and report, to say nothing to Clara. But knowing the key was out there would niggle at Susan like a hangnail, she knew that. She hated loose ends. She liked knowing where everything of hers was. A control issue, her friends might chide her, and Susan could acknowledge that it was, without being embarrassed.

She adjusted the backboard on the quad machine, then pulled and reset the pin in the weights. Why did she always seem to follow a six-foot-five,

250-pounder who lifted three times the weight she did?

So, Clara had a key. It was impossible to imagine her having anything to do with this drug fiasco. Clara was a shy, quiet schoolteacher in her fifties. Susan's information came partly from dyke community sources, partly from Martin. Clara had lived with her parents until about five years ago, when they both died of something or the other, still lived in the same house she was born in. Most of her friends were nuns, since she taught at a Catholic girls' school. She might have gone that way herself if her parents had ever released their grip enough for Clara to leave home. That Clara had come out about the time of her fiftieth birthday had astonished the few friends who knew. It seemed an act of assertion beyond anything they could imagine for Clara. An equally shy and quiet nun who taught at the high school started sharing Clara's home. End of chapter, as far as dykes went.

Still, Clara wasn't finished making changes. Tired of teaching fifth-graders, she applied to and was accepted at the state university's political science Master's degree program for women interested in working in government or running for office. When Susan asked Clara to visit her cat, Clara had been an intern working for one of the state senators. But in spite of these apparently radical changes, nothing about Clara suggested she had changed enough to be involved in drug use or sales or anything vaguely illegal, overt or covert.

Susan lay on her back and pushed her feet against the 120-pound weights hanging on the end of the chair, first one, then the other. Ferociously she pedaled, concentrating on making her muscles do exactly what she expected of them. God knew, not much else in her life was going the way she'd planned.

"Did you plan Rachel?" Carmen's voice came into her thoughts as she rested between sets. No, in fact, she hadn't. She told Carmen she'd pursued Rachel, and that was true, as far as it went. But she had never imagined she would be so ready to have Rachel be a part of her life, to share Rachel's life however she could. As much as she would like to believe she was in control, she knew she hadn't planned on Rachel either.

Leave it, she told herself, as she got up off the machine and wiped away the sweat running down her face. Don't try to figure it out. Time is not at fullness. Did the *I Ching* really say that or was she making it up? She could concentrate when she had to, and she made her way through the biceps/triceps machines with quiet fierceness.

"Not bad," Jorge, the trainer, told her as she panted between sets. "Did you double your weights on purpose today, or were you just not paying attention?" He went behind the machine and readjusted the pin to Susan's usual weight level. "There. Try that."

Susan looked at him for a moment, her mind blank. Then it registered and she decided to laugh. "I think it's time for the whirlpool, Jorge. Check in a few minutes and make sure I haven't drowned, okay?" He grinned, gave an obliging wave and moved on.

Back home, her sweaty clothes thrown in the

172

washing machine, Susan pondered two courses of action: walking down the block to get her key back from Clara or calling Debora. For once, discretion won.

"Susan, don't you dare go up there and ask for that key back." Debora was even more pissed off at the suggestion than she'd imagined. "I don't want you to say a thing to her, not a word, do you hear me?"

"Debora, relax. It's not like this is a hot lead or anything. Clara Moynihan never did a drug stiffer than aspirin in her life. It's a fluke. I just thought I'd tell you since you've been asking and asking about that key."

"I hear you. But just remember that the police couldn't find any evidence of a break-in, not a single nick or scar to say somebody came in the window or even used a pick on your door lock. You say her girlfriend's a nun? Carol used to be a nun," she was talking about the new lawyer working part-time in her office, the one who was looking for Astrid. "I'm going to put her on it right away, so don't you . . ."

"Debora, you're overreacting." Susan snapped, then paused, expecting an argument. But there was silence. Shit, she'd done it again. "I'm sorry," she apologized. "I think I've discovered something new that's going to be helpful, then I deny it's any use at all and my adrenalin goes crazy."

"It's okay, Susie." Debora accepted the apology and turned the moment around. "What do two Jewish girls know about nuns, anyway? I mean, did you ever think this would be a meaningful topic of conversation between us?"

Susan had to laugh. They talked for a few more

moments, and then Debora hung up. Susan wandered around her apartment, lonely, more depressed than she'd been since the night after the indictment, the night she spent in the county jail. She wished Rachel were there to talk with, to comfort her, and she was also glad Rachel was with Richard. She wanted to be alone, and she didn't want to be alone. She thought Carmen might be right about what was happening to her, and she was furious at Carmen. There was only one thing that made any sense at midnight on a Thursday. She picked up the phone and dialed her son Jacob in Washington state. It was only nine o'clock his time and talking with Jacob always seemed to calm her down.

"Susan." He sounded surprised. "What's up?"

"Not much," she said. "Am I bothering you? You guys busy?" She knew the girls would have been in bed for a couple of hours and Laurie was probably doing classwork for the next day.

"Nah," he said easily. "Laurie's reading and I'm watching a delayed-broadcast football game, so I already know Seattle isn't going to win." He didn't seem particularly upset about this, and she wondered for the millionth time how she'd ever produced a son who was so easy-going. "How's the case?" He wasn't sure he should bring it up, she could read that in his voice. "Anything new yet?"

"Not really." She told him about remembering the key and Clara Moynihan and the cat and before long they were both laughing — just a little — at a shared memory of Toklas and her catnip eccentricities. Toklas and Jacob had moved into Susan's house in the same year and they'd grown up together — all three of them, Susan used to tell friends, she and Jake and the kitten.

"It just feels more than a little out of control, Jake," Susan told him finally. "I'm on one of those kid's merry-go-round things that spin faster and faster and I can't get my feet on the ground to brake it, to slow it down. Know what I mean?"

There was another silence as Susan realized what she'd just asked her child who had once been spun so far out of control she'd nearly lost him. Shit, she breathed to herself. Shit, shit, shit. She didn't mean to bring that up.

"Yeah, Mom, I do know what you mean." His tone was not accusatory, she noticed, and he almost never called her mom, only in their closest moments. "And you know what? The merry-go-round almost always comes to a stop by itself. You've just got to hang in there until inertia takes over, okay? You'll get your feet on the ground again. I know you will. You always have."

He was right, Susan thought, and she went to bed that night with the image of the merry-go-round slowing down, slowing down, until her life began to come into focus again and she could distinguish trees and buildings from the blur that had circled her and gradually she could even see the ground and know that in a little while she would be able to put her feet down on it and walk away without tumbling head-over-heels into the darkness.

CHAPTER EIGHTEEN

By Tuesday afternoon Richard had been moved out of intensive care and onto a general ward. The oxygen tent over his bed had been dismantled and a tank with a mask substituted so that he could use it whenever he needed it. Pentamidine still dripped through the IV into his arm.

"We're sort of getting the hang of this, aren't we?" he asked Rachel with a weak smile. He breathed heavily, deliberately, as though he were practicing a new skill.

"Sort of," she agreed, holding his free hand

loosely in hers. This was his third bout with pneumocystis. During the first one, Colin had been alive, just barely, in the same hospital. The second time was eight months later, during the summer. This attack seemed too soon, too sudden to Rachel.

"Carmen left Saturday morning," he said, giving Rachel the background she needed. "I was fine then. I did the hotline for a few hours Saturday night and felt more tired than usual. I asked John to come and stay over. He brought me in Sunday morning."

So much between them was unspoken. Rachel nodded slightly at the mention of John. If Richard had been truly ready to quit, as he often claimed he was, he wouldn't have asked John. John was insurance, an AIDS buddy who'd seen three men through these stages to the inevitable end. John knew to set the alarm for every two hours so he could go and check Richard's breathing. John knew when the labor of breathing had gone beyond deep sleep.

"How was the weekend?" Richard asked slowly. "Are my mountains still there? Did you ski?"

Rachel nodded, tears clogging her throat.

"Good," Richard whispered. "I dreamed about you being there."

When Rachel left the hospital, she went back to her own home for the first time since Thanksgiving night. It was dark and cold and very neat. John had gone back and washed the dishes, made Richard's bed with fresh sheets, creating the future with small concrete acts. It was a ritual Rachel understood well.

Her pack with her mother's letters was on her desk. She hadn't told Richard about them yet but she would, as soon as he had the energy to listen. The message light on her phone machine was blinking persistently. Rachel sighed and pushed the play button, not ready to be reconnected to this life but unable to leave it behind.

The first voice was Angie's. "Rachel, I know you're away for the weekend, but I have to talk with you as soon as you get back. It's urgent, you understand? Very urgent." Angie's voice went from self-important to hushed. "It's about Susan and her case. I have to talk with you."

Fine, Rachel thought, but not now, Angie.

The second message was from Debora. "Rachel, I need someone to make an inquiry for the case. It occurred to me you might know Clara Moynihan or her lover Donna Kaminski. Either way, would you give me a call when you get it. It's Tuesday morning."

Rachel looked at the answer machine as though it might have more questions for her, but it burped and shut off. "I do know Donna actually," she told Debora. "We were on a task force on abortion rights together, about ten years ago."

"A nun was on a task force on abortion rights," Debora said, disbelieving.

Rachel smiled. "Uh huh. She represented a group called Catholics for Choice. What's up? What do you need me for?" She knew about the key. Susan had told her this afternoon when she called from the hospital to check in.

"Catholics for Choice." Debora hadn't quite caught up yet. "Does the Pope know about this group?"

"Yes, to his regret." Rachel laughed.

"Okay." Debora let it drop and came around to business. "Did Susan tell you about her key?"

"Yeah. She didn't think it was very important."

"Probably it isn't, but I need to check it out. Do you think you could go around there and ask them about it. I'd rather you got at it kind of indirectly. I'd send a paralegal, but I think it would be better coming from someone who knows her. Or can at least talk the same language."

"Okay. I guess we can talk first and see what her reaction is when I ask about it. Is that the sort of thing you want to check on?"

"Exactly. I'd go myself, Rachel, but I can't think of a thing I'd say to her before I'd say, 'So, you got the key or what?' "

"Anything else turn up yet?" Rachel wasn't sure she was allowed to ask Susan's lawyer questions like this, but she tried it anyway.

"Yes, actually. Carol has been asking around and it seems like Astrid just disappeared. She talked to three of her lovers, fifteen ex-lovers, her housemate and a couple of women who work with her at the store. No one who ought to know where she is does know. The women at the store are sure it's a new affair with somebody famous and that's why it's all hush-hush."

"Right." Rachel let the sarcasm seep in. She hadn't met Astrid yet, but she knew her well, thanks to Susan. "That would be my first choice."

Debora snorted back a laugh. "Her lovers think it's a family related crisis and her roommate is just enjoying the unnatural calm. No one seems worried."

"So it's not much, really, except that she's left town?"

"Not quite. Carol has a couple of buddies in the police department and one in the prosecutor's office.

She can't be positive, but she thinks she got a response when she asked about her by her real name — made up some story about a small claims adjustment she was trying to collect from Jeanette Larson."

"Hmmm. What kind of a response?"

"I think he started to answer that he'd heard of her, but he didn't quite get it out and it turned into a choke and then a no."

"Does it mean she's an informant?"

"How do you know about all this stuff?" Rachel laughed at Debora's surprise. "No. Stop. Don't tell me. I know too much already. If nuns can be on abortion task forces, who knows what a Unitarian minister might be doing. I gotta go. Call me when you talk to this Clara, right?"

Rachel was still laughing when she hung up, shaking her head. What had she gotten herself into now? And what could Angie want? May as well get that over with too.

Half an hour later, agitated, Rachel called Susan. "Susan," she demanded. "Did you tell anyone except me and Debora about the envelope J. Lawrence got? Anyone?"

"No." Susan sounded tired. "What do you mean? Why do you ask?"

"It's probably nothing," Rachel heard an edge of irritation and automatically switched into soothing mode. "I just had this really weird talk on the phone with Angie."

"Angie?" Susan sounded like she barely remembered who Angie was.

"She's the one you met at Thanksgiving. Who does the AIDS training for Glenda Mathis. She's a consultant, basically. To train the new trainers Glenda's hiring." This had been the ostensible reason for Angie's call, to ask Rachel to congratulate her on this coup. Angie wasn't giving up her job in the schools, but Glenda had recognized that her expertise would make this whole project go more smoothly.

"Ah ha, yes. Angie. The subtle one." There was a smile in Susan's voice.

"The very same."

"So what about Angie and the Commissioner, Rachel? What are you saying?"

"Angie seemed to know your job had been threatened by more than the indictment. That you were at risk as a lesbian, too. She said Glenda had implied it, and Angie was using it to tell me she was worried about you and to include her, Angie, in your support network." Rachel paused. "And then it came to me. How could Glenda know about the homophobia? How could Glenda have heard a rumor, even, about someone trying to discredit you with the Commissioner?"

"She said what?" Susan was clearly tired and a little confused, but not so defensive. "That I was going to lose my job because I'm a lesbian? I wish that was the most I had to worry about right now."

Rachel tried to explain it again, using Angie's exact words. "It didn't strike me as odd at first. Then I realized you told me Debora had said to tell no one about the envelope. Could the Commissioner have told someone? Someone he was working with, perhaps, about the threat?"

Susan explained that as far as she knew, J. Lawrence had said nothing about the envelope to anyone. "He has an investment in being quiet about it, I think. He has enough trouble, politically, just keeping up business as usual, given that three of his people are under this kind of a shadow." She paused for a moment, then said, "My brain must be wrapped in cotton. Glenda knew about those photos and the threats?"

"That's what it sounded like. Any ideas?"

"Too many."

Rachel heard the hesitation in Susan's voice, the unease. Last week she would have let it go, continued the soothing, withdrawn herself from the tension. "I know it's late," she said suddenly, "but I want to see you. I want to hear what you're thinking about, but not on the phone. Can I come over?"

"Rachel," Susan began to protest. Rachel waited. "Yes. Come as soon as you can," she said.

CHAPTER NINETEEN

The Susan who stepped confidently off the elevator that next Friday morning and let her long stride carry her down the length of the gray hallway to her office was a very different woman than she had been a week ago. Her body seemed charged with a suppressed energy, like a spring wound taut, but not too tight. She had never given in to despair, but the unresolved tension had sapped her energy, her vitality. Today, it was back. Her authority was back. This was her department, and she was going to run it. That message was in her footsteps and the tilt of her chin. Martin was waiting in her office, and behind him slouched the figure of her former employee, Tom Brady.

"Susan, good morning," Martin greeted her briskly.

"Thanks for coming in, Susan." As though she were doing him a favor. As though she shouldn't have kept him waiting. Tom kept his sneer just this side of blatant. She was prepared for it, but the audacity of the man still stunned her.

Susan looked Tom in the eye without returning his greeting or insult. She had been planning this confrontation since Tuesday night, and now she felt almost as though she didn't know what to say. Physically, she thought he looked better than he had for a while, although it was hard to tell. His belly hung over his belt, even when he stood up straight, and the veins across the bridge of his nose were reddened. At thirty-eight, his hair had mostly thinned, leaving a fringe around the edges and a bushy black mustache with a few gray hairs for emphasis. His eyes met hers and seemed clear, which was an improvement. But he also seemed nervous and ill at ease. Not surprising, she guessed, for the situation in which he found himself. He was awaiting sentencing, and conventional wisdom had it that he was going to jail, maybe for a long time, though his cooperation might buy him something.

She turned away from Tom and stepped behind her desk, opening her briefcase and bringing out the files she would need.

Martin cleared his throat and nodded. The tape recorder was running. Time for her to begin.

"Tom," she addressed him for the first time, "the

Commissioner has asked me to debrief you, basically, and take over the contracting process you've been working on for the AIDS/DASA curriculum. Mark and Josie have finished putting together the curriculum and training requirements, but they couldn't finish the contracting without you." She paused, wondering how he would take the rest of what she was planning to say. "They would have gone ahead with that too, but they needed access to your computer files and I guess you forgot to leave them the password for those tentative contract agreements."

To say that Tom looked surprised would have been an understatement. Then he managed a look of superiority, quite a feat under the circumstances, Susan thought.

"I'm afraid you're mistaken," he said, trying for polite. "J. Lawrence brought me back to finish these contracts. My understanding was that I would take them directly to him for his signature."

He heaved himself to his feet, and nodded dismissively to her to indicate the discussion was over. "I'll be at my desk. Working." The word was almost a snarl.

Before he could turn away, Susan handed him a piece of paper. "J. Lawrence is out of town this week," she informed him quietly, "but this memo should serve to remind you that you work for me, you report to the Commissioner through me. His instructions are very clear." She paused, giving him time to scan the short memo. "You are here today to finish up business. Today is your last day at DASA. The legal department won't allow anything else, under the circumstances." If he balked she would remind him he was a convicted felon.

Tom turned on her furiously. "You don't know what you're doing with this. You'll fuck up a year's worth of negotiating. I cleared all of this with J. Lawrence's office last week. What the hell have you been doing?" He sounded almost self-righteous as he threw out that last question.

Tripping you up, hopefully, Susan thought to herself. She remained silent for a moment to see what else he might say, but he subsided into his chair, his arms folded defiantly across his chest.

"If you'll give us the passwords, Tom, we can get on with this and get it finished before the end of the contract year. Oh, yes, and I think Josie had some questions about the software she and the interns have developed for the curriculum. She's not sure what the protections you wrote into it mean. We did develop the program here at DASA, right? I mean," she paused, then said casually, "it does all belong to the division, doesn't it?"

"You are such a fool." This time he was venomous and there was no trace of righteousness. Understanding began to dawn in his face as Susan watched him. He's figured it out, she realized; he knows we know.

"No, you're not a fool, are you? You want a piece of it, that's it, isn't it? You can see how big this is going to be."

"Tell me what you mean," Susan prodded.

Tom looked nervously at Martin, then dismissed him as a nonthreatening flunky. "I'll give you ten percent of my cut. That's all. You haven't done any of the work on this. In fact, Glenda knew you would fuck it up if you got the chance." He paused, hearing himself, trying to recover. "Look, it's foolproof. I've got all the copyrights and contracts tied up. She's going to sell the division the software as part of her training contract. It's all in her name already. All we need to do is get J. Lawrence to approve the contracts. Legal won't have a thing to say about it, I promise you." He stopped, checking Susan's face for a response.

"So how much are we talking about, Tom?" Susan asked quietly. "What's your cut? What would I be getting ten percent of?"

"I wrote the contract for five million. Her costs over three years won't amount to more than a million a year for the trainings. The other two mil is for the software she's supposed to develop. That's the slush."

The software Josie and her interns spent two years developing, Susan thought, trying not to let her anger show.

"I'm taking a third, as a consultant, you know." He looked at her for a moment, then added bitterly, "At least I'll have something to build on when I come out of prison." Still Susan didn't respond. "You'll need it too," he sneered at her, beginning to sense her resistance. "Don't be so goddamned above it all. Your ass is on the line just like mine is."

"You're offering me about sixty thousand dollars to sign off on these contracts, lie to the Commissioner and help Glenda Mathis sell back software to the division that we developed ourselves during the last two years, is that about what you're offering?" She hoped she hadn't said that so bluntly that he'd suspect the wire Martin was wearing.

"That's right." He was proud of it, not suspicious. God, coke heads are such arrogant fools, she thought tiredly. She turned slightly toward Martin, ready for the wrap-up, but Tom wasn't quite finished.

"Ten percent is all I'm offering, Myers, so don't try and stall me for more. It won't work."

She heard Martin stifle a snort. Time to end this charade. "Tom, your offer is not one I can accept." Her words and voice were formal. "We did, in fact, get into your contract files last week, in spite of your password." That had been Mark's success. "Legal has been through them and invalidated them. The division has also begun copyright proceedings on the software. Legal says there's no problem with that, given all of the backups showing the development of the program during the last two years. There's no way Glenda Mathis can hope to lay claim to that work. We know she used some of the same interns during that time, which is no doubt how she got access to the programs, but if she ever tries to use that material, the division will have her prosecuted. She will be informed of that by Legal next week when we draw up new contracts for one of the legitimate bidders."

Tom's hope for his future was fading. His face went from anger to contempt to rage. Never once did she see a moment of regret or fear or humiliation. So much for rehab, she thought. He stood, his fist clenched in front of her. He couldn't have stopped using. His responses were too classic. Arrogant. Sure he was powerful enough to control it all, even when he was staring out at the world from the bottom of a deep, deep well.

"You are a fool," he snarled. "I'll get you. That's one thing you can count on. You're finished too, Myers." Then he turned and left the office.

Martin smiled at her, reached inside his jacket and brought out the tape recorder, which he switched off. "You were great, Myers. Just great."

Susan grinned at him, elation beginning to seep through her. "That boy is still using, isn't he?"

Martin nodded. "No question. Did you see his face when he figured out we knew something and he decided to try and con us. I'd love to play poker with that guy. Dead giveaway!"

"Typical coke head. He thinks he's the only one holding any cards." She stretched. "I loved telling him we broke his password." She was remembering the euphoria she and Martin and Josie felt when Mark finally brought up the files. And the tension until they convinced the Commissioner to let them handle it without creating more scandal for the division. It was over, as far as the division was concerned. Tom was gone. Eduardo, in the Commissioner's office, would handle the new contracts, exactly as planned. Glenda Mathis would be warned, politely.

Susan took the tape out of Martin's recorder and put it in her pocket. She would make copies. One for Legal, one for the Commissioner and one for Debora. The division might be finished with Glenda Mathis, but she was not.

"Not a bad morning's work, Myers." Martin couldn't keep himself from grinning and Susan found it contagious.

"Not bad," she agreed. "Now maybe we can get back to the work we're supposed to be doing here. Let Mark and Josie know how it went, will you?"

When Susan left work that evening, she carried her copy of the microcassette tape tucked deep in her skirt pocket. She had no idea when Glenda would find out what had transpired that morning in her office, but she'd had visions all day of Glenda slugging her with her heavy purse as Susan came off the elevator, shaking her down for the tape and making off with it.

CHAPTER TWENTY

When Susan opened the front door, her whole house smelled of a pungent curry. Rachel was puttering around the kitchen like she belonged there. Susan stood in the front hall, savoring the moment. She had a premonition then, a flash, that everything was going to be okay. She hadn't felt like this since before the day of her indictment. She walked into the kitchen and put her arms around Rachel. "Hi. Some superior sense tells me you've made dinner."

"Mmmm. What was your first clue?"

"Clue. You said the magic word, lady. Want to

hear about it?" Rachel did, of course, want to hear every word, but she insisted on serving dinner while Susan told her.

She knew parts of it. By the time Rachel called Susan on Tuesday night with the information about Glenda from Angie, Susan was actually close to beginning to figure out what Glenda had been up to.

"I think the first clue was that conversation Debora overheard at Thanksgiving —"

"When she started grilling you about your history with Glenda?"

"Right. After work Monday, I stayed late and went into all of the computer files on Josie's machine. Everything seemed in order and up to date. It's pretty hard to hide a whole curriculum, and that wasn't what this was about. I wondered why Glenda seemed so sure she was going to get the contract, when several of the bidders were companies we'd worked with before and had a much larger capacity than Glenda's small consulting firm — which seemed to me to rely far too much on student interns and minimum-wage teenagers. It didn't inspire confidence, let's put it that way." She took a forkful of curry and rice. "So I started looking at the bids and the contract proposal our division had put out. Still nothing out of the ordinary, except Glenda didn't seem to have a completed bid in the computer file."

"That's sort of where I got left off," Rachel reminded her.

"When I went in Wednesday morning I got another strange piece to figure in to the puzzle. I got a note from the Commissioner that Tom was coming back to work Friday — after a month in rehab and two weeks' vacation time. I headed straight for J. Lawrence's office. Technically, Tom didn't have a job anymore, because of the plea bargain. J. Lawrence hemmed and hawed about some internal departmental difficulties, but when we finally talked, it was very interesting indeed." Susan felt a little smug, remembering the conversation with J. Lawrence. "I called in every single favor I'd ever done for him. He couldn't ignore me. Though he was tempted. He thought if he did it Tom's way the problem would just disappear."

"Oh, boy." Rachel stared at her in disbelief. "He's been a bureaucrat too long, hasn't he?"

"He said something to that effect, actually. I think this whole experience has been something of a sea change for him. I can't quite imagine what he'll do with it, but I bet it's going to be interesting."

J. Lawrence and Susan had decided it was time to bring Martin in. Susan would have been happy being a manager back in the days when memos were written neatly in pen and ink. Martin, on the other hand, turned on his computer in the morning before he had his first cup of coffee. "It's how he gets the news, chats with his buddies, finds out what's on the local gay social calendar. Sometimes," Susan waved her fork for emphasis, "I swear it brushes his teeth for him." Rachel snickered at that and Susan realized how relieved she was to be at a place where this could all be amusing. "I'll tell you what kept me going on Wednesday and Thursday, if you *won't* laugh."

"Cross my heart." Rachel grinned at her.

"A lesson from my grandmother Yetta that I take very seriously. She used to say, 'Sometimes people *are* out to get you.' Her voice was very clear in my mind as I walked up the hill to work on Wednesday.

'Susie, you can assume people are good, you can assume they want to help you, but don't ever rely on it.' "

"Cover your ass, right?"

Susan laughed. It still surprised her when Rachel talked like normal people. "You got it."

"Martin didn't think I was crazy. Quite the contrary. You should have seen it. His eyes began to gleam and his fingers twitched. 'There have to be records somewhere,' he said. 'Let's start in the memo file memory documents.' Like I'd know what that was."

"I know you're going to tell me," Rachel protested, "so let's take our coffee in the living room first."

"Good. That's where I've got exhibit A. It's in my briefcase." Settled with coffee, she continued, "Every memo that goes through our system on the office memo template gets backed up on the hard drive, which gets dumped into a library tape system every three months or so. Martin thought we could get a trail out of the backups." She didn't tell Rachel how she'd left him working and gone back into her office, suddenly depressed at the realization that none of this was going to explain how the kilo of cocaine had come to rest under her radiator cover.

Susan showed Rachel the batch of memos Martin had retrieved for her, starting with the earliest dated last July when the contract proposals were issued. It was written in Susan's name, labeled EXTREMELY CONFIDENTIAL and advised Tom that Susan was putting Glenda Mathis's proposal on a fast track, since her firm clearly had the personnel and background to complete the trainings in the three-year period. It noted her already advanced work in creating a software program to train the trainers for this curriculum.

"This is what really got me." Susan pointed to a personal note, added almost as an afterthought, if a casual observer were looking at the memo: *Glenda Mathis will be given every consideration by the Ed Department; please provide her with any information she requests.* "Signed with my name. Do you believe it?"

"Wow." Rachel was properly impressed. "How did they think they'd get away with it? Didn't anyone ever refer to this memo? Why didn't Josie come to you about it at some point? Why didn't it come up in a staff meeting?"

"Keep reading," Susan told her.

It was clever. It could have fallen apart at any moment, but they'd been lucky as well as clever. The next "memo" told Tom he was to handle everything, that Susan was working on other projects and would leave the completion of this one entirely to him. Toward the end there was even one from the Commissioner, thanking Tom for his work and telling him to send the contracts up to Legal for review. That one was written the day before Tom's arrest.

"How did Martin and you know it wasn't the Commissioner?" Rachel asked.

"Each memo that goes out on that template has a code that tells what work station it originated from. Martin called up all the memos from Tom's station. I don't think the Commissioner would trot down to Tom's desk to write him a memo."

"Hardly. What about your other staff? Was Tom entirely on his own?"

"Entirely. Josie believed the memos he showed her were from me. Why would she think otherwise?" Susan hesitated, then went on. "It's what I said before, when we were up at the cabin. She's very angry at me, has been for months. So she was ready to believe the worst. I didn't realize how badly Tom was abusing his position. She couldn't quit. She's a single mom with three kids. Things are tight, so she couldn't even get transferred. I found out yesterday that she was prepared to file harassment charges against Tom with the division."

"Sexual harassment?"

"Sexual and racial. Tom made her life hell. Josie thought I should have intervened a lot sooner. She's right. I should have."

"I'm sorry."

After a moment Susan said, "I think this explains the photographs."

"What was the point of that? I don't quite see it," Rachel was still flipping through the memos, shaking her head in disbelief.

"They didn't want J. Lawrence to consult me about that project. Tom was off in rehab trying to figure out how he could get those contracts up to Legal without me seeing them. One of those memos — there, that next-to-last one —" She shuffled through the pages Rachel was holding. "That's a real one. The Commissioner gave me a copy for my collection. Glenda sent it to him, saying she'd been notified the contract was hers last month and she had already done a lot of work on the curriculum and was concerned about the delay in forwarding her the completed papers."

"She has balls," Rachel said. "Did he know

anything was wrong? I mean, bureaucracy like this is a kind of haze to me. How could a contract of this size have been promised without him knowing it?"

"It wouldn't have been. She was baiting him. Betting he would react by sending the papers and covering up the apparent slip."

"Would he have?"

"He says not, but there's been a lot of slippage recently and the publicity over the indictments hasn't helped. I think that's why he was going to allow Tom to come back to work for a few days. Until our talk Wednesday morning."

The last memo in the pile was the one written by J. Lawrence himself, the one Susan had shown Tom. Rachel read through it, shaking her head.

"What?"

"It's so hard to believe. I mean, it's not hard to believe on some level. But it's so complicated, and so underhanded. What was she doing? Making her interns steal the training software from you? One of the terms of their employment with a so-called feminist business — rip off the establishment."

"I think so. Martin says Tom probably caught Glenda at it, which is maybe how he got in on the deal. He thinks they were planning on selling the software nationwide. It's that timely."

"Ugh. It makes me furious. But there's nothing you can do now, is there?"

"Not really. Glenda didn't get the money, but she's not going to be punished for this, not in any real sense. It may be a while before DASA would work with her again but she can do the same thing tomorrow with any other agency."

Rachel looked pensive. "She'll be punished." When

Susan raised a questioning eyebrow, she said, "I watched her at Thanksgiving. She wants approval. She wants to be part of the in-group. She may not face court appearances, but remember what the hardest part of this ordeal was for you, early on?"

Susan did remember. "The walk up the hill, past my co-workers and into my office."

"I don't think this was just about the money for Glenda, though she does seem to use money to define herself. I thought about that when I saw her house last August. I imagine she thought this contract was going to put her in the middle of the dialogue about AIDS and AIDS education — at a policy level, probably."

"Basically," Susan agreed, "it would have done just that."

And that was where they left it. Some of Susan's celebratory feeling after the confrontation with Tom had slipped away. She slouched on the sofa next to Rachel. What had she accomplished? She was still under indictment. Debora didn't know how they could even begin to explain the cocaine in her house. The January trial date was racing closer and closer. Her flash earlier this evening — that everything was going to be all right — must have been wishful thinking. She could be looking at some very serious jail time.

Rachel, lost in her own world, hadn't noticed. She was still thumbing through the memos.

Susan moved closer, twined her arms around Rachel, and started nibbling on her ear.

She was pretending not to notice. "It's so interesting..." She continued looking at the papers and Susan knew she wasn't referring to the tongue traveling around the rim of her ear.

"Ummhmm?"

"It's almost like we both got messages from the past this week — stored, saved for us, hidden until we found them."

Amused, Susan decided to test Rachel's powers of concentration. Her mouth was moving down along the muscle on Rachel's neck now. She was thinking more about unbuttoning Rachel's shirt — so this journey didn't get interrupted — than about messages.

Rachel continued, "Of course the messages you got, these memos, Tom didn't mean for you to see them. It's more like the universe was saving them for you." She looked down at Susan speculatively. By then Susan had transgressed her collarbone, opened her shirt to the waist, and was moving toward Rachel's nipple. "You were meant to stop Glenda, weren't you?"

"Mmmhmmm," Susan agreed, happy to participate as long as she could keep circling the nipple, nibbling on it, gently, until it was small and hard.

Rachel had put the papers down now and her hands were on the back of Susan's head, pulling her closer, saying, at the same time, "All week I've felt like I was talking with my mother."

Was she serious? Susan ignored her since Rachel was unbuttoning her own pants, not the act of someone who would rather talk than fuck.

"But it isn't my mother, no matter how much I want that fantasy, no matter how much I might wish it were her." She slid her pants down over her hips in one smooth motion. She was half-sitting, half-lying on the couch now, her legs spread, her ankles trapped in her tangled clothing.

Susan was beginning to enjoy the conversation and wondered how much longer it could go on. She ran her fingers up Rachel's thigh and trailed them lightly over her curly hair. Rachel's legs moved a little farther apart.

"Do you know what I think it is?"

No, Rachel, Susan breathed silently, hoping she wouldn't need an answer. Her mouth was occupied and on its way down Rachel's belly.

But Rachel was going to tell her anyway. "It's this. This energy. The spirit of the universe. Whatever we want to call it."

Susan raised her head, looked at her. "Rachel, you're right. Now be quiet." She was kneeling between Rachel's knees, "This message is from the present, not the past, okay?"

Rachel smiled. "Whatever you say, dear." She sighed, then moaned softly as Susan's tongue pressed down on her throbbing clit. Her hands in Susan's hair trembled, her legs opened wider, wider. She took one of Susan's hands off her breast and led it down to her crotch. "Oh, yes." Susan slid her fingers inside her. "Deeper," she breathed, "deeper. Fill me up."

CHAPTER TWENTY-ONE

As Rachel drove toward the hospital the next morning, the scent of Susan still on her hands, she wondered if the book she had been going to write still existed somewhere in her consciousness. She hadn't thought about it seriously in weeks; so much had been happening. And yet she knew that if she'd meant to be writing that book, she would have been taking notes, jotting down thoughts as they occurred to her, rather than letting images come and go.

What's my goal? she asked herself, as she rode in the elevator up to Richard's room on the fifth floor of the hospital. She walked into Richard's room, carefully holding onto her mood. He was sitting up in the bed, wearing the lavender terrycloth bathrobe he had given Colin several years ago.

"Whoa," she said, surprised, pleased. "You look like you're feeling better."

"I am," he agreed. "I want all the gossip. I could tell you've been holding back all week, and I'm dying to know the dirt." He grimaced at his choice of words. "Well, not dying exactly, dear, but you know what I mean."

"So you could tell?" she asked happily, taking his hand.

"Rachel, to me you broadcast everything. How anyone could miss it, I don't know. But they must, because I've heard in some circles you're considered fairly subtle." He was laughing at her and her heart lifted a notch. She could tell he was going to be all right, this time.

Rachel took the letters out of her pack and told him where she had found them. Then they went over them, piece by piece. Richard was furious when he read her father's letters stating the terms for this "marriage."

"But I don't know why," he said after a moment. "It's something to feel sad about, I guess. He set up a situation that would limit him his whole life. As long as your mother lived and abided by his terms, he was trapped in this bargain too."

Rachel hadn't seen it that way initially, but it made sense to her when Richard said it. "I don't know if my father was ever challenged in his work life, but certainly nothing in his personal life ever seemed to challenge him."

"Sort of guaranteed to keep him mediocre, isn't it?"

Rachel nodded, thinking.

"What are you going to do about your sister?"

Her head jerked up from the letter she'd been studying for the hundredth time. *Sister.* What a shocking word that seemed.

Richard ran his bone-thin hand through his sandy gray hair and waited to see if Rachel would answer his question.

"I guess I haven't figured out what to do, if there is anything I can do," she told him finally. "I've kind of been holding it close, until I know where I am." As she said that, she realized she'd been carrying the letters around with her like a shield or talisman since the night she came back from the cabin. "Any advice?"

"You could probably get in touch with the agency again," he said slowly, looking at Enid Flint's business letter to the adoption agency. "Laws have changed a lot since the fifties. They may be doing some kind of registry now. You know, keeping lists of parents who are willing to be known and matching them with children who inquire and vice versa. Our agency gets involved in this kind of inquiry occasionally. There are no guarantees, but you could try if you want." He looked at her closely. "Do you want?"

"To know if I have a sister, to know who she is? I've wanted it my entire life without knowing it was what I wanted. If you think there's a chance the agency keeps a list like that, I'll write tomorrow. I guess my only question is whether or not they'd reveal it to me, since I'm not the primary party — the parent or the child."

"I don't know." Richard smiled at her. "But it shouldn't be hard to find out. Talk to Debora."

Before she left, Rachel had promised Richard and herself she would take at least the next step toward finding her sister. *Sister.* She tried the word out loud once or twice in the empty elevator. Richard had called her *sister.* She had called some of her close friends *sister.* But this was different. She felt quite tentative about the word.

All that day, Rachel had been thinking about her upcoming visit to Clara and Donna to ask about the key. It wasn't that she was putting it off, exactly, she argued to an imaginary Debora. When she'd called on the pretense of wanting to discuss her possible career change, they'd said they wouldn't be home together until later on Saturday, and since Debora wanted this to be a "social visit" she could hardly say to Clara, "Well, never mind Donna, I just want to know what you did with the key." She and Susan had gotten up late, enjoyed the rare leisure of a Saturday morning just like two lovers anywhere might. Then there had been time at the hospital with Richard, who was going to be released on Monday, his doctor promised, if everything continued well.

And then there was a phone call to Carmen, a longer conversation than Rachel had planned on. Carmen had to hear it all, of course. "A sister, Rachel, to think you might have a sister." There was reverence in her voice. Carmen, more than anyone in

Rachel's life, knew what this would mean to her. And finally, Rachel told her what Susan had discovered at work.

"Glenda?" Carmen was astonished. "That woman whose house I ate dinner at? She would invite us to eat in her home when she was doing things like that to Susan?" Rachel loved the predictability of Carmen's sense of propriety — that Glenda had violated hospitality laws outraged her. The scam about the contracts was much less interesting to her; it was more within the bounds of human nature, Rachel guessed.

They talked for so long that Rachel was late getting to Clara's. She parked in front of Susan's house and walked quickly down the block to Clara's, sure this was a waste of time, wishing she could just duck into Susan's and forget the whole thing. But they were expecting her.

"Is it too late, or could I interest you in a cup of coffee?" Clara sounded apologetic.

"I'd love a cup of coffee," Rachel insisted. "It doesn't seem to matter when I drink it. Nothing keeps me awake at night."

"Coffee in the evening is a habit I picked up in Mexico," Donna said, her voice stronger than her serene, nearly gray, facade. Looking at her now, Rachel remembered that same quality from the task force meetings, a firm position coming out of this apparently acquiescent nun. "Coffee with milk and a piece of bread was a before-bedtime ritual for the whole family."

"So let's be family and move this ritual into the kitchen," Clara suggested comfortably, "so I can talk and fix at the same time."

"You were in the refugee camps, weren't you, Donna?"

"For three years. Then I came down with a bug I couldn't get rid of. Some intestinal thing." She was shaking her head as though she still couldn't quite believe it. "I felt like such a wimp."

"Hardly," Rachel disagreed. "The wimps were those of us who didn't go and live like that. It wasn't your fault you had an *estomago norteamericano*, was it?" Rachel was remembering how much she liked Donna.

Clara's back was to them as she poured coffee into the filter, but her comment was aimed at Rachel. "You said on the phone you were thinking about making some permanent changes in your professional life, that it was a bit unsettling. We thought you probably meant you were thinking about more than a leave of absence from the ministry."

Rachel's head came up sharply. No mincing around politely here.

"It's an enormous step," Donna said, "so it's not surprising you're having some reaction to it."

"I guess not, but I'm not very far along in the process. It's been hard for me to even think about it."

"What's hardest about it? Losing the sense of belonging? Or something else?" Clara came back and sat with them at the table while the kettle heated.

"Something else, I think." Rachel noticed she was tapping her spoon nervously on the empty cup in front of her and set the spoon down. "Even when the work I do as clergy is mundane, not glamorous, like changing a bedpan, I still had the sense it was connected to something larger." She stopped. She hadn't expected to step into this dialogue quite so rapidly.

Clara got up to pour the coffee and Donna sat quietly. Finally she said, "I guess that's why I haven't left the convent. That and the practical. I'm fifty-six years old and I have nothing, no savings, no pension. If I'd known at thirty what I know now," she shrugged, "I'd probably have left. Some say I should, even now, that this way of living in two worlds is dishonest."

"I wondered about that." Rachel was glad to shift the focus of the conversation. This *was* a rather unusual arrangement for a nun who was still part of a community. "I wondered whether you'd gotten any flack for it."

"Most of the questions aren't to my face." Donna's smile was ironic. "So I haven't had to answer them for anybody but myself."

"Always an important first step, I'd say." Clara passed a plate of cookies to Rachel.

"Right." She looked down at the cookie in her hand as though it held some answers. "That's what I have to do, I guess. My work isn't any less important even if it's no longer in the context I thought it was when I was clergy — the context of working for justice, I mean, worldwide. And working with a sense that my spirit was — I don't know — connected somehow to my work."

"Of course it isn't less important," Clara said impatiently.

"But, Clara," Donna intervened, and Rachel could see they'd had this conversation before, "it isn't about what's real, it's about how we see ourselves, our spiritual selves. That's the adjustment Rachel's having trouble with. It's a heart adjustment." She added, "Didn't you say you were writing a book? Won't that help you make this transition? Keep you focused on your work? I'd think writing a book would keep you connected."

"Every time I sit down to look at my notes for this book, my head goes about a thousand miles away. That's been a problem for me, I guess, in trying to understand whether I can write this book or not. How can I write it if I can't concentrate for five minutes?"

"Doesn't sound very promising," Donna said.

Rachel stared at her. She had expected Donna to tell her, "Oh, sure you can do it, don't worry."

"She just means it doesn't sound like you want to write a book now," Clara explained gently. "Maybe that's not the work you're going to be doing."

Rachel felt as if the small table they were sitting at was a life boat that had suddenly drifted out into an enormous uncharted water. She had not realized she was holding on to the notion of writing a book like a lifeline, something that would keep her connected to her life in the church.

When Carmen had helped her redefine the subject and context of the book, she'd thought the problem was solved. Yes, she'd told Carmen, I could write a book that included my feelings about loving Susan. But that had been weeks ago, before the tensions of the indictment had escalated, before she'd found the letters from her mother. Tonight she couldn't even remember what Carmen had thought the book might be about. Tonight she was sitting with two women who didn't seem to care whether she wrote a book or not, and they assumed, it seemed, that she could find meaningful work to do even if she didn't write a book.

Rachel drew a deep breath and looked at Donna, some of the tension in her shoulders lifting. "Maybe a book isn't what I need to be doing now."

By the time they finished talking, it was very late. Rachel looked at her watch. She had told Susan she'd be back tonight, long before now.

Then she remembered the other reason for this evening's visit, the real reason. She'd nearly forgotten it.

"Clara," Rachel blurted out. "Do you still have the key to Susan Myers' house? From when you were feeding her cat?" So much for subtlety, she laughed at herself. Even Debora could have been more circumspect than that.

Clara looked at her with surprise, wondering, no doubt, why this might be Rachel's concern. "I gave it to Astrid," Clara said casually. "She said she needed to leave Susan some confidential documents for a project they were working on. So I gave the key to her."

CHAPTER TWENTY-TWO

"Wow!" Debora sounded energized for the first time since the indictment. "We've got the lead we need. I'm sure of it. Tell Rachel she does good work. I may have to put her on my permanent investigation staff."

"Do you think so? That it will help, I mean?" Susan had gone from excitement when Rachel first came in with the news to gloom and despair that the news wouldn't matter since no one could find Astrid.

"It will help, Susie. You're allowed to be excited

over this one. Maybe if you pump some adrenalin into it, you'll find some more answers."

"Like what?" Susan couldn't even muster sarcasm.

"We *have* to find Astrid now," Debora said. "But how? Every lead I've followed up has been a dead end."

They decided a full committee meeting was essential — tomorrow — even if it was already ten o'clock on Saturday night.

"I'll make the calls," Debora said.

The next morning, Debora, Susan and Rachel were munching bagels in Susan's kitchen, planning the meeting.

"Are you going to say anything about why Glenda wasn't invited?" Rachel asked the obvious.

"No," Susan said.

"Yes," Debora answered in the same moment.

"Ah hah." Rachel smiled. "Let's hear it. We better have just one agenda for this meeting."

"We have to say something," Debora was in charge again. "We have to be careful, though. There won't be any formal or legal proceedings against Glenda. Which means she can't be found guilty. But it also means she can't face her accusers and offer her side of the story. And," she waved a knife on its way from the cream cheese to her bagel, "we don't know for sure that she isn't buddies with someone else on the committee."

"I don't know what to say about her," Susan said, feeling defensive. "I haven't had a chance to talk with her in person. I don't want to say anything until then."

"Talk with her in person? You can't do that," Debora protested.

"Of course I can do that. If I don't, what am I going to say to her the next time I see her at a concert or a United Way meeting?"

"Do what everybody else does. Nod at her and walk by. Or pretend you don't know her. Or pretend you don't see her." Debora looked at Rachel in exasperation. "Why? Why? The one person who wants to handle conflicts in a grown-up way and she has to be my client."

Rachel laughed. "I don't know the answer either, but I don't see why you can't just say she couldn't be here today. I mean, that's the truth, isn't it? She couldn't be here."

They agreed, it was the truth.

After the meeting convened and Rachel's discovery about the key had been explained, Susan asked Debora again, "Do you think the D.A.'s office could be hiding Astrid?"

Debora shrugged. "I thought so for a while, but Amanda seems to have a different opinion."

"I've gotten all the witnesses' names from discovery," Amanda said, "and she's not on the list. They've built their case without her. At least that's what they want us to believe."

"If they're not hiding her, she's taken off on her own and we'll have to find her by figuring out her natural cover," Bill Pritchard, the physician, said, crossing his long legs and leaning back in his chair. "What community she'd go to in order to hide, I mean." He cleared his throat. "I feel a little at a loss about how I can be helpful here. Now, if she were a doctor, I might have a network that would be useful.

I could call places where she used to work, track down who she associated with, that sort of thing. But you say she's mainly functioned in the women's," he hesitated again, "the lesbian community. Most of us here wouldn't know where to begin finding her. It's a pretty specific network." His chair clunked down to the floor on all four legs.

"I think you're right," Debora said glumly, some of her energy fading. "We've followed every lead and gotten nowhere. Carol's been working hard on it."

"Have you checked back?" Dolores Young asked. "These younger ones seem to move around a lot. No matter what community they're part of."

"True." Debora smiled at Dolores. "But Astrid seems to be the exception. She went to the university here and stayed. Before that it was high school, and we found nothing around her family or hometown."

"Where's she from?" Jimmy Bonito wanted to know.

"Rochester," Amanda said.

"I think we're missing a bet here." Everyone looked at Charlie Leitman expectantly. It was the first time he'd spoken that morning. "This Astrid person. You say she's not stupid and she's not mean. Generally, you say she's community-minded and all that." He paused and Debora and Susan nodded confirmation. "And you say she's selling drugs to people in her community?" They nodded again. "What does that tell you about her?" He didn't wait for an answer this time. "It tells you she's using the stuff herself. And if she's doing things you wouldn't expect her to do, pretty sure she's an addict. Right?"

"Sure makes sense to me," Martin said quietly.

"And if she's got a habit that's out of control and she's in trouble, what's she going to do?" He shrugged, waiting for them to catch up.

"She might go home," Debora said slowly. "But Carol tried her there and her mother didn't seem to know where she was. Really didn't seem to know."

"You mean she's going to look for help, don't you, Charlie?" Susan was beginning to make sense of it now. "You mean we're overlooking the recovery network, right?"

"I think it's worth a try. You never know who'll show up in an AA room, do you?"

A while later, as the group filed out of Debora's conference room, Rachel and Susan sat waiting.

"What do you think?" Susan demanded of Debora as soon as they were alone. "What do you really think?" She leaned forward intently, as though her attention could direct Debora's answer.

"I think we're on an edge," Debora said without hesitation. "At this point, it could fall either way. If we go to court with nothing more than this and a little luck, I might win. And I might not. Reasonable doubt? We can't explain the cocaine in your house, but we're closer to having a reasonable scenario. Much closer. Would a jury buy it? I just don't know."

"But it's much better than it was," insisted Rachel.

"Yes." Debora looked pleased. "It's much better than it was." She reached across the table and squeezed Susan's hand. "We'll think about what Charlie said. He may be on to something, but I'm not sure how to follow up on it. Let's talk tomorrow."

Susan and Rachel walked out of Debora's building into a weak December morning. "It seems appropriate," Rachel said, nodding toward the sun.

"I beg your pardon? The sun seems appropriate?" Susan was laughing at Rachel's internal ellipses. Figuring out the hops, skips and jumps kept Susan active, she told herself.

"Sorry, dear. I mean it seems appropriate that we're nearly at the solstice and the sun will be coming back to us. I get nervous in late November as it retreats and retreats. I understand why early people told stories about the underworld and making bargains with the gods to bring the sun back."

"Mmm. Did you make any bargains?"

"I did, actually. And when I see you tonight, I might be persuaded to tell you about them."

"Deal," Susan promised. "I'll be my most persuasive. Now I have to go clean up a mess of paperwork at my desk so that Monday morning can happen normally."

Rachel watched Susan as she climbed the hill toward her office building. Hemmed in on all sides by tall buildings and the dome of the Capitol, Rachel wondered what would make this landscape feel like home to her. She tried to imagine herself embraced, comforted by the closeness of these building canyon walls. Out on the Cape, there were no tall buildings, only miles of windswept dunes. She wandered down the street in the opposite direction Susan had taken, keeping amid the buildings. At times, in her dunes, she had felt vulnerable and frail. During a hurricane one August, the wind had blown the sand so hard it bit viciously into her body through her skin. But wind there was normal. Rachel didn't know what normal was here, among the unfamiliar tall buildings and narrow streets.

How did a place become home, she wondered. Had it been so long that she'd forgotten the process even? She had gone to Provincetown in 1984 because the congregation had invited her. She could see the work she would be doing in bringing together an incredibly diverse community. She immersed herself from the first day she arrived, before she unpacked her books, practically before she had a place to stack her boxes. That place had been as foreign to her then as the streets she was walking now. Before her first interview with the congregation, she hadn't known a single person.

Here, she knew Susan. Several other women too. But it was different, not being brought by a ready-made community. And her work on the book was so solitary . . . She remembered her discovery last night. She didn't want to write a book. Writing was not how she encountered the world; it never had been, not even when she was giving sermons. She had prepared by walking, finding out what was in her thoughts as she walked the beach, flinging an occasional stone into the water. Back at her desk she would write down two or three key phrases that would guide her as she spoke. Sometimes on Sunday, after a sermon, she would look at the words written on her cue card and laugh. Posterity would have a hard time figuring out those clues. But Rachel had never lived for posterity, she knew that. Being remembered in a hundred years was not the least bit important to her. Being thought of by the people whose lives she entered today was very important.

Rachel wandered slowly on down the hill, scuffing the dirty, week-old snoew. She found the elusive underpass that let her cross the highway to the river. Three homeless men huddled in the lee of a cement buttress, sipping out of a bottle wrapped in the inevitable brown paper bag. That scene never changed, Rachel thought, whether it was Albany or Boston or the smallest village on the Cape. And the river itself was timeless, dark black with cold, flowing sluggishly as it approached freezing. Shards of ice clung like transient memories to the riverbank and to pieces of tree branches floating on the surface.

As a young woman, Rachel had always been slightly amazed at her friends' easy mobility. They followed school openings, jobs, lovers or just whim from one end of the country to the other. Stuck, as she thought of it, with an ailing mother, then father, Rachel had never ventured farther than when she left home to go to college in central Massachusetts and that was only because she was expected to go to one of the seven sisters. Until seminary. Until she cut all of her roots by selling the family home in Saratoga and trying to imitate those wandering, apparently free-spirited friends.

But Rachel knew she had never floated lightly on the surface of anything. Her need to settle was as basic to her as breathing, and so picking up, leaving a community like the one she had grown deeply attached to in Provincetown, felt like an amputation, like some part of her was dying. She knew too that there would also be a sense of liberation, a freedom in starting over, but that was never as obvious to her, never as easy a feeling to tap into.

She wrapped her down parka more tightly and stood staring at the water until her toes went numb. Then she turned and began to climb the hill back up to the city.

CHAPTER TWENTY-THREE

Susan rubbed her ear then cradled the phone back in the crook of her neck and dialed again. "Hi," she began, "this is Peggy Larson. My daughter Jeanette Larson left this number and said I could leave a message for her with you if anything came up while she was away. Is this the right place?" She paused as the voice on the other end of the line denied any knowledge of Jeanette Larson. "Oh," she sounded doubtful. "Maybe I misunderstood her. Sorry to bother you."

She hung up and handed the phone to Martin who dialed a new number. Jimmy sat on the couch in Susan's living room, sorting through a dozen lists, making notes and adding a new number to a pad of paper on his lap. In the middle of the afternoon, Martin and Jimmy had called Susan at work with an idea about how to find Astrid. It had sounded good at the time, and she had rushed home to meet them. Rachel arrived just before dinnertime. There was no dinner, just lists of hospitals and rehabilitation centers from every county in the state which Martin had pulled off his computer.

Rachel sent out for pizza when she could get to the phone between calls.

"Short of calling every rehab in the state," Martin said glumly, "I don't know how we're going to find her."

"Do you really think you're going to get anything this way?" Rachel asked. "Aren't they supposed to keep anonymity?"

"Yes, of course they're supposed to keep clients anonymous," Susan answered, tired. "It's just that I don't know what else to do. When we finish this, we've got no other way to even think we might track down Astrid."

"And of course," Martin added, "we might already have gotten the right one and they've denied —" He stopped talking to them and began speaking into the phone. "Hi, this is Martin Larson. My daughter Jeanette Larson left this number — I beg your pardon?" He looked stunned, then confused. "But we haven't, I mean . . ."

The others could hear the click of a phone being

slammed down. "Wow. What was that about?" Rachel asked curiously. "Pissed about anonymity, or what?"

"I found her." Martin sounded as though he didn't quite believe it. "She must be there. This woman told me to leave her alone and stop calling her. She said, 'You people stop bothering her, she needs to be left alone to work on her recovery.'" He was starting to sound excited.

"What did she mean? Leave her alone? It's not like you've tried them five times tonight. Haven't we kept track of the ones we've called?"

"Yes. I don't know what she meant. This place is near Rochester. Maybe Astrid really did give someone this number, someone who's bugging her."

Susan dialed Debora's familiar number and told her the news.

"She's under her own name and near Rochester," Debora mused. "It has to be her. There aren't coincidences like that. Good work, Susan. When you and Martin told me what you were going to try, I didn't think you had a chance. But now this worries me a little."

"Me, too," Susan said impatiently. She wanted to say, "I'm leaving for Rochester, I have to talk to this woman right now," but she knew what Debora would have to say about that. "I don't like it, but I don't know why. Do you?"

"Well, let's see. First it means she's not a witness they're hiding from us. It may mean she's running because she knows the D.A. is trying to catch up with her. But I guess what makes me uneasy is wondering who else is calling her. Who else is trying to find her, I'd like to know."

"The D.A. might not have caught up with her yet? But wouldn't there be a warrant out for her arrest? We'd have heard about that. And then she'd have to be using a different name."

"Right. But I doubt if it's the D.A. calling to locate her. That's hardly the way he'd do it. He'd just send a local man over there to pick her up." There was a long pause as they both thought about that scenario. "What I guess I'm more concerned about," Debora continued as though she weren't concerned at all, "is the drug connection. She was obviously selling. If she's checked into a rehab, she's trying to break away from the drugs. Maybe . . ."

"Maybe what?" Susan snapped. "Are you saying she might be in danger? *Someone* knows where she is besides us."

"I'm going to call her mother again, Susan." The deliberate slowness was gone from Debora's voice. "I want to know if she's been in touch with Jeanette today. I want to rule out a family fight before we push the panic button, okay?"

Rachel, Martin and Jimmy were sitting still, their attention riveted on Susan and Susan's half of the conversation. She looked at their expectant faces, then explained Debora's concerns.

The phone rang again. "She did talk to her today. Jeanette called her and said she was afraid. I had to tell her mother I didn't know why she'd be afraid. I don't know who might be calling her there. And I don't. But I think I have to go find out."

"Not without me," Susan said firmly.

"Susie, we can't argue about this now and you can't go, you just can't."

"Debora, cut the crap. We won't argue about it,

I'm going. That's all. This is my life, in case you've forgotten."

"And I'm supposed to keep you from spending the next bit of your life in jail," Debora said fiercely, "which is where you will be if you're seen as intimidating this witness."

Susan was about to scream at Debora in frustration when Rachel took the phone out of her hand. "Debora, it's me, Rachel. Maybe we could work a compromise here?" She paused. "Not if she lets you be the only one who has contact with Astrid. We'll come with you, both of us. You'll need help with the driving. It's late already and I assume you mean to go tonight. We'll wait in the car and you can see what's happening for yourself. If you need to call the D.A., that sort of thing, we'll make ourselves scarce until you're ready to leave. Promise. Susan will promise, too."

Susan nodded and Debora apparently agreed because Rachel was smiling. Finally she said, "It is her life, Debora. She has to choose her risks." Then she hung up the phone.

"She'll pick us up in an hour."

Susan and Rachel were waiting outside in the lightly falling snow when Debora pulled up in front of the house. They jumped into the car and pulled away into the darkness.

"Thanks," Susan said after a moment.

Debora nodded. The argument was over. "I know this is nuts. It's a five-hour drive at least. It's starting to snow and we'll be driving right into it.

And I can't imagine what we're going to do at this place when we get there." She looked at the car radio's clock. "It's after eleven now."

"Don't apologize," Susan insisted, settling into the back seat. "If you hadn't said you were coming, I'd probably have rushed over by myself. I don't exactly know why we're going either, and I certainly don't know why we want to get there at four in the morning, but I know I couldn't stay home. It's too eerie. Something tells me we've got to get there."

After the first hour, Debora couldn't peer through the blowing snow anymore and Rachel took over the driving. The Thruway stretched straight ahead for miles, through the low hills west of Albany, then past the snow belt of Syracuse. They traded drivers every hour and kept one another awake by speculating about what had happened, what might happen when they arrived.

Coming down one of the long hills outside of Syracuse, they saw flares and flashing lights on the opposite side of the road. Susan slowed the car to a crawl as they went by. Several cars were on the shoulder of the road and a large semi was jackknifed across most of the road, lying on its side.

"It's treacherous," Susan muttered through clenched teeth as their car swerved trying to go up the next hill.

"Oh, God, this is nuts," Debora was clearly having second thoughts. "What *are* we doing?"

"Covering ourselves against a worst case scenario, I imagine," Rachel said softly. For a while they drove on in silence.

The rehab was on the south side of town and they took the bypass around Rochester, looking for the exit. Martin had gotten explicit directions from a friend who'd been in that rehab. More than a few gay people go there, he'd explained, they're better than average on gay issues.

"Count on Astrid to know that." Susan sighed.

The place, when they found it, was enormous. Surrounded by a crumbling old wall, lawns sprinkled with tall pines, the snow drifting across the circular driveway, they might have been driving into another era. The original ancient brick building was imposing enough, but the additions had been built in the same red brick, and the effect was fortress-like. They drove through the main entrance, out past the parking lots, and into the service road behind the building. Another car had made deep ruts in the snow ahead of them. Susan pulled over to the curb, turned the car lights off, and turned back to look questioningly at Debora.

"I don't know," she said. "I really don't know."

They sat, watching the snow fall. Another car's lights pierced the snow out on the perimeter road then disappeared around the bend. Five minutes passed, and the car lights reappeared, traveled around, disappeared.

"Is that the same car?" Rachel asked. "I wonder if they have some kind of patrol."

"You aren't exactly locked up in rehab," Susan reminded her. "It's voluntary. People can leave anytime."

As she spoke, a door opened fifty yards away and a crack of light appeared. Someone came out, closed the door, looked around and started to walk toward their car. When the car lights out on the perimeter road reappeared, the figure ducked back behind a service truck and waited until they disappeared again. Then it came cautiously their way.

"What in the world?" Susan breathed softly. "This is nuts. You really can leave whenever you want."

"That's not what this looks like," Debora muttered. "I don't think he knows we're here."

The figure sprinted for the shelter between their car and the building and bent down to hide, lifting for a second to survey the terrain before sprinting again. In that second, with her face only inches away from the dark, shrouded figure, Susan recognized her. "My God, it's Astrid," she said loudly.

Whether Astrid heard her name, or only saw movement in a car she had presumed empty, she turned and ran back toward the building.

"Oh, no, you don't," Susan opened her door and raced after Astrid, her promise to let Debora handle Astrid completely forgotten.

She slipped in the snow, regained her balance, and caught up with Astrid at the self-locking door to the rehab.

"Damn." Astrid was pulling on the door blindly, panting as though she'd run much farther.

"Astrid. I just want to talk with you. Please." Susan took her arm and pulled Astrid around to face her.

"You're not Glenda." The relief on her face shifted to fear as the headlights from the other car came around again. "Hide," she said urgently, and she started to pant again with fear.

Susan pulled Astrid down flat in the snow and lay down beside her, hoping the car was too far away to see them prone, hoping Rachel and Debora wouldn't give them away. Her own breathing seemed noisy to her, and she could hear her heart pounding in her chest. Why? Why should she be afraid of Glenda Mathis? Glenda might be weird or even unethical. Susan couldn't quite see her as dangerous. But Astrid's fear was real, and contagious, and they stayed huddled in the snow until it was dark again. Then she pulled Astrid up and pushed her toward the car.

Debora had been watching them and opened the door as they approached. Susan pushed Astrid into the back seat with Debora, then got in and started the car. With the lights off, she started for the exit.

"What in the world is going on?" Debora's whisper seemed directed as much toward Susan as to Astrid who was sobbing loudly between long drawn breaths in the back seat.

"She thinks Glenda Mathis is in that car. She's afraid of her," Susan told them. She looked toward Astrid for confirmation, but she shook her head no, and kept trying to control her deep gasping breath.

"Does that mean no, she's not afraid, or no, we're not getting it, I wonder." Rachel was turned around, staring at Astrid as though she couldn't believe this apparition that had appeared in their car.

Susan turned onto the main road outside the rehab and switched on her headlights. As soon as her lights went on, another car turned on its lights and followed them. "Shit," she muttered. "I thought I'd lost it. Should I be worried, Debora? What's the deal here?" She couldn't quite bring herself to accepting that it was Glenda they were fleeing from.

Astrid twisted around in her seat, saw the lights

behind them, and started wailing hysterically. "She'll kill us. I know she will. She'll kill us all." She lunged toward the door.

Debora grabbed her arm and pulled her back. "Astrid, for God's sake, cool it. Glenda Mathis is not going to hurt us."

"Oh, good, more traffic," Susan muttered as a large delivery truck came over the hill toward them.

She clutched the wheel tightly and steered toward the right side of the road, the dividing line and the shoulder both being invisible in the driving snow. Suddenly the car lurched and swerved. "Jesus!" Susan glanced quickly over her shoulder, then back at the road. "She's nuts. She's trying to run us off the road!" The car lurched again as Glenda's car hit them from behind. This time Susan couldn't control the skid. "Shit, shit, shit," she muttered as the car began to slide into the path of the oncoming truck.

With a last wrench of the wheel and a sudden acceleration, she managed to swing the car into an opposite skid, and slid away from the truck, toward the ditch as Astrid continued to scream, "She'll kill us, she'll kill us."

In the dark, the truck horn blared, and they heard the crunch of metal on metal and glass breaking on the road behind them, and then there was a breathless silence as their car spun slowly around and settled into the ditch, resting against a tree.

It was quiet in the car and quiet outside. Rachel drew a deep breath. She could see that Susan was all right, leaning against the steering wheel, panting. She turned around to make sure Debora and Astrid were also unhurt. Astrid seemed to have been shocked into silence.

The car was a two-door and Susan's door was jammed against the tree. Rachel tried hers. It wouldn't open. The frame seemed to have been skewed and she didn't have the leverage to push up and out at the same time. She tried the window. It had cracked but responded when she turned the handle. Snow blew in the opening. Outside, there was still silence.

"I have to see ... Maybe I can help." She put her head and shoulders through the window and let her upper body fall against the side of the car, then slid the rest of the way out, falling in the soft snow. Their headlights illuminated a few feet in front of them, but behind, where they had heard the sound of metal and glass, there was only dark swirling snow. Rachel stayed close to the ditch, afraid of other cars fighting through the blinding snow. Down the hill a few hundred yards, the rear of the delivery truck loomed out of the snow in front of her.

"Hello," Rachel called, her voice lost in the wind. She went forward and saw a light flashing at the front of the truck. It was the driver of the truck, flashlight in hand, trying to find his way out of the cab. The truck had gone into the same ditch, Rachel saw, and crushed under the heavy semi's cab was Glenda Mathis's small car.

CHAPTER TWENTY-FOUR

Debora nodded at Astrid, who began to speak as though she had rehearsed. "I put the cocaine in your apartment," she said to Susan. "Glenda told me I had to. I didn't know why. I found out later about the contract with your agency and that she wanted you discredited and out of the way."

"Why don't you start at the beginning?" Debora suggested. They were seated in her office back in Albany. It was Monday afternoon. A few hours and a lifetime away from the snowy road outside of Rochester where Glenda Mathis had died.

Astrid started with a cocaine habit that had been recreation, something that was cool, a way to prove she was not one of the Twelve Step groupies who had no mind of her own. Astrid could find her own way. But the way led past Glenda Mathis.

"Glenda?" Susan couldn't help interrupting.

Glenda. Astrid had done some work for her, arranging the sound system for a leadership training conference Glenda was running. Glenda flattered her, told her she wasn't limited politically like so many of the other dykes in the community. Glenda was older, she had a kind of authority. Astrid liked that. And when Glenda said she had a source for some recreational drugs, Astrid liked that even more. It had been gradual, her growing dependence on Glenda. Glenda started asking Astrid to represent her point of view in the community. Casually. Then she began to push. By the time Glenda suggested Astrid might use Susan's backyard as a drop for some of the drugs she was selling, Astrid couldn't say no.

"Where was Glenda getting drugs? Did she use? I mean, it's just hard to imagine." Susan still felt dazed.

Glenda was getting drugs from one of her sons, Astrid thought, who was a big-time dealer in the city. Every six months or so, he'd come up, and then Glenda would tell Astrid there was a supply to sell. Recently, he'd been coming up more often. Every month at least.

"I can see why the D.A.'s office wanted to talk to you," Debora said.

"That's why I'm in trouble. More trouble than you know," Astrid told her. Mark Raskin, one of Debora's friends who had agreed to represent Astrid,

231

nodded in confirmation of that. "I was arrested when I sold coke to an undercover guy and offered a contract. If I gave them other names, if I talked to the grand jury —" She didn't look happy, saying this out loud. "They told me they'd drop the charges against me if I could lead them to some other sources, but Glenda started threatening me. I was really fucked up. I put the stuff in your apartment," she said to Susan, "just to get Glenda off my back for a while. Then I lied to the grand jury. I told them I was getting the stuff from you."

There was silence for a moment. Shocked, Susan was staring at Astrid. Rachel was shaking her head sorrowfully.

"Somewhere in the fear, though, I kept hearing a voice that told me I didn't have to do this. It wasn't a very strong voice, but I could hear it." Astrid looked proud for a moment. "I ran away to get myself straightened out so I could think. I would have come back. I meant to be back before your trial and tell the truth. But Glenda . . ." She paused, and the fear came back into her eyes. "She knew I was slipping away from her. She got really mean. She told me I was disgraced in this community and I ought to just kill myself. I was in such bad shape, I nearly believed her. When I left town, I couldn't tell anyone where I was. But she found me anyway. She called the rehab." She started to cry. "She was so angry at me. She said her son was coming up, and I'd have a lot more to worry about if he found me. I had to get away. I just wanted to be left alone. How did this happen to me?" Her sobs were the only sound in the room.

Susan and Rachel left Debora's office together and

went, without discussing it, to Susan's house where they watched the evening news in silence. In the television picture, it was still early morning, and the two cars were being towed away. It was snowing, and the desolation of that little piece of back road south of Rochester was chilling. No mention was made of Glenda's attempt to run another car off the road into the path of the oncoming truck. They hadn't told the police about that at the scene of the accident, and so the reporter just reeled off the gory details of the accident — the snow and ice delaying a rescue effort, jaws of life cutting Glenda out of the car, but by then it was too late. Glenda was pretty well known in Albany, and there was a picture of her, one of her professional mug shots where she looked bright and intelligent and cheerful. Debora said she didn't know how much else would eventually be reported about what Glenda was doing. That was pretty much up to the D.A. and how much of Astrid's testimony would be made public.

When the news ended, they walked to a small restaurant around the corner for dinner. Susan was kicking the soft snow aside — "It seems so benign now," she said to Rachel — but she couldn't help remembering what it was like to be driving a car through it and see the truck coming toward her and think she couldn't get out of the way. There had been times in her life, she was thinking, when events collided out of control and she felt like she *was* being run over by a truck. Those times had mostly ended when she quit using drugs.

"It's not your fault," Rachel said. "I know you know that, but sometimes it's hard to believe."

They talked about Glenda over dinner, how she

had gotten to that point of desperation, to that place of violence out on a snowy road. There had been no weapon in her car. Had she meant to harm Astrid, or did she only want to talk with her? Was Astrid's fear reasonable, they wondered, or had paranoia pushed her into hysteria? Who did Glenda think was in the car when she rammed it from behind? She must have seen Astrid and someone — she couldn't have known it was Susan — lying in the snow when they thought they were hiding.

"I wonder if she asked the same question Astrid was just asking," Rachel said softly. "How did this happen to me? I can't imagine that this was how Glenda intended her life to be." But there were no easy answers.

Rachel had tried to help Glenda while the truck driver went back up to the rehab for help. When Susan finally struggled out of the car window, she found Rachel down in the ditch by Glenda's car. She shook her head when she saw Susan and climbed out of the ditch.

"You were sure there was nothing we could have done for her?" Susan asked now. "Maybe I should have gone down in that ditch myself with the flashlight, so I wouldn't have to imagine her trapped in the car, slowly bleeding to death, cursing me for all of her imagined — or real — grievances."

"She must have died instantly. I couldn't get inside — close enough to tell. But there's no way she could have been alive."

"I know. I do believe you. It's just that I had unfinished business with her." Susan was still sorry she hadn't confronted Glenda, talked with her about the contracts, instead of letting Tom call her, or some bureaucrat from the Commissioner's office. "What if? What if?" she muttered.

"Say it," Rachel demanded.

"Would Glenda have gone looking for Astrid if we had talked? Would she have told me about the drugs? Maybe she was as exhausted by running away from it all as Astrid had been. She could see it was out of control, that she'd lost control of the web she'd been spinning." She leaned back in her chair, exhausted. "Or maybe it was only myself I was thinking of, that past self that had come back from a crazed life of drugging and unimaginable consequences because I simply couldn't deal with the uncertainty anymore. I know you say I'm not responsible, Rachel, but in someplace less than rational I feel like Glenda would be alive today if we'd only had the chance to talk."

"Maybe." Rachel conceded. "But we'll never know. We'll never know."

Later, walking home in the fresh snow, their boots scuffed a path along the unshoveled walks. The crescent moon hung low on the western horizon. Susan thought she ought to be celebrating. After all, it was over. Debora had said the indictment would be dropped. It was over. But she couldn't get to the relief and joy she had expected to feel if this could only be resolved.

"You didn't make Glenda choose that path." Rachel's hands were tucked deep in her pockets and she was looking at the moon as she spoke. Susan wondered if she was talking to her. "You insulted her once, fifteen years or so ago. Her son didn't become a drug dealer on the strength of that. Her anger at you festered and became something grotesque. It didn't have to be that way. It wasn't your fault, Susan. Believe me."

"I know what you're saying. It's going to take some time for me to figure out what I'm feeling. I hate that you and Debora might have gotten killed because you were trying to help me. Do you understand that?"

"Oh, yes, very well." Rachel was quiet for a moment. Then she took Susan's hand. "Take all the time you need. We have time now, don't we?"

And Susan agreed that they did. She thought they did. "I'll be back," she told Rachel. "But right now I need some time alone."

The next day, Glenda's son Michael was picked up in New York City as part of a huge drug bust. They found him in a crack house with several kilos of cocaine in addition to the crack. The marks on the bags matched the one that had been hidden under Susan's radiator cover.

Alone in front of her television, she watched him being led into a courtroom in New York in handcuffs. He glowered at the camera through two days of unshaven beard. When Susan had known him as a boy, she thought he had a better chance than her own son. His mother wasn't an addict, didn't drag him around the streets with her, feeding a habit, didn't hang out in strange houses. Her son never woke up and wondered where he was and who the people sitting in the room with him were. Her son was never the subject of a bitter custody battle, and as far as Susan knew Glenda had never been alienated from her son, never had to meet him again as an adolescent, a young man, and learn who he had become apart from her. Now her son was in jail and Jake was leading an exemplary life as a conservation specialist for the National Forestry Service.

What kept coming back to her was an image of herself and Glenda fifteen, maybe seventeen years ago, in Boston, in Glenda's living room. They were arguing about whether women who lived in the suburbs and had husbands could ever be feminists. Susan was sure they could not. There were too many easy things about their lives. How could anyone understand the revolution from inside a comfortable life? In retrospect, she knew she had been arguing about her mother, of course. But Glenda didn't know that. Glenda said she was being ridiculous, that any woman who lived closely with a man knew what it was to be a second-class citizen, knew what a power differential was. She was arguing about herself, and she was furious.

For a few months then, Susan and Glenda had been held together by a band that didn't have much stretch in it. Susan never could say exactly what Glenda might have been attracted to in her, but she was sure that she had seen in Glenda a mother who would fight with her, and fight they did. Until the inevitable — the band broke. Susan left in a fury one night after saying searing, horrible things to Glenda. The role Susan had assigned to her didn't include sex, that was beyond imagining.

What was bothering her, she realized as she watched the rest of the news without seeing it, was that she had never brought Glenda out of that "bad dream" place in her life. With Glenda, she'd never gone through that process they call "making amends" in AA. She and Jacob had that conversation, in a formal way first, and later in any interaction where they clashed or disagreed, where they had to go back to what had been and try to create the present out of something different from the past.

But Glenda? Susan got up restlessly and turned off the television. In all of their later interactions she was still the person Susan had to fight, if only in her imagination. She'd just ignored the past.

However the world might come to judge it, Susan believed that she and Glenda shouldn't have ended in two cars chasing down a dark snowy road. Glenda may have thought she was chasing Astrid, but in some way, Susan felt Glenda knew who she was really chasing.

The next day Susan went to work, walking up the hill in the snow, holding her hood closed against the wind. No one in her office was pretending nothing had happened. The entire staff was already there, waiting for her in the large conference room, and when she stepped out of the elevator they started to applaud. Susan felt like she was still living in some other dimension, and then she remembered they were applauding because the indictment had been dropped, not because Glenda was dead. Only a few knew how Glenda had been connected to the indictment. So she thanked them, shyly, unsure for the first time of her relationship to her own staff. When Martin suggested an informal half-day vacation, Susan was relieved. The snow was supposed to start again that afternoon. She needed more time to think, to be alone.

Susan's favorite reading for years had been accounts of explorers and adventurers who went off and did it alone. Byrd in the Arctic, Mowat among the northern wolves — too few women among these intrepid solitary explorers, she admitted, but nonetheless she always imagined herself in that way. Alone. Self-sufficient. Serene. Eventually, she began to notice that none of those explorers was really alone. Incredible teams made their adventures possible. Not one of them could have survived out there without the pilot who dropped off supplies, the graduate students who analyzed data and sent new directions, the grants and book contracts that supported the adventurers financially. True, that was all on the sidelines. The hero was out there alone. But Susan finally had to admit, alone is relative. When you stand on top of the mountain, there is a broad base beneath you, no matter how narrow and isolated the view from the summit.

CHAPTER TWENTY-FIVE

Rachel hadn't thought about what faith was for years. Even for clergy, faith is not an item of everyday conversation outside of seminary. For Rachel, generally, faith meant believing in the possibility of love, in the healing power of love. And so, during that week after Glenda's death, she wrestled herself into an attitude of faith. It took all her strength and even then she doubted she would have made it without Richard's encouragement.

"Of course she loves you," he'd reassure her. "Why not believe she'll be back. She told you she would. What do you gain by giving up and pulling back inside yourself? Do you really want to let go of her, of the possibility of this relationship?"

No, she didn't. And so she let his words play over and over again in her head whenever she began to doubt, whenever the pain of missing Susan became too strong.

In the back of her mind, she could occasionally hear a bright cheerful voice saying, "Never say never." Those words, she thought, were the mantra of faith. She knew she hadn't heard those words from her parents. Each of them said never with great frequency — it was certainly a concept her mother knew intimately — never see her family again, never tell about her secret child, never, never, never. Rachel's father used it to give orders: You will never do that in my house, my business, my state. And Rachel herself had said her share of nevers. Never be loved, really loved. Never have a family. Never have a sister. She'd fought the pessimism of her nevers for years, but simple faith, believing in, was not an attitude she learned in her family.

While she was struggling with her own definition of faith, somewhere amid the events of that last week, Rachel also realized that she was ready to stop being a minister to a congregation. Permanently. The conversation with Donna and Clara had only clarified what she must have known when she asked for this leave. She was tired and she didn't want to answer to anyone or want anyone to think she had the answers.

"Are you leaving the church, then?" Carmen's voice, distant across the phone wires, didn't convey to Rachel whether she was pleased or upset.

241

"I guess I am," she admitted. "I don't want my roles defined for me anymore." She had gone to seminary to find her spirituality. It hadn't been there. What she had found was a format for how she could take care of people. Not that she couldn't use that. After nursing both of her parents, she needed to have a defined role in relationship to others. Dutiful daughter? It didn't fit her. Minister to a congregation with all of the rituals and duties already set for her? She'd needed that.

"I found a community, a family, in the church," she told Carmen. "It was a way of being with a group of people that I had never experienced in my family. That's what brought me my spirit self. It came with working with people who weren't perfect, like I wasn't perfect." Carmen was still silent. "And now I've learned how to create my own community, my own family."

"Yes," Carmen agreed finally, "you have. And you'll be fine, Rachel, wherever you decide to work."

As she hung up the phone, Rachel wondered whether her mother's letters might have freed her, in a sense — freed her to believe in love, not just love given, but love received.

She remembered years ago telling an elderly member of her congregation in Provincetown that no, she didn't believe in life after death. The old woman fixed Rachel with a stern eye and corrected her. "Young woman," she said, "of course there is life after death. It is here. The dead always stay around to remind us of who we are."

* * * * *

"How's the book coming?" Richard asked Rachel innocently one morning over breakfast.

She stared at him as though he were speaking a foreign language and then realized from the quizzical look on his face that he had no idea how far away from writing a book she'd gone in the last few days.

"It's not coming," she told him and felt no regret. "I think I've decided I'd rather live my life than write about it."

"Some people think they can do both."

"True. But not me. Not now. I don't know exactly what I need to do, but the book isn't right. I'm not sure why, but I do know it's not right, not for me, not now."

Richard was listening and nodding, and he didn't seem surprised. "I've always seen you in the middle of things," he said slowly. "I've wondered how you'd manage alone at your desk for as long as it takes to write a book. Not that you couldn't do it if you wanted to," he added.

"What kind of work do you see me doing," Rachel asked him out of curiosity, "if you don't see me sitting alone at my desk?"

He settled back in his chair as though she'd given him a long assignment and he needed to get comfortable. He'd grown so thin since his hospitalization that Rachel was sometimes afraid she'd see his bones push through his pale, luminous skin. He saw her look of concern and brushed it away with a shrug.

"Well, let's see, Sis. One thing I'd be sure of is that you'll be preaching. That's why I thought you might do the book, actually. It's another way to tell the world what's going on. But so is teaching. I could see you holding forth in a classroom, you know." He crossed his arms and went on. "You're too plain spoken for mass media."

She snorted a laugh and wished for a moment that Susan was there to enjoy this, but Richard wasn't joking.

"But I do see you with a much wider venue than being in the church gave you. State government? I'm not sure they're ready for you there yet either? But maybe an alternative agency of some kind. Healing? You're a healer, you know, as well as an activist. Yes, you're an activist," he preempted her protest, "you're just a little tired right now. Ask yourself — what needs organizing the way services for AIDS needed organizing when you first went out to P-town?" He gave her a crooked smile. "I know better than to tell you what it is. You'll find it yourself. When it's time."

"Thank you, Richard." She found his matter-of-factness calming.

Rachel sat down at her desk after their talk and looked at her notes for the book. Her definition of spiritual journey had been wrong, she decided, when she first conceptualized it. She'd been thinking then of women who knew they had spiritual missions in life, women who were conscious missionaries to the world, even though the women she wanted to write about were for the most part not connected to formal religious traditions. Then Carmen had told her that loving Susan was part of her spiritual journey, part of the book. It was a thought to hold on to during these days when Rachel was missing her so fiercely, but it seemed to have nothing to do with a book.

Besides, no one listens to sermons any more. And why should they? There was more theology in a horror film than in the average sermon, if theology was meant to lift the veil between the physical and spirit worlds.

She put her old notes aside. The streets had been plowed, the snow was melting. She got out her jogging shoes. A run would do more good than staring at the wall above her desk or waiting for the phone to ring with Susan's voice asking for her.

She slogged through the wet snow, six times around the long block, uphill, then down, uphill, then down.

CHAPTER TWENTY-SIX

Carmen stood at the sink in Richard's kitchen, waving a long thin knife around while she talked. "Now, Susan, has Rachel given you my recipe for curried jalapeño cream dip?"

Christmas had arrived and with it Richard's annual holiday party. Susan and Rachel had talked every day since Glenda's death but spent nights in their own homes. Susan wasn't ready to celebrate anything and yet she knew that it was time to try and move out of her solitude.

"Curried jalapeño? Isn't that overkill? I mean, we want people to enjoy this party, not leave in pain."

Rachel laughed. "Actually, Carmen's dips are a multi-cultural experience all by themselves," she insisted, and Susan appreciated her light-hearted tone. They were all trying.

Gradually the warmth of the kitchen began to work on them. Carmen needed to hear more about what had happened. They started to talk about Glenda, indirectly at first, between the chopping and stirring. Was she evil? What was evil anyway? How does one come to the place where murder seems a solution?

"I can't make her evil," Susan confessed. "Even when I'm most furious at her. Ambitious, yes. Greedy. Unscrupulous. All of that. But evil?"

"Even after seeing how afraid of her Astrid was?" Rachel wondered.

"Even. It doesn't compute for me."

"I can understand that," Carmen said slowly. "She was someone you knew for a long time, wasn't she?"

"In a way, yes."

"We shouldn't look for one reason Glenda did what she did. Our whole past shapes our present. You were part of Glenda's past, maybe more than you knew."

"That terrifies me more than evil," Susan tried to be flip, but she didn't quite carry it off.

"Tell us what you mean, Susan," Rachel came up to the table where Susan sat and put her hand on Susan's shoulder.

Wishing she had said nothing, and yet wanting to explain, Susan told them how she used to think she

247

was safer being alone, that no one else could get hurt by her actions if she didn't let them in close. "That was my first lesson from losing Jacob," she said bitterly. "The judge told me that I was harming my son by 'proximity.' Having you and Debora in the car when I began to lose control of it," she put her hand over Rachel's. "The sense of proximity, you know. It was too close for me."

"Susan, we're grown-ups. You aren't responsible for us. We chose to take that trip."

"I know that, Rachel." Her voice was miserable. "But my feelings don't."

Carmen sat at the table with them. "Have you seen those children's books that have the transparencies in them. You know, when you open it you're looking at a jungle filled with fierce, threatening monsters. If you lift up the first overlay, the monsters are really only a cat and her kittens. Then you pick up another and all of a sudden the dark shadows are gone and the cat is in a familiar back yard. The shapes stay the same, it's just a matter of perspective." She looked at Susan. "Your experience is the same shape as one that happened to you a while ago. We all have appointments in life we have to keep, and that judge was one of yours. You just don't have the new perspective on it yet. It will come, Susan, I think it will come."

Rachel was nodding, and Susan could see her imagining all the sets of overlays her past had given her.

"And besides," Carmen got up from the table with emphasis, "you've been learning a new shape altogether this time around."

Susan looked at her with raised eyebrows.

"You're learning about letting other people be there for you. Now where's the rest of the fruit for this punch, Rachel? Folks will be arriving before too long." The doorbell rang as Rachel was giving directions and Susan fled to answer it.

She didn't remember much of that evening later. There were hugs and good wishes. For a while she had the sense that Debora was watching her worriedly from across the room. And then, Susan felt something rigid in her spine begin to relax — not all at once, but gradually. "I'm really pissed they didn't take me along," she heard Martin say at one point. He was talking to Carmen. "I missed seeing Susan tackle Astrid in the snow. Can you imagine?" Carmen gave him one of the quizzical looks that Susan was beginning to recognize.

Later, it was Charlie Leitman watching her from across the room, but he waved and came over. "You're doing okay," he said, and Susan began to believe that perhaps she was.

The evening came into focus for her again briefly when Josie and Mark came stomping into the living room, knocking snow off their boots, shaking it off their hats. "Martin told us this was a not-to-miss party," Mark said, greeting Susan. Since he'd helped them get access to the files that blew Tom and Glenda's scam off the map, Mark had a new confidence. Josie hung back a bit, shaking more snow off her hat than was on it. Here we go, thought Susan as she introduced them both to Rachel. Mark was pleased, very pleased, and breezed off to find Martin. Josie looked from Susan to Rachel and back to Susan. "I wanted to thank you," she said. "I should have known — Tom said some things that made me think you wouldn't care what happened —"

Susan would have helped her finish a sentence, but she truly did not know what Josie wanted to say. She had spoken to Josie at the office right after Tom's dismissal and apologized for not having kept a closer watch on him. This seemed to be about something else.

"He said terrible things about you being gay," she blurted out finally. "How I shouldn't get too close to you because you'd hit on me. I just wanted you to know I like working for you." She raced to the finish and closed her mouth abruptly.

"Thank you, Josie," Susan managed before Josie fled, "and I like working with you."

When someone put an arm around her waist, she half turned and saw Rachel. She leaned further into Rachel's arms and brushed her lips across the gray fringe of hair at the side of her face. "Hi," she said, newly shy. "I do love you, you know?"

Rachel was quiet for a moment as the party pulsed around them. "Yes," she said. "Yes, I do know."

"Come home with me? This will go on for hours."

Rachel wasn't hard to persuade.

They woke up together the next morning. The sun was taking its time rising, shining weakly through high thin clouds, burnishing the icy windows with a pale glare. Susan let herself fall back into sleep several times, hugging Rachel, pulling the blankets around them.

They finally woke to talk, to plan a future that did not include an indictment, the prospect of prison. For the first time Susan appreciated how much lighter her heart was with that threat removed. Their conversation carried them down to the river, walking, talking. The nights had been cold and only a single dark channel of water ran down the center of the river. Susan listened to the deep crunch of ice floes rubbing together and wished the river would talk to her.

"I mean to find my sister." Rachel was looking upstream beyond the bridge. "I don't know how, but I have to try."

"I expect that. How could you not?"

Rachel told her about Richard's balloon, how he'd put everything from his painful childhood in the balloon, including the need for his parents to love him, and he'd taken it down to the river and let it go. "I can't do that. I need to know where she is, who she is."

"I agree with you. I think Richard is wrong. I don't think we can choose when we're finished with the past. At some point, maybe, it's finished with us. Then we move on. We have to move on or get mired down. But we have to let it finish with us first. You'll find your sister before you let go of that balloon."

She paused. "This afternoon ... this afternoon is the Commissioner's staff and family Christmas party."

Rachel looked up. "Really?"

"I want you to come with me. Will you come with me?"

"Do you think Josie is ready for this?" Rachel was joking, but she looked very pleased. "You've moved on, at any rate," she said finally. "Do you think I can keep up with you?"

"Do you want to try?"

"Yes. Oh, yes," she said. "Yes, I do."

A few of the publications of
THE NAIAD PRESS, INC.
P.O. Box 10543 • Tallahassee, Florida 32302
Phone (904) 539-5965
Toll-Free Order Number: 1-800-533-1973
Mail orders welcome. Please include 15% postage.
Write or call for our free catalog which also features an
incredible selection of lesbian videos.

DEATH AT LAVENDER BAY by Lauren Wright Douglas. 208 pp.
1st Allison O'Neil Mystery. ISBN 1-56280-085-X $10.95

YES I SAID YES I WILL by Judith McDaniel. 272 pp. Hot
romance by famous author. ISBN 1-56280-138-4 10.95

FORBIDDEN FIRES by Margaret C. Anderson. Edited by Mathilda
Hills. 176 pp. Famous author's "unpublished" Lesbian romance.
ISBN 1-56280-123-6 21.95

SIDE TRACKS by Teresa Stores. 160 pp. Gender-bending
Lesbians on the road. ISBN 1-56280-122-8 10.95

HOODED MURDER by Annette Van Dyke. 176 pp. 1st Jessie
Batelle Mystery. ISBN 1-56280-134-1 10.95

WILDWOOD FLOWERS by Julia Watts. 208 pp. Hilarious and
heart-warming tale of true love. ISBN 1-56280-127-9 10.95

NEVER SAY NEVER by Linda Hill. 224 pp. Rule #1: Never get involved
with . . . ISBN 1-56280-126-0 10.95

THE SEARCH by Melanie McAllester. 240 pp. Exciting top cop
Tenny Mendoza case. ISBN 1-56280-150-3 10.95

THE WISH LIST by Saxon Bennett. 192 pp. Romance through
the years. ISBN 1-56280-125-2 10.95

FIRST IMPRESSIONS by Kate Calloway. 208 pp. P.I. Cassidy
James' first case. ISBN 1-56280-133-3 10.95

OUT OF THE NIGHT by Kris Bruyer. 192 pp. Spine-tingling
thriller. ISBN 1-56280-120-1 10.95

NORTHERN BLUE by Tracey Richardson. 224 pp. Police recruits
Miki & Miranda — passion in the line of fire. ISBN 1-56280-118-X 10.95

LOVE'S HARVEST by Peggy J. Herring. 176 pp. by the author of
Once More With Feeling. ISBN 1-56280-117-1 10.95

THE COLOR OF WINTER by Lisa Shapiro. 208 pp. Romantic
love beyond your wildest dreams. ISBN 1-56280-116-3 10.95

FAMILY SECRETS by Laura DeHart Young. 208 pp. Enthralling
romance and suspense.   ISBN 1-56280-119-8   10.95

INLAND PASSAGE by Jane Rule. 288 pp. Tales exploring conventional & unconventional relationships.   ISBN 0-930044-56-8   10.95

DOUBLE BLUFF by Claire McNab. 208 pp. 7th Detective Carol
Ashton Mystery.   ISBN 1-56280-096-5   10.95

BAR GIRLS by Lauran Hoffman. 176 pp. See the movie, read
the book!   ISBN 1-56280-115-5   10.95

THE FIRST TIME EVER edited by Barbara Grier & Christine
Cassidy. 272 pp. Love stories by Naiad Press authors.
                                              ISBN 1-56280-086-8   14.95

MISS PETTIBONE AND MISS McGRAW by Brenda Weathers.
208 pp. A charming ghostly love story.   ISBN 1-56280-151-1   10.95

CHANGES by Jackie Calhoun. 208 pp. Involved romance and
relationships.   ISBN 1-56280-083-3   10.95

FAIR PLAY by Rose Beecham. 256 pp. 3rd Amanda Valentine
Mystery.   ISBN 1-56280-081-7   10.95

PAXTON COURT by Diane Salvatore. 256 pp. Erotic and wickedly
funny contemporary tale about the business of learning to live
together.   ISBN 1-56280-109-0   21.95

PAYBACK by Celia Cohen. 176 pp. A gripping thriller of romance,
revenge and betrayal.   ISBN 1-56280-084-1   10.95

THE BEACH AFFAIR by Barbara Johnson. 224 pp. Sizzling
summer romance/mystery/intrigue.   ISBN 1-56280-090-6   10.95

GETTING THERE by Robbi Sommers. 192 pp. Nobody does it
like Robbi!   ISBN 1-56280-099-X   10.95

FINAL CUT by Lisa Haddock. 208 pp. 2nd Carmen Ramirez
Mystery.   ISBN 1-56280-088-4   10.95

FLASHPOINT by Katherine V. Forrest. 256 pp. A Lesbian
blockbuster!   ISBN 1-56280-079-5   10.95

CLAIRE OF THE MOON by Nicole Conn. Audio Book —Read
by Marianne Hyatt.   ISBN 1-56280-113-9   16.95

FOR LOVE AND FOR LIFE: INTIMATE PORTRAITS OF
LESBIAN COUPLES by Susan Johnson. 224 pp.
                                              ISBN 1-56280-091-4   14.95

DEVOTION by Mindy Kaplan. 192 pp. See the movie — read
the book!   ISBN 1-56280-093-0   10.95

SOMEONE TO WATCH by Jaye Maiman. 272 pp. 4th Robin
Miller Mystery.   ISBN 1-56280-095-7   10.95

GREENER THAN GRASS by Jennifer Fulton. 208 pp. A young
woman — a stranger in her bed.   ISBN 1-56280-092-2   10.95

TRAVELS WITH DIANA HUNTER by Regine Sands. Erotic
lesbian romp. Audio Book (2 cassettes)   ISBN 1-56280-107-4   16.95

CABIN FEVER by Carol Schmidt. 256 pp. Sizzling suspense
and passion.   ISBN 1-56280-089-1   10.95

THERE WILL BE NO GOODBYES by Laura DeHart Young. 192
pp. Romantic love, strength, and friendship.   ISBN 1-56280-103-1   10.95

FAULTLINE by Sheila Ortiz Taylor. 144 pp. Joyous comic
lesbian novel.   ISBN 1-56280-108-2   9.95

OPEN HOUSE by Pat Welch. 176 pp. 4th Helen Black Mystery.
                                           ISBN 1-56280-102-3   10.95

ONCE MORE WITH FEELING by Peggy J. Herring. 240 pp.
Lighthearted, loving romantic adventure.   ISBN 1-56280-089-2   10.95

FOREVER by Evelyn Kennedy. 224 pp. Passionate romance — love
overcoming all obstacles.   ISBN 1-56280-094-9   10.95

WHISPERS by Kris Bruyer. 176 pp. Romantic ghost story
                                           ISBN 1-56280-082-5   10.95

NIGHT SONGS by Penny Mickelbury. 224 pp. 2nd Gianna Maglione
Mystery.   ISBN 1-56280-097-3   10.95

GETTING TO THE POINT by Teresa Stores. 256 pp. Classic
southern Lesbian novel.   ISBN 1-56280-100-7   10.95

PAINTED MOON by Karin Kallmaker. 224 pp. Delicious
Kallmaker romance.   ISBN 1-56280-075-2   10.95

THE MYSTERIOUS NAIAD edited by Katherine V. Forrest &
Barbara Grier. 320 pp. Love stories by Naiad Press authors.
                                           ISBN 1-56280-074-4   14.95

DAUGHTERS OF A CORAL DAWN by Katherine V. Forrest.
240 pp. Tenth Anniversay Edition.   ISBN 1-56280-104-X   10.95

BODY GUARD by Claire McNab. 208 pp. 6th Carol Ashton
Mystery.   ISBN 1-56280-073-6   10.95

CACTUS LOVE by Lee Lynch. 192 pp. Stories by the beloved
storyteller.   ISBN 1-56280-071-X   9.95

SECOND GUESS by Rose Beecham. 216 pp. 2nd Amanda Valentine
Mystery.   ISBN 1-56280-069-8   9.95

THE SURE THING by Melissa Hartman. 208 pp. L.A. earthquake
romance.   ISBN 1-56280-078-7   9.95

A RAGE OF MAIDENS by Lauren Wright Douglas. 240 pp. 6th Caitlin
Reece Mystery.   ISBN 1-56280-068-X   10.95

TRIPLE EXPOSURE by Jackie Calhoun. 224 pp. Romantic drama
involving many characters.   ISBN 1-56280-067-1   10.95

UP, UP AND AWAY by Catherine Ennis. 192 pp. Delightful
romance.   ISBN 1-56280-065-5   9.95

PERSONAL ADS by Robbi Sommers. 176 pp. Sizzling short
stories.   ISBN 1-56280-059-0   10.95

FLASHPOINT by Katherine V. Forrest. 256 pp. Lesbian
blockbuster!   ISBN 1-56280-043-4   22.95

CROSSWORDS by Penny Sumner. 256 pp. 2nd Victoria Cross
Mystery.   ISBN 1-56280-064-7   9.95

SWEET CHERRY WINE by Carol Schmidt. 224 pp. A novel of
suspense.   ISBN 1-56280-063-9   9.95

CERTAIN SMILES by Dorothy Tell. 160 pp. Erotic short stories.
                                            ISBN 1-56280-066-3   9.95

EDITED OUT by Lisa Haddock. 224 pp. 1st Carmen Ramirez
Mystery.   ISBN 1-56280-077-9   9.95

WEDNESDAY NIGHTS by Camarin Grae. 288 pp. Sexy
adventure.   ISBN 1-56280-060-4   10.95

SMOKEY O by Celia Cohen. 176 pp. Relationships on the
playing field.   ISBN 1-56280-057-4   9.95

KATHLEEN O'DONALD by Penny Hayes. 256 pp. Rose and
Kathleen find each other and employment in 1909 NYC.
                                            ISBN 1-56280-070-1   9.95

STAYING HOME by Elisabeth Nonas. 256 pp. Molly and Alix
want a baby . . . or do they?   ISBN 1-56280-076-0   10.95

TRUE LOVE by Jennifer Fulton. 240 pp. Six lesbians searching
for love in all the "right" places.   ISBN 1-56280-035-3   10.95

GARDENIAS WHERE THERE ARE NONE by Molleen Zanger.
176 pp. Why is Melanie inextricably drawn to the old house?
                                            ISBN 1-56280-056-6   9.95

KEEPING SECRETS by Penny Mickelbury. 208 pp. 1st Gianna
Maglione Mystery.   ISBN 1-56280-052-3   9.95

THE ROMANTIC NAIAD edited by Katherine V. Forrest &
Barbara Grier. 336 pp. Love stories by Naiad Press authors.
                                            ISBN 1-56280-054-X   14.95

UNDER MY SKIN by Jaye Maiman. 336 pp. 3rd Robin Miller
Mystery.   ISBN 1-56280-049-3.   10.95

STAY TOONED by Rhonda Dicksion. 144 pp. Cartoons — 1st
collection since Lesbian Survival Manual.   ISBN 1-56280-045-0   9.95

CAR POOL by Karin Kallmaker. 272pp. Lesbians on wheels
and then some!   ISBN 1-56280-048-5   10.95

NOT TELLING MOTHER: STORIES FROM A LIFE by Diane
Salvatore. 176 pp. Her 3rd novel.   ISBN 1-56280-044-2   9.95

GOBLIN MARKET by Lauren Wright Douglas. 240pp. 5th Caitlin
Reece Mystery.   ISBN 1-56280-047-7   10.95

LONG GOODBYES by Nikki Baker. 256 pp. 3rd Virginia Kelly
Mystery.   ISBN 1-56280-042-6   9.95

FRIENDS AND LOVERS by Jackie Calhoun. 224 pp. Mid-
western Lesbian lives and loves.   ISBN 1-56280-041-8   10.95

THE CAT CAME BACK by Hilary Mullins. 208 pp. Highly
praised Lesbian novel.   ISBN 1-56280-040-X   9.95

BEHIND CLOSED DOORS by Robbi Sommers. 192 pp. Hot,
erotic short stories.   ISBN 1-56280-039-6   9.95

CLAIRE OF THE MOON by Nicole Conn. 192 pp. See the
movie — read the book!   ISBN 1-56280-038-8   10.95

SILENT HEART by Claire McNab. 192 pp. Exotic Lesbian
romance.   ISBN 1-56280-036-1   10.95

HAPPY ENDINGS by Kate Brandt. 272 pp. Intimate conversations
with Lesbian authors.   ISBN 1-56280-050-7   10.95

THE SPY IN QUESTION by Amanda Kyle Williams. 256 pp.
4th Madison McGuire Mystery.   ISBN 1-56280-037-X   9.95

SAVING GRACE by Jennifer Fulton. 240 pp. Adventure and
romantic entanglement.   ISBN 1-56280-051-5   9.95

THE YEAR SEVEN by Molleen Zanger. 208 pp. Women surviving
in a new world.   ISBN 1-56280-034-5   9.95

CURIOUS WINE by Katherine V. Forrest. 176 pp. Tenth Anniver-
sary Edition. The most popular contemporary Lesbian love story.
                                         ISBN 1-56280-053-1   10.95
         Audio Book (2 cassettes)   ISBN 1-56280-105-8   16.95

CHAUTAUQUA by Catherine Ennis. 192 pp. Exciting, romantic
adventure.   ISBN 1-56280-032-9   9.95

A PROPER BURIAL by Pat Welch. 192 pp. 3rd Helen Black
Mystery.   ISBN 1-56280-033-7   9.95

SILVERLAKE HEAT: A Novel of Suspense by Carol Schmidt.
240 pp. Rhonda is as hot as Laney's dreams.   ISBN 1-56280-031-0   9.95

LOVE, ZENA BETH by Diane Salvatore. 224 pp. The most talked
about lesbian novel of the nineties!   ISBN 1-56280-030-2   10.95

A DOORYARD FULL OF FLOWERS by Isabel Miller. 160 pp.
Stories incl. 2 sequels to *Patience and Sarah.* ISBN 1-56280-029-9   9.95

MURDER BY TRADITION by Katherine V. Forrest. 288 pp. 4th
Kate Delafield Mystery.   ISBN 1-56280-002-7   10.95

THE EROTIC NAIAD edited by Katherine V. Forrest & Barbara
Grier. 224 pp. Love stories by Naiad Press authors.
                                         ISBN 1-56280-026-4   14.95

DEAD CERTAIN by Claire McNab. 224 pp. 5th Carol Ashton
Mystery.   ISBN 1-56280-027-2   9.95

CRAZY FOR LOVING by Jaye Maiman. 320 pp. 2nd Robin Miller
Mystery. ISBN 1-56280-025-6   9.95

STONEHURST by Barbara Johnson. 176 pp. Passionate regency
romance. ISBN 1-56280-024-8   9.95

INTRODUCING AMANDA VALENTINE by Rose Beecham.
256 pp. 1st Amanda Valentine Mystery. ISBN 1-56280-021-3   10.95

UNCERTAIN COMPANIONS by Robbi Sommers. 204 pp.
Steamy, erotic novel. ISBN 1-56280-017-5   9.95

A TIGER'S HEART by Lauren W. Douglas. 240 pp. 4th Caitlin
Reece Mystery. ISBN 1-56280-018-3   9.95

PAPERBACK ROMANCE by Karin Kallmaker. 256 pp. A
delicious romance. ISBN 1-56280-019-1   10.95

MORTON RIVER VALLEY by Lee Lynch. 304 pp. Lee Lynch
at her best! ISBN 1-56280-016-7   9.95

THE LAVENDER HOUSE MURDER by Nikki Baker. 224 pp.
2nd Virginia Kelly Mystery. ISBN 1-56280-012-4   9.95

PASSION BAY by Jennifer Fulton. 224 pp. Passionate romance,
virgin beaches, tropical skies. ISBN 1-56280-028-0   10.95

STICKS AND STONES by Jackie Calhoun. 208 pp. Contemporary
lesbian lives and loves. ISBN 1-56280-020-5   9.95
Audio Book (2 cassettes) ISBN 1-56280-106-6   16.95

DELIA IRONFOOT by Jeane Harris. 192 pp. Adventure for Delia
and Beth in the Utah mountains. ISBN 1-56280-014-0   9.95

UNDER THE SOUTHERN CROSS by Claire McNab. 192 pp.
Romantic nights Down Under. ISBN 1-56280-011-6   9.95

GRASSY FLATS by Penny Hayes. 256 pp. Lesbian romance in
the '30s. ISBN 1-56280-010-8   9.95

A SINGULAR SPY by Amanda K. Williams. 192 pp. 3rd
Madison McGuire Mystery. ISBN 1-56280-008-6   8.95

THE END OF APRIL by Penny Sumner. 240 pp. 1st Victoria
Cross Mystery. ISBN 1-56280-007-8   8.95

HOUSTON TOWN by Deborah Powell. 208 pp. A Hollis
Carpenter Mystery. ISBN 1-56280-006-X   8.95

KISS AND TELL by Robbi Sommers. 192 pp. Scorching stories
by the author of *Pleasures*. ISBN 1-56280-005-1   10.95

STILL WATERS by Pat Welch. 208 pp. 2nd Helen Black Mystery.
ISBN 0-941483-97-5   9.95

TO LOVE AGAIN by Evelyn Kennedy. 208 pp. Wildly romantic
love story. ISBN 0-941483-85-1   9.95

IN THE GAME by Nikki Baker. 192 pp. 1st Virginia Kelly
Mystery. ISBN 1-56280-004-3   9.95

AVALON by Mary Jane Jones. 256 pp. A Lesbian Arthurian
romance.   ISBN 0-941483-96-7   9.95

STRANDED by Camarin Grae. 320 pp. Entertaining, riveting
adventure.   ISBN 0-941483-99-1   9.95

THE DAUGHTERS OF ARTEMIS by Lauren Wright Douglas.
240 pp. 3rd Caitlin Reece Mystery.   ISBN 0-941483-95-9   9.95

CLEARWATER by Catherine Ennis. 176 pp. Romantic secrets
of a small Louisiana town.   ISBN 0-941483-65-7   8.95

THE HALLELUJAH MURDERS by Dorothy Tell. 176 pp. 2nd
Poppy Dillworth Mystery.   ISBN 0-941483-88-6   8.95

SECOND CHANCE by Jackie Calhoun. 256 pp. Contemporary
Lesbian lives and loves.   ISBN 0-941483-93-2   9.95

BENEDICTION by Diane Salvatore. 272 pp. Striking, contemporary romantic novel.   ISBN 0-941483-90-8   9.95

BLACK IRIS by Jeane Harris. 192 pp. Caroline's hidden past . . .
                                            ISBN 0-941483-68-1   8.95

TOUCHWOOD by Karin Kallmaker. 240 pp. Loving, May/
December romance.   ISBN 0-941483-76-2   9.95

COP OUT by Claire McNab. 208 pp. 4th Carol Ashton Mystery.
                                            ISBN 0-941483-84-3   9.95

THE BEVERLY MALIBU by Katherine V. Forrest. 288 pp. 3rd
Kate Delafield Mystery.   ISBN 0-941483-48-7   10.95

THAT OLD STUDEBAKER by Lee Lynch. 272 pp. Andy's affair
with Regina and her attachment to her beloved car.
                                            ISBN 0-941483-82-7   9.95

PASSION'S LEGACY by Lori Paige. 224 pp. Sarah is swept into
the arms of Augusta Pym in this delightful historical romance.
                                            ISBN 0-941483-81-9   8.95

THE PROVIDENCE FILE by Amanda Kyle Williams. 256 pp.
2nd Madison McGuire Mystery.   ISBN 0-941483-92-4   8.95

I LEFT MY HEART by Jaye Maiman. 320 pp. 1st Robin Miller
Mystery.   ISBN 0-941483-72-X   10.95

THE PRICE OF SALT by Patricia Highsmith (writing as Claire
Morgan). 288 pp. Classic lesbian novel, first issued in 1952 . . .
acknowledged by its author under her own, very famous, name.
                                            ISBN 1-56280-003-5   9.95

SIDE BY SIDE by Isabel Miller. 256 pp. From beloved author of
Patience and Sarah.   ISBN 0-941483-77-0   9.95

STAYING POWER: LONG TERM LESBIAN COUPLES by
Susan E. Johnson. 352 pp. Joys of coupledom. ISBN 0-941-483-75-4   14.95

SLICK by Camarin Grae. 304 pp. Exotic, erotic adventure.
                                            ISBN 0-941483-74-6   9.95

NINTH LIFE by Lauren Wright Douglas. 256 pp. 2nd Caitlin
Reece Mystery.   ISBN 0-941483-50-9   8.95

PLAYERS by Robbi Sommers. 192 pp. Sizzling, erotic novel.
                                                  ISBN 0-941483-73-8   9.95

MURDER AT RED ROOK RANCH by Dorothy Tell. 224 pp.
1st Poppy Dillworth Mystery.   ISBN 0-941483-80-0   8.95

LESBIAN SURVIVAL MANUAL by Rhonda Dicksion. 112 pp.
Cartoons!   ISBN 0-941483-71-1   8.95

A ROOM FULL OF WOMEN by Elisabeth Nonas. 256 pp.
Contemporary Lesbian lives.   ISBN 0-941483-69-X   9.95

THEME FOR DIVERSE INSTRUMENTS by Jane Rule. 208 pp.
Powerful romantic lesbian stories.   ISBN 0-941483-63-0   8.95

CLUB 12 by Amanda Kyle Williams. 288 pp. Espionage thriller
featuring a lesbian agent!   ISBN 0-941483-64-9   8.95

DEATH DOWN UNDER by Claire McNab. 240 pp. 3rd Carol
Ashton Mystery.   ISBN 0-941483-39-8   9.95

MONTANA FEATHERS by Penny Hayes. 256 pp. Vivian and
Elizabeth find love in frontier Montana.   ISBN 0-941483-61-4   8.95

LIFESTYLES by Jackie Calhoun. 224 pp. Contemporary Lesbian
lives and loves.   ISBN 0-941483-57-6   10.95

WILDERNESS TREK by Dorothy Tell. 192 pp. Six women on
vacation learning ''new'' skills.   ISBN 0-941483-60-6   8.95

MURDER BY THE BOOK by Pat Welch. 256 pp. 1st Helen
Black Mystery.   ISBN 0-941483-59-2   9.95

THERE'S SOMETHING I'VE BEEN MEANING TO TELL YOU
Ed. by Loralee MacPike. 288 pp. Gay men and lesbians coming out
to their children.   ISBN 0-941483-44-4   9.95

LIFTING BELLY by Gertrude Stein. Ed. by Rebecca Mark. 104 pp.
Erotic poetry.   ISBN 0-941483-51-7   10.95

AFTER THE FIRE by Jane Rule. 256 pp. Warm, human novel by
this incomparable author.   ISBN 0-941483-45-2   8.95

THREE WOMEN by March Hastings. 232 pp. Golden oldie. A
triangle among wealthy sophisticates.   ISBN 0-941483-43-6   8.95

PLEASURES by Robbi Sommers. 204 pp. Unprecedented
eroticism.   ISBN 0-941483-49-5   8.95

EDGEWISE by Camarin Grae. 372 pp. Spellbinding
adventure.   ISBN 0-941483-19-3   9.95

FATAL REUNION by Claire McNab. 224 pp. 2nd Carol Ashton
Mystery.   ISBN 0-941483-40-1   10.95

IN EVERY PORT by Karin Kallmaker. 228 pp. Jessica's sexy,
adventuresome travels.   ISBN 0-941483-37-7   10.95

OF LOVE AND GLORY by Evelyn Kennedy. 192 pp. Exciting
WWII romance.   ISBN 0-941483-32-0   10.95

CLICKING STONES by Nancy Tyler Glenn. 288 pp. Love
transcending time.   ISBN 0-941483-31-2   9.95

SOUTH OF THE LINE by Catherine Ennis. 216 pp. Civil War
adventure.   ISBN 0-941483-29-0   8.95

WOMAN PLUS WOMAN by Dolores Klaich. 300 pp. Supurb
Lesbian overview.   ISBN 0-941483-28-2   9.95

THE FINER GRAIN by Denise Ohio. 216 pp. Brilliant young
college lesbian novel.   ISBN 0-941483-11-8   8.95

OCTOBER OBSESSION by Meredith More. Josie's rich, secret
Lesbian life.   ISBN 0-941483-18-5   8.95

BEFORE STONEWALL: THE MAKING OF A GAY AND
LESBIAN COMMUNITY by Andrea Weiss & Greta Schiller.
96 pp., 25 illus.   ISBN 0-941483-20-7   7.95

OSTEN'S BAY by Zenobia N. Vole. 204 pp. Sizzling adventure
romance set on Bonaire.   ISBN 0-941483-15-0   8.95

LESSONS IN MURDER by Claire McNab. 216 pp. 1st Carol Ashton
Mystery.   ISBN 0-941483-14-2   10.95

YELLOWTHROAT by Penny Hayes. 240 pp. Margarita, bandit,
kidnaps Julia.   ISBN 0-941483-10-X   8.95

SAPPHISTRY: THE BOOK OF LESBIAN SEXUALITY by
Pat Califia. 3d edition, revised. 208 pp.   ISBN 0-941483-24-X   10.95

CHERISHED LOVE by Evelyn Kennedy. 192 pp. Erotic Lesbian
love story.   ISBN 0-941483-08-8   10.95

THE SECRET IN THE BIRD by Camarin Grae. 312 pp. Striking,
psychological suspense novel.   ISBN 0-941483-05-3   8.95

TO THE LIGHTNING by Catherine Ennis. 208 pp. Romantic
Lesbian 'Robinson Crusoe' adventure.   ISBN 0-941483-06-1   8.95

DREAMS AND SWORDS by Katherine V. Forrest. 192 pp.
Romantic, erotic, imaginative stories. ISBN 0-941483-03-7   10.95

MEMORY BOARD by Jane Rule. 336 pp. Memorable novel
about an aging Lesbian couple.   ISBN 0-941483-02-9   10.95

THE ALWAYS ANONYMOUS BEAST by Lauren Wright Douglas.
224 pp. 1st Caitlin Reece Mystery.
                                       ISBN 0-941483-04-5   8.95

THE BLACK AND WHITE OF IT by Ann Allen Shockley.
144 pp. Short stories.   ISBN 0-930044-96-7   7.95

SAY JESUS AND COME TO ME by Ann Allen Shockley. 288
pp. Contemporary romance.   ISBN 0-930044-98-3   8.95

MURDER AT THE NIGHTWOOD BAR by Katherine V. Forrest.
240 pp. 2nd Kate Delafield Mystery.   ISBN 0-930044-92-4   10.95

WINGED DANCER by Camarin Grae. 228 pp. Erotic Lesbian
adventure story.   ISBN 0-930044-88-6   8.95

PAZ by Camarin Grae. 336 pp. Romantic Lesbian adventurer
with the power to change the world.   ISBN 0-930044-89-4   8.95

SOUL SNATCHER by Camarin Grae. 224 pp. A puzzle, an
adventure, a mystery — Lesbian romance.   ISBN 0-930044-90-8   8.95

THE LOVE OF GOOD WOMEN by Isabel Miller. 224 pp.
Long-awaited new novel by the author of the beloved *Patience
and Sarah*.   ISBN 0-930044-81-9   8.95

THE HOUSE AT PELHAM FALLS by Brenda Weathers. 240
pp. Suspenseful Lesbian ghost story.   ISBN 0-930044-79-7   7.95

HOME IN YOUR HANDS by Lee Lynch. 240 pp. More stories
from the author of *Old Dyke Tales*.   ISBN 0-930044-80-0   7.95

PEMBROKE PARK by Michelle Martin. 256 pp. Derring-do
and daring romance in Regency England.   ISBN 0-930044-77-0   7.95

THE LONG TRAIL by Penny Hayes. 248 pp. Vivid adventures
of two women in love in the old west.   ISBN 0-930044-76-2   8.95

AN EMERGENCE OF GREEN by Katherine V. Forrest. 288
pp. Powerful novel of sexual discovery.   ISBN 0-930044-69-X   10.95

THE LESBIAN PERIODICALS INDEX edited by Claire Potter.
432 pp. Author & subject index.   ISBN 0-930044-74-6   12.95

DESERT OF THE HEART by Jane Rule. 224 pp. A classic;
basis for the movie *Desert Hearts*.   ISBN 0-930044-73-8   10.95

TORCHLIGHT TO VALHALLA by Gale Wilhelm. 128 pp.
Classic novel by a great Lesbian writer. ISBN 0-930044-68-1   7.95

LESBIAN NUNS: BREAKING SILENCE edited by Rosemary
Curb and Nancy Manahan. 432 pp. Unprecedented autobiographies
of religious life.   ISBN 0-930044-62-2   9.95

THE SWASHBUCKLER by Lee Lynch. 288 pp. Colorful novel
set in Greenwich Village in the sixties. ISBN 0-930044-66-5   8.95

SEX VARIANT WOMEN IN LITERATURE by Jeannette
Howard Foster. 448 pp. Literary history. ISBN 0-930044-65-7   8.95

A HOT-EYED MODERATE by Jane Rule. 252 pp. Hard-hitting
essays on gay life; writing; art.   ISBN 0-930044-57-6   7.95

AMATEUR CITY by Katherine V. Forrest. 224 pp. 1st Kate
Delafield Mystery.   ISBN 0-930044-55-X   10.95

THE SOPHIE HOROWITZ STORY by Sarah Schulman. 176 pp.
Engaging novel of madcap intrigue.   ISBN 0-930044-54-1   7.95

THE YOUNG IN ONE ANOTHER'S ARMS by Jane Rule.
224 pp. Classic Jane Rule.   ISBN 0-930044-53-3   9.95

OLD DYKE TALES by Lee Lynch. 224 pp. Extraordinary stories
of our diverse Lesbian lives.   ISBN 0-930044-51-7   8.95